P9-DDG-132

VOODOO MOON

ED GORMAN

St. Martin's Minotaur ⚌ New York

VOODOO MOON. Copyright © 2000 by Ed Gorman. All rights reserved. Printed in the United States of America. No part of this book may be used or reproduced in any manner whatsoever without written permission except in the case of brief quotations embodied in critical articles or reviews. For information, address St. Martin's Press, 175 Fifth Avenue, New York, N.Y. 10010.

www.minotaurbooks.com

Book design by Clair Moritz

Library of Congress Cataloging-in-Publication Data

Gorman, Edward.
    Voodoo moon / Ed Gorman — 1st ed.
        p. cm.
    ISBN 0-312-24271-9
    1. Payne, Robert (Ficticious character)—Fiction. 2. Police psychologists—Iowa—Fiction.   3. Serial murders—Iowa—Fiction.   I. Title.
PS3557.O759 V66 2000
813'.54—dc21

                                                            00-24754

First Edition: August 2000

10 9 8 7 6 5 4 3 2 1

TO SUE REIDER,
who puts up with me

VOODOO MOON

PROLOGUE

THIRTY-SOME YEARS ago, the fireman found the skull. He was searching through the debris left in the ruins of the psychiatric hospital.

This was a routine part of his job and nothing special. Firehouse lore had it that once in every firefighter's life, he would find something valuable. A diamond. Rubies. A stash of money.

But on this particular day, in this particular circumstance, in the mind of this particular firefighter, there was no thought at all of riches. There was thought only of his wife and the arduous pregnancy she was enduring. The doctor had said that a third pregnancy could be troublesome, maybe even dangerous, for her. But she was adamant. They had two girls. She knew how badly the firefighter wanted a boy.

He'd kill himself if she died in childbirth. That was what he told himself, anyway. In truth, Amy and Cindy would need a dad more than ever. And so he'd be there for them. But he'd be lonely. Miserable.

Please, God, he prayed, as he and six of his fellow firefighters sifted through the debris. The fire marshal followed in their wake.

☾

WHAT HE DID was trip over the skull.

He was in what had been the subbasement of the psychiatric hospital and tripped right over it.

His rubber-gloved hand dipped to pick it up.

Ash and dust had blackened the otherwise white skull.

Behind him, the fire marshal said, "Let me see that. You keep on looking."

In the next ten minutes, he found the rest of the skeleton. By this time, everybody had gathered in the subbasement area per the instructions of the fire marshal. They searched the rubble, too.

☾

THERE WERE A lot of weird stories about the psychiatric hospital. Halloween campfire stories for adults.

About how madmen with butcher knives frequently raped the attractive female patients.

About how some patients were tortured with whips and arcane devices from the Inquisition.

About how lesbian nurses took advantage of some of the patients.

And how strange Haitian voodoo rites were frequently held in the subbasement.

The stories flourished, as gossip always does, irrespective of the fact that they weren't true. A madman with a butcher knife would never get far in the heavily patrolled halls. Whips would tend to leave telltale signs for visiting family members to see. And crazed lesbian nurses played well in the steamy thirty-five-cent paperbacks of the day but were mere fantasy.

But strange Haitian voodoo rites . . .

THE STATE POLICE lab was run by a man named Dick Hampshire. He was, in order of preference, a University of Iowa Hawkeye fan (football, basketball, swimming, marbles, he didn't give a shit), a husband, a father of four, and a member of the American Legion.

He was also a skeptic when it came to the bombastic assertions frequently made by his bucktoothed assistant, Tom Watson. Watson loved high drama. He'd even once suggested that a rather routine homicide had been committed by space aliens, owing to the appearance of crop circles near the murder. A most fanciful lad was he.

Hampshire put up with him because he made for good brewski stories. "You know what that dumb sumbitch told me today?" or "Listen to this one. That dumb asshole really topped himself this time," or "You're not gonna believe this one; I swear to God, you're not gonna believe it." His crowd loved hearing his Tom Watson stories as much as Hampshire loved telling them.

SO A FEW days after the skull and bones were found in the rubble of the asylum, and after twenty-six hours of examining the bones, Watson knocked on Hampshire's office door and said, "Those bones?"

"Yeah."

"Cannibalism."

"Aw, shit, Tom. Please. I'm not up for it today. I'm really not. I've got that asshole from the Highway Patrol crawlin' all over me."

Of course, all the time Hampshire's thinking, *What a great Watson story this'll make. Cannibalism. You don't get much better than that.*

"And that isn't all."

Hampshire sighed. This one was going to be even better than the crop circle deal. "OK, Tom. Lay it on me. I'll forget all about how well that Highway Patrol captain knows the governor. Just tell me."

"One of those odd necklaces we found on one of the bodies?"

"Yeah."

"Guess what it was made of?"

"Just tell me, Tom. Skip the buildup."

"Human vertebrae."

"Bullshit."

"I've got it all set up for you to see."

"This is crazy."

"Well, there were a lot of rumors about voodoo being practiced there by some patient name Renard."

"This is all I need," Hampshire said. "The Highway Patrol accuses us of sloppy lab work that cost them an important case in court—and now we're gonna start talking about voodoo and human necklaces?"

"It's true," said young Tom Watson. "It's absolutely true."

AND IT WAS.

Hampshire spent the next four days examining various bones, teeth marks, gashes, and the pattern of human bite marks and concluded . . .

But that wasn't all.

One of the firefighters had found a small oval-shaped metal canister filled with a soupy mixture of some kind.

The stench was so bad, Hampshire skipped not only lunch but dinner, which his wife, who'd fixed a roast, was not happy about.

Hampshire spent two days breaking down the contents of the canister, and when he had drawn his final conclusion, he said, "Watson, c'mere."

"You OK, chief?"

"No, I'm not."

Watson stood next to the canister and bent to peer inside. "Oh, God, that smells awful."

"You wanna know *why* it smells awful, Tom?"

"Why?"

"Because it's not soup. At least not as we think of soup. It's a kind of stew made of a human heart, genitals, and a human spine ground to a fine powder. Then stirred up with human blood."

"Oh, God."

THEY WEREN'T GOING to be telling Tom Watson stories anymore.

They were going to be telling Dick Hampshire stories . . .

ONE

WAY UP HERE, at certain times of year, you can sometimes hear them screaming, more than twenty people who died in the asylum fire over thirty years ago.

At least, that's what some of the locals tell you, about the screaming, I mean.

I thought about that as I steered my rental Chevrolet through the countryside that graceful, warm autumn morning. It was weather so gorgeous, it made you a little crazy. You didn't quite know what to do with yourself, it was so exhilarating. Green rolling hills, trees still full and furious with color, black and white dairy cows, green John Deere harvesters, and lazy silver creeks winding past small, white, tidy farmhouses and clean red barns. Hard to imagine the screams of the dying up in these smoky hills on such a day.

The fire-gutted Sterling Psychiatric Hospital wasn't difficult to find. It sat on top of a very high hill. And it had a TV production van from Dubuque parked in front of it. Tandy West was already at work.

You probably know the name. The waif on *Mind Power*, cable

TV's second most popular show a few years back, as the publicists had been eager to tell you then. They weren't so eager to tell you that now, since the show had slipped to the midtwenties in the ratings and was facing cancellation.

Five years ago, a year after my wife died, I was asked by a law firm to investigate the murder of which their very wealthy client had been accused by an exceedingly ambitious county attorney. Said wealthy client wanted a bona fide FBI psychological profiler to work for him, which was me, or at least was me when I worked for the bureau; he also wanted a psychic who'd worked successfully with police departments before, which was Tandy West, who was twenty-one years old at the time. That's how Tandy and I met.

She'd phoned me last night in Cedar Rapids and asked, somewhat desperately, I thought, if I could fly up in the morning and "help out." She wouldn't say any more. I had some time off coming at the law firm where I worked as a legal investigator, and she'd given me a perfect excuse to take my ancient and beloved biplane to the northern part of the state. So why not? It wasn't as if the fetching Tandy had ever quite left my memory. There'd been a sweetness about her that had comforted me even more than the gentle sex she'd had to offer.

I was curious about seeing her. See if she'd gained any self-confidence. She was the opposite of her beautiful, brilliant, and brittle older sister Laura. Timid, anxious, and self-deprecating. That was Tandy. The first time I'd ever slipped her bra off, she'd said, "Don't look at them, Robert. They're too small. If they were fishes, I'd throw them back in." That had been only the beginning, I was to learn. By dawn, she had commented that her feet were too big, her ribs too bony, her nose too pugged, her eyes too big, and her bottom like a middle-aged woman's. I'd returned the favor by saying I wished my nose weren't so big, my penis so small, my ears not quite so jugged. To which she'd said: "Your nose is fine, your penis is average sized, and your ears aren't jugged at all. You're just trying to make me feel better. But unfortunately, it didn't take. I just wish I looked like Laura. No, I wish I *was* Laura." I was glad she wasn't. Laura the Invincible could've given Benito Mussolini a few lessons in arrogance. I liked Tandy. She was cute and sexy in a teenage sort of way, and she was fun as hell in the sack.

So I'd set off at dawn this morning, rented a car on landing, and now here I was.

☽

LAURA WEST SAID, "I hate using local crews. They're never very good. But Chicago didn't want to pay the freight to send out a crew of our own."

Mind Power was produced by a Chicago cable network that did a lot of infomercials and some of the wilder religious programs. One of their more popular pastors always proclaimed that there was nothing wrong with smiting sin. Toward this end, he packed, a .357 magnum, which he kept on his pulpit right next to his Bible. You know, the way Jesus did.

"Well, this is a pretty easy shoot, I guess," Laura said, trying to reassure herself. "I mean, we just need a couple of establishing shots of the asylum and then an interview with the kid."

"The kid?"

She smiled. She was tall, regal, slender, shapely, beautiful in an icy blond way, and utterly without humility or humor. She was in all likelihood the forerunner of a master race that would someday seize all the skyscrapers in all the countries that mattered and take over the human species. Even her tampons were probably Armani. She'd never liked me, and I'd never liked her right back. Maybe it was her Phi Beta Kappa key. She and Tandy had grown up in one of those Walt Disney Iowa Mississippi river towns where you can easily imagine the steamships churning upriver in all their ostentatious glory, and where they'd been cheerleaders and fun dates and B+ students and good daughters.

Tandy had secretly grown up with a headful of talents that scared both herself and her parents. Even as a five-year-old, she could "find" things that neighborhood people had lost, including a little girl who had fallen down a sewer. She could also occasionally "picture" the person who had robbed the local 7-Eleven, or snatched an old woman's purse, or, when she was twelve, the man who had murdered the town's one and only professional streetwalker. She often crudely sketched out the pictures she saw. The local gendarmes and her parents agreed to keep Tandy their secret. The folks didn't want her exploited; the cops didn't want their enviable arrest record attributed to a little girl. Then, when she joined her sister at the University of Iowa, Tandy "pictured" the rapist who had been terrifying the campus. He was arrested, and confessed. Tandy was a secret no more. It was at that point that Laura became Tandy's official protector: if you wanted anything with Tandy, you had to go through Laura first. And going through Laura was oftentimes hard on both mind and soul. Two years later, the rich man the ambitious county attorney was after hired both Tandy and me to prove him innocent.

☾

"OH, SHIT, THAT guy is an idiot. We got to town here two days ago and he was the only one we could turn up."

Laura was watching the small monitor sitting on top of the large black metal trunk the video equipment was stored in.

The setup was simple. Tandy, with a hand mike, walked around the ash-gray remains of the psychiatric hospital, telling her viewers what had happened here. All the camera needed to do was follow her. Stay wide enough to keep her in focus with the asylum clearly in the background. TV Cinematography 101. For some reason, though, the cameraman had elected to stay very tight on Tandy's face. Lovely as it was, we also needed to see the burned hulk for reference to what Tandy was talking about.

"I'll be right back," Laura said.

There were a number of ways Laura could have handled the situation diplomatically. She declined to use any of them.

The camera operator was one of those lumbering, shaggy, overgrown boy-men with a face of twenty and a belly of forty. He wore Elvis sideburns and a Marilyn Manson T-shirt. He undoubtedly considered himself a part of showbiz. He looked sad and put-upon and utterly incompetent. He also looked scared as hell of Laura, and I didn't blame him.

I saw all this in pantomime: her angrily wagging her finger at him; him hangdog defending himself with slow useless words and downcast defeated eyes; him reluctantly taking the camera clamp off his shoulder; him handing over the camera like a disgraced pitcher handing the ball to the manager who has just pulled him out of the game; and her expertly mounting the camera on her own shoulder and then going over to talk to Tandy.

He shambled over to the van where I was standing. He looked embarrassed. I felt sorry for him.

"Cal won't like this," he said.

"Who's Cal?"

"The boss. Tri-State Video. The deal is, nobody's supposed to touch the equipment except us. He's gonna kick my ass, I tell him what she did."

"Maybe you shouldn't tell him."

"Cal's got this way of finding stuff out."

The blue van with TRI-STATE VIDEO painted red-white-and-blue on the driver's door had a sliding back door that was partly opened. He dug into a cold chest and retrieved an ice-dripping can of Diet Pepsi. He held it out to me. "Want one?"

"No, thanks."

We leaned against the front of the truck watching them work. He worked on his Diet Pepsi.

Laura had set the camera down. She was blocking out the shot. Rehearsing words in relation to action.

The kid said, "Just because you live in Chicago doesn't necessarily mean you know more than somebody who lives in Iowa."

"Right."

"Cal, he shot this kung fu movie with this guy who's really big in Taiwan. It's been on cable and everything. I bet Cal's got a lot more credentials than she does. And I got to shoot the governor of Missouri when he was here one time. He said I did a real good job." Then, "You know her?"

"A little bit."

"She always like this?"

"She's under a lot of pressure." I looked over at him. He was still embarrassed. "It's nothing to get upset about. Nobody needs to know what happened. I'll ask her not to say anything to Cal."

He looked relieved. "Hey, really?"

"Really."

" 'Cause Cal might fire my ass, she makes a big deal of it. And I'm supposed to get married in the spring. And there just aren't that many video jobs around. I'd have to go back to Best Buy. You know, on the floor. I worked there four years."

"I'll talk to her."

He gunned the rest of his pop and said, "Mother Nature's calling me. I'm gonna take a pee in the woods over there."

I went up the incline to where the asylum had once stood. Judging by the width and length of the foundation, it had been a large wooden building. The charred chimney indicated that it had been three stories tall. The place had the air of ancient ruin, a tumbledown monastery in the south of France, perhaps. Until you looked at the ground, anyway. Gold Miller beer cans and red Trojan condom wrappers and crumpled Camel cigarettes told of some very modern teenagers. A crow was perched on the top of the chimney, gleaming sleek and black. He did not seem unduly impressed with the human activity going on beneath him.

Laura and Tandy continued their blocking. The camera sat atop a small boulder. Tandy saw me and waved. Her fiery hair was made even more fiery by the sunlight, fierce red Irish hair that marked women capable of magic in ancient Celtic warrior tribes. In her blue turtleneck and fawn-colored suede jeans, she was as elegant and elegiac as always—elegiac because, like all women possessed of magic, there was an air of sorrow about her that never quite faded. I could see it—even feel it—even from this distance.

I sat next to the camera. Watched them. Laura was doing a much better job than the kid had done. I understood now why she'd been so unhappy.

"Let's try one," she said.

She came over to get the camera.

"Hi, Robert!" Tandy called to me and waved again. I waved back.

Laura hefted the camera. Got it ready to shoot.

"I told the kid you wouldn't say anything to his boss."

"He's an idiot, Robert."

I shrugged. "Maybe he'd be an idiot in Chicago. But out here he's probably just fine."

She laughed coldly. "You should be a union representative, Robert. They always say things like that."

"He's getting married in the spring."

"Isn't *that* just ducky?" She smiled sarcastically.

"You're a hard woman." I tried to kid the line but we both knew I was serious.

"I know I am, Robert. And I intend to stay that way in order to protect my sister." She paused. "I don't know why the hell she called you, anyway. Nothing personal."

"Of course not."

"She's the star now. She doesn't need to share the spotlight anymore. And anyway, things are going just fine."

"I can see that."

"Except for that incompetent fucking cameraman. And I *am* going to tell his boss."

Then she went to work.

"OVER THIRTY YEARS ago, on this ground where I'm standing, was an experimental, cutting-edge psychiatric hospital called the

Sterling Institute, named after its founder, a psychiatrist named J. K. Sterling.

"The hospital treated many of the most violent criminals in America, studying them, trying to quantify them as to types of psychological disorders. Sterling was cited here and in Europe as one of the most important medical men of his time. He was regarded as the Freud of criminology.

"Here is what's left of his hospital. A burned-out hulk over which crows and coyotes and the occasional wolf now have domain. His career came to a violent end one day over a quarter a century ago when a patient named Renard—a sadomasochistic rapist and murderer—slashed Sterling's throat and then doused much of the first floor with gasoline and set it ablaze. More than twenty patients and staff perished in the fire.

"A manhunt found Paul Renard the next day, hiding in a cave. But he managed to elude them once again. He was never found. There were rumors he made it to Europe; rumors he's now living in South America; even rumors that he's living in Brenner again. In disguise, of course. Most officials seem to think he's dead.

"The land around the remains of the asylum seems barren compared to other land nearby. It even seems several degrees cooler—a clammy kind of chill—when you stand near the charred foundation—like that of Poe's description in 'The Fall of the House of Usher.'

"I'm here at the request of a local teenage boy who is about to go on trial for first-degree murder in the death of his girlfriend. The boy, Rick Hennessy, claims to be possessed by the spirit of the killer Paul Renard. He claims he explained this many times to a counselor his parents had sent him to but that the counselor refused to take him seriously.

"The Hennessys have asked *Mind Power* to come here to this small Iowa town and talk with Rick Hennessy and see if we can help him in any way. We thought we'd give you a look at the notorious asylum from which Paul Renard escaped nearly thirty-five years ago, leaving twenty people dead in his wake.

"Now, we go into town and talk to the Hennessy boy."

"Cut!" Laura said. "Great, Tandy! Let me check it on playback. But I think we've got it."

Tandy brought her microphone over to Laura and then turned and looked at me. Her smile was a heartbreaker.

TWO

SHE WAS FIVE-FOUR and maybe one hundred pounds. Next to her, Laura, all of five-six and maybe one-ten, looked like a giant.

The way she walked gave an impression of struggle, as if everything she did were difficult. And maybe it was. She was child-size in an adult world.

She was three, four feet away when I noticed the difference in her face. Five years ago, she could have posed for those sentimental paintings you see of young saints—fresh of complexion, innocent of gaze, and with a kind of radiance that truly did reflect the soul.

That was all gone. The smile was still there, and so was the quirky, impish beauty and gentle but powerful eroticism. But there was a frantic quality to the gaze and no radiance at all.

It was the weight loss and the attitude of the gray-green eyes. She probably hadn't lost more than four or five pounds, but on her the loss was noticeable. The bones were too sharp, especially the facial bones, and up close there was a cynicism and distrust in the gaze that would have been unthinkable when I'd first met her. She reminded me of the few models I'd known, all coffee nerves and cigarettes to repress the normal need for food, and a sense of anxiety that was almost violent.

She said, "Hug?" But it was more formal than truly friendly.

"You bet."

She slid into my arms. I felt as if I were holding somebody who was seriously ill. I'd given my favorite aunt a clinging hug the night before she died in the hospital. The cancer had worn her down to bone. There was some of that in holding Tandy now.

"It's really good to see you, Robert. I'm glad I called you."

"I don't think Laura is."

She squeezed me. At least her strength was intact. Her arms were strong and agile.

Then, "Oh, God, I forgot about him." She eased away from me and said, "I'd better go say something to him."

She was talking about the cameraman. He was down leaning against his truck. I followed her. There was a breeze suddenly, cool but fragrant with smokiness. Jack-o'-lantern weather. Beasties and ghoulies weather. Thousands of miniature Draculas prowling the streets for candy bars and taffy apples—hopefully the kind without razor blades secreted inside.

She said, "I'm sorry if my sister was a little rough on you."

His male pride took over. He shrugged, the gesture saying it didn't matter to a master like himself. That amateurs could do what they wanted. No skin off his nose. Or ass. Or balls.

"She's under a lot of pressure."

He started thinking about his job. Forgot about his pride. "Your friend here says you won't mention this to the boss. How she took the camera from me."

"I'll make sure she doesn't."

"A guy in a production company in Des Moines told me anytime I want a job all I need to do is call him."

"I'm sure you're very good. She's just a little nervous is all."

He nodded uphill to Laura. She was checking things on playback. "How much longer she gonna be?"

"I think she just wants to check the tape, make sure it's all right. Then she'll bring your trunk back and you can go."

"How'll you get back?"

"Our friend Robert here'll give us a ride."

"Five bucks," I said.

"A comedian," she said.

"What about the videotape?"

"Oh, she'll keep that."

"Won't she want to edit it?"

"Yes, but we'll do that back in Chicago."

"Oh." He looked at me and then at her. "And she really won't say nothing to Cal?"

"I'll see to it," she said again.

THE TRUNK WEIGHED seventy pounds. I found out the hard way. I went up to give Laura a hand. The cameraman was by now duly afraid of her. He sat in the van. He was packed up. He had some heavy-metal station on. He could go when I shoved the trunk in the back. I hefted the trunk by the handles. He made no offer to help.

As we were coming downhill, she said, "I'm going to call his boss and tell him what a moron that kid is."

"No, you're not."

"What the hell's that supposed to mean?"

"The kid's getting married. I told you that already."

"So?"

"And if he loses his job, he'll have to go back to Best Buy."

"That's not exactly my problem, Robert. He's incompetent."

"You get what you pay for. Your company didn't want to spring for a Chicago outfit so you hired some small company out here. They do a lot of cornball commercials and probably even a wedding or two when things get really thin. That's what I mean. You get what you pay for."

"You should've been a priest."

I laughed. "I'm holding out for pope."

"The kid's an idiot."

"Well, if he is, we'll let his boss find that out for himself."

THE KID GOT out of there as fast as he could. As he ground the stick shift into reverse, he rolled down the window and said to me, "Remember what you promised. You know, about Cal."

I nodded. He backed up all the way to the blacktop road. He kept the heavy metal up good and loud. Now, *there* was something worth bitching to Cal about—the kid's taste in music.

Tandy had walked back up to the ruins. She looked frail against the chimney. There was a sense of isolation up here. The burned-out asylum made the isolation ominous.

"She doesn't usually do stuff like this, does she?"

"What 'stuff' are you talking about?" Laura said.

"Seeing if someone is possessed."

"She sees it all of a piece, the whole thing. As Dr. Rhine at Duke always insisted, paranormal powers tend to come in clusters. People gifted with clairvoyance also seem to have the facility for other forms of ESP. You have a problem with that?"

"I asked a civil question."

"No, you didn't. You asked a cynical, snotty one. That's one of the reasons I don't want you around. Your skepticism gets in the way. And she doesn't need any more skepticism at this stage of her life."

"She doesn't need any people exploiting her, either."

"What the fuck is that supposed to mean?"

The breeze was stronger now and muffled the sound so that it didn't register true.

The second sound that came right on top of the first was unmistakable. "Hit the ground!" I shouted up to Tandy.

"God," Laura said, "what's going on?"

"Gunshots."

I took off running the long way up the hill and around the far side of the asylum. Since I'm a reasonably faithful jogger, the run was easy. The hard part was dodging the two shots that were directed at me, the second of them pinging off a small pile of native stone and stirring up a whirl of dust.

Hitting the ground so fast and hard shocked my bones. It took me half a minute to adjust to the impact. The sunburnt grass smelled dusty. Hard nuggets of animal feces were almost decorative. A 7UP bottle cap glistened in the sunlight.

The ruins and the surrounding forest—where the shots had come from—were silent. So were all the humans.

I listened to the wind. The Mesquakie, Iowa's indigenous people, believe that the wind speaks to those who know how to listen. But if the wind was speaking, it was whispering. It gave me neither information nor solace.

I don't know how long I lay on the ground. Enough to feel the dampness just beneath the surface of the soil from a recent rain. The crow started up, that lacerating caw that is somehow half joyous and half mournful. Druids believed that crows were divine messengers.

I got to my feet.

No gunshots.

I started around the back of the asylum.

Tandy had managed to crawl inside the foundation and hide behind a line of broken concrete, only inches from the lip of the hole which was filled with debris from the fire.

She said, "God, those were gunshots, weren't they?"

"They certainly were."

"I can't believe it. Who'd want to shoot me?"

I held out my hand and helped her over the rubble. "That's something we'd better find out."

Laura joined us, breathless from her run up the hill. "Oh, Lord, hon, are you all right?"

She grabbed Tandy and held her tight, the irony being that she seemed far more upset than Tandy did. Perhaps she was holding herself by proxy.

"Those were really gunshots," she said. She tenderly stroked the back of Tandy's head. "I just don't understand why anybody'd want to hurt you."

I said, "Maybe they didn't."

They both looked at me.

"There's the possibility that this was just random."

"Random meaning what?" Laura said.

I shrugged. "Two high school kids with a rifle out hunting and deciding to have a little fun."

"Not even knowing who Tandy is?" Laura said.

"Right."

"You really think so, Robert?" Tandy said.

"Not really. But it's a possibility that can't be ruled out. Sometimes, there really are simple explanations for things."

Laura looked around at the forest to the west of us. "I was going to go for a walk in there when we wound things up here. I used to love to walk in woods when we were little girls. Remember?"

"I used to leave bread crumbs on the trail," Tandy said. "I was very taken with 'Hansel and Gretel.'"

"Now it looks scary," Laura said. "No woodsy walk for Laura today."

"Or Tandy."

"I'll have to take a little stroll," I said.

"Really?" Tandy said.

"Yeah. See if I can find anything. First, I want to walk around up on the hill."

"How come?"

"Look for shell casings." Then, "Either of you know anything about guns?"

"Laura does a little bit," Tandy said.

"Dad gave me some lessons when I was a teenager. Tandy always hated guns."

"You two go down to my car and lock yourselves in. There's a police special thirty-eight in the glove compartment if you need it. Think you can handle it?"

Laura nodded. "One of the guns Dad taught me on was a Smith and Wesson thirty-eight."

"Then you won't have any trouble."

"You want us to go with you?"

I shook my head. "Faster if I go alone. If I'm not back in half an hour, use my cell phone and call the local law."

"God, Robert, you sure you want to do this?" Tandy said. She sounded young and fresh again. The old Tandy. Not the celebrity Tandy.

Nice to see you back, I wanted to say. "I'll be fine."

TWO TOWERING GNARLED bur oaks formed an entrance to the woods. A broad, sandy path wound through sections of golden maples and sycamore, then hackberry and elm. The land on either side of the path was busy with squirrels and foxes and rabbits and tangled up in shrub stratum that ran from gooseberry to viburnum to dogwood, brightened with coralberry and hazelnut. Gray prehistoric bedrock could be seen beneath its cover of autumn-rotted vegetation, lichenlike beards of growth that had likely first appeared soon after the Ice Age. The forest smelled of birth and death and a baffling ten million years of history. An angled beam of sunlight streamed down through the canopy of leaves above me. It was so lovely and powerful and mythic, I wondered if it might beam me up to heaven, if you'll forgive me mixing *Star Trek* with Christianity.

There were a lot of caves in this part of the state. I'd assisted in two manhunts over here right after leaving the FBI. An escaped killer had been able to hide out in a cave for more than a month. He'd been caught through his own stupidity. He just couldn't resist firing at a deputy sheriff who was getting too close. He must have studied the Watergate manual on how to conduct successful burglaries.

A mother raccoon and one of her babies watched me from a branch above. For me, they're the nobility of the forest, combining as they do intelligence, cleanliness, inventiveness, and the occasional tendency to the comic pratfall. Jim Carrey has nothing on these folks. I wanted to stop and look up at her. But this wasn't the time for it.

In all likelihood, the shooter had fled. Then again, since we knew nothing about him, maybe he had a reason to wait for me in the woods. Unarmed, uncertain of the geography, I'd be easy prey.

I had an instinctive sense of the general direction where the bullets had been fired from. I wondered if I'd gotten myself lost. Then I started seeing the clear, cleated impressions on the damp path.

The shooter made it easy for me. Near a small clearing, I saw a pine tree that heavy hiking boots had chafed. Whoever had shot at us had climbed up several feet on the lightly branched tree. The tree was next to the path. The angle gave him a good, almost direct shot at the asylum. The boot wound on the pine was damp and fresh.

The prints showed three rows of deep V-shaped rubber cleats on the soles. Whoever it was had left a clear impression. I'd never seen this particular formation before. I doubted it was common.

I spent ten minutes rooting around in and off the path looking for shell casings. A rifle had been used. A bolt action, the shooter could easily keep track of the casings. A semiautomatic, they'd kick out and be difficult to find. I worked deeper off-trail, scattering a number of animals in the undergrowth, foliage and shrubbery rattling frantically in their wake.

I reached down through years of rotted vegetation. Sort of like reaching into a corpse. The undergrowth held an amazing number of pop bottles and Twinkie wrappers and exploded firecrackers. There were even a few mud-streaked photos from some of the more downscale men's magazines. Apparently, the male forest animals had a great interest in the siliconed ladies of the human species.

I gave up. The gods never allotted you two pieces of luck in the same day. I was starting back toward the path when it glinted, winking, in a stray angle of sunlight. There was just one of them but that was all a lucky man needed.

It was bottleneck shaped and the same chamber as the M1 bullets used in WW II, 30.06. I wasn't an expert, but I'd seen enough Ruger 77 shell casings to recognize it with no trouble.

I dropped it in my pocket. Then I pushed the hell out of my luck by looking for another piece of evidence. Maybe he'd dropped his wallet. Or maybe he'd even left me a note: I DEEPLY REGRET FIRING AT YOU PEOPLE. HERE'S MY ADDRESS AND PHONE NUMBER.

A few minutes later, the gods no doubt chiding me for my foolish luck-pushing, I walked back to my car.

THREE

"OF COURSE ROBERT needs to tell the local police," Laura said on the way back to town.

"I just want to go back to Chicago," Tandy said from the backseat. "I just want to forget this whole thing."

"Sweetie," Laura said, "may I remind you that sweeps are less than five weeks away in most of our major markets and that if we don't get back up to our old share, they're going to put us out on the street?"

"You don't take it as a bad omen?" Tandy said. "Somebody *shooting* at us?"

"Omens I leave to you," Laura said. "My job is to see that we get renewed for next season. Because if we don't, there goes the three-book hard/soft deal Lloyd is trying to set up for us at Random House. And that means there'll be no book to tour with when we go to England next summer. And if we don't do well in England, we can just forget about the rest of Europe."

"God, I don't know how it ever got so screwed up."

"What got so screwed up, hon?" Laura said.

"You know," Tandy said, sounding eleven or twelve, "everything."

☾

LAURA HAD BEEN tilting her face to the backseat. She turned frontward now. Her jaw muscles tensed. She stared at the countryside.

The town was coming in view. Three structures were tall enough to rise above the rest of the town: a silver water tower with BRENNER painted in black on the side, and two church steeples, one with the traditional cross on the tip, the other with a simple, yearning spire.

To the east you could see a giant shopping center of some kind. "What's that?" I said.

"Factory outlet," Laura said. "Eighty stores. Gucci. Neiman Marcus. Ralph Lauren."

"Out here in the boonies?"

"People come from all over the state. It's open twenty-four hours. You should see that place on weekends. You wouldn't believe it."

"What happened to the town?"

"Antiques," Tandy said from the backseat. "I've never seen so many antique stores in a small town before." She seemed happy, as if her sisterly spat hadn't happened. I'd been right to change the subject away from the shooting.

"That's all that they had left," Laura said. "The factory outlet wiped out all the merchants, so everybody converted to antiques and boutiques. There's even a head shop; you know, like in my mom's hippie days. The chamber of commerce type who showed us around said that they're actually making more money than ever."

Then came the town itself. The fall trees, burning fires of yellow and russet and red leaves, painted the flame-blue sky and lent a watercolor perfection to the small frame houses on the edge of the town limits. The houses got bigger the closer we got to town. I'd checked up on Brenner last night. It had come into being shortly after the Civil War, when returning soldiers had formed a co-op of sorts to store, process, and ship grains. The trouble was, the towns along the Mississippi had not only trains but steamboats for their cargo. Brenner never had the growth and expansion opportunities of the river cities.

The houses got bigger as we neared the downtown area, Victorians and colonials and even a vast, marbled Italianate-style house that looked like something Busby Berkeley and George Lucas had designed during a long session of drinking cheap liquor. This was no doubt the area where the local gentry lived. Ancient servants' quarters could be seen on a few of the estates.

Downtown was three blocks running north-south. Most of the businesses were housed in two-story buildings with dates chipped somewhere into their fronts. For some reason 1903 had been a big year; three of the buildings bore that date. Video Village was housed in a store that had been built at the turn of the century and had probably had a hundred different tenants in that time. How could you have explained to a person of the early 1900s that someday you could buy these little cassettes, you see, and take them home and play them on your TV set? He'd be just as baffled as I would be if a man from 2098 tried to explain to me some of *his* times' inventions. The library was an Andrew Carnegie, a tiny red-brick Grecian-style structure on a busy street corner. The date 1911 was above the door. It would be quiet inside, and a dusty reverence would have settled lightly upon all the books. Maybe even upon the people themselves.

I was about to say something about a time warp when our part of the century came rushing to brash, plastic, fat-sodden life. Pizza Hut, Burger King, McDonald's, and Arby's lent the local air dash, splash, and trash. Lunchtime cars filled the various parking lots and drive-up windows.

"Turn up here—on the left—for the police station," Laura said. I turned left.

☾

THE BUILDING WAS new and strictly functional. The bond issue had probably been passed but by a small enough margin to send a clear signal to the local law people: nothing fancy. For all the bull-market bravado of this decade, taxpayers are ruthlessly cheap. And most times with good reason. Courthouse, jail, police station in a gray, squarish, three-story concrete building with no style whatsoever. The taxpayers had no doubt been mollified. Presumably there was indoor plumbing.

Inside, a receptionist directed us to the left side of the building where, behind a glass wall, several people in khaki police uniforms worked at various tasks—typing on computers, talking to citizens, talking on the telephone, and using, with great dispatch, a communications computer board that linked them with the officers in the field. For such a small town, the way the officers conducted themselves—and used their equipment—was imposing. They probably *did* have indoor plumbing.

We walked through the door. I went over to an officer who had just hung up his phone. I said we'd like to see the chief. He asked what it was about. I told him we'd been shot at. He looked genuinely shocked. "What the hell is that all about?" he said. Then he went to see if the chief could see us.

Two, three minutes later, we walked into the chief's office. I could tell you about the neat and tidy desk; the various law enforcement plaques and awards on the wall; the photo cube bearing the image of a lovely, dark-haired teenaged girl, the same girl in infancy, at the high school prom, and more recently hang gliding. But walking into the office of Susan T. Charles, the first thing you noticed was her.

And for two reasons.

One, female police chiefs weren't supposed to be so pretty. And two, women so pretty weren't supposed to have scars that stretched from their right temple all the way down to the edge of their full and sensual mouths. The contrast between her green-eyed, brunette loveliness and the ugly knife scar was stunning.

She watched us watch her. She was used to this. She didn't like it but she'd learned resignation long ago. She even managed a sweet, tolerant little smile for us as she shook our hands and let us unfasten our gaze from the half-moon scar.

The same uniformed cop who'd escorted us in now brought us coffee. He'd taken our order previously.

When he was going, Chief Charles said, "Close the door, would you, Mike?"

"Sure."

He closed the door.

She said, "Let's get right to it. Somebody shot at you this morning?" She sounded as startled as Mike had.

So I told her our story. And explained why Tandy and Laura were here.

Chief Charles smiled. "*That's* who you are. Several of my friends watch your show all the time. Love it."

Tandy returned the smile.

"And you would be who?" the chief said to me.

I told her my name and what I did.

"He's here to help us with the story," Laura said. "Give us a profile of the type of person likely to commit such a murder."

"You don't believe it was Rick?"

Laura shrugged. "Actually, we don't have an opinion. But it's an interesting story. Renard burning the asylum down. I'm told he even got several of the patients into voodoo."

"That's my understanding," the chief said. "In fact, there were certain voodoo symbols found on the grounds. He must've left them behind right before he escaped."

Tandy said, "We'd like to interview Rick Hennessy, if we could."

" 'Interview' means what exactly?"

"Talk to him," Tandy said.

"Put him on videotape?"

"If we could."

The chief sighed. "I don't have to agree, you know." Her tone was as crisp as the white button-down shirt she wore beneath her blue blazer. She had a sporty flame-blue scarf tied around her neck. Very decorative. She was quite lovely.

"We know," Laura said. And smiled.

"What are your objections?" Tandy said.

"Well, we already have people from just about every major tabloid in the country camped out here, waiting for the trial to start next week. And they're all over the air and the newsstands talking about the 'Devil trial.' I grew up here. I know the pride this town has. We don't like to look like buffoons. Rick Hennessy killed his ex-girlfriend by strangling her. Then he took his knife and cut several voodoo symbols into her. But there was nothing 'supernatural' going on at all. She'd been unfaithful to him. He couldn't deal with it. He stalked her for several months. We arrested him twice. Then he started reading about Renard. I'm still not sure how that came about. But anyway, he became as obsessed with Renard as he was with his girlfriend, Sandy Caine. She was a straight-A student and a very nice kid. Pretty, too. Had everything going for her. Had already signed up for the U. of Iowa. Was going to major in history. Very serious kid. And a sweet one, too. Her mother was dead, and her dad will never recover. I wouldn't, anyway." She sighed. "Anyway, Rick—who isn't a bad kid, either, for that matter—managed to convince himself that Paul Renard demanded some kind of 'voodoo sacrifice,' as Rick put it. So he killed Sandy. I don't believe in pop psychology but it seems to me that this was an example of somebody who couldn't deal with the fact that he'd killed somebody he loved—so he blamed it on someone else. In this case, a man who is probably dead."

"Some people think he's living here right now."

She grinned. It was a kid-sister grin and it was fetching as all hell. "You sure you're not a tabloid reporter, Mr. Payne?"

"Not the last time I looked."

"That's the 'theory' they're pushing. That Renard didn't really die and has come back here. And that *he* killed Sandy, not Rick."

Then she looked at Tandy. "But I'll bet you're pushing the super-natural angle, aren't you?" There was an edge in her voice now. "And you'll take your camera along the street and interview people until you find a few idiots who believe in the supernatural theory, too. And there we'll be, on the tube, Brenner, Iowa—or 'Ioway,' as the hicks say—talking about spooks and demons and nasties."

"You've really got me wrong, Chief," Tandy said quietly. She sounded hurt. And looked hurt, too. "I'm not a fake. I'm a serious psychic investigator. You may not believe that, but anybody who has ever worked with me will tell you that. And I'm certainly not here to make fun of your town."

Apparently sensing Tandy's pain, Chief Susan Charles said, "I'm sorry. I went over the top a bit, I'm afraid."

"I'm not a cynical person, Chief. I'm really not."

The chief nodded. "All right. I accept that—if you'll accept the fact that I'm very protective of this town."

"That means we can't see him?" Laura said.

"That means you can't see him alone. I want my deputy Bob Fuller in there at all times."

"All right," Laura said.

"And I want to see the segment before it goes on the air."

"That we won't do," Laura said.

Susan Charles smiled again. "I didn't figure you would."

Laura laughed. "You're one hard lady to read."

At just this moment, my eyes happened to be concentrating on Susan Charles's facial scar. I was wondering how it had happened. And when.

She caught me. Our eyes met. She seemed to be as curious about me as I was about her.

"Are you going in with them, Mr. Payne?"

"I thought I would."

"I need to talk to one of you about the shooting this morning."

"Listen," Tandy said. "Why don't Laura and I go ahead and get set up and introduce ourselves to the Hennessy boy. You can come down after a while, Robert."

"Fine with me."

The chief touched a button on her intercom system. "Would you tell Bob Fuller to come to my office please, Am? Thank you."

☽

DEPUTY FULLER WAS a burly, balding, fortyish man who might have passed himself off as just another small-town cop. But the eyes belied that. Sharp, steady, quick in appraisal, full of hard intelligence. He looked us over as the chief explained who we were and what we wanted. He seemed less than overwhelmed. "UFOs, huh?" he said, giving us a haiku version of his judgment. His khaki uniform had been dry-cleaned and faintly crinkled starchily when he moved. His black oxfords were so shiny you could use them for shaving mirrors.

"Mr. Payne was with the FBI," Susan Charles said.

"I'll try not to hold that against him." He didn't even try to make a joke out of it. He had the sometimes deserved animus of most cops for the *federales*.

He led Tandy and Laura away.

Susan Charles said, "He doesn't talk much."

"He doesn't need to. His opinion was loud and clear."

"He's a very practical man. Doesn't go much for theoretical stuff." Then, "I wouldn't think FBI men would go much for theoretical stuff, either." I liked her euphemism for "crazy." Theoretical. Nice civilized touch.

"If you mean Tandy, there's nothing 'theoretical' about her. She helped me on two very important cases when I was still with the bureau. In both cases, she found bodies we'd been looking for for weeks."

"Wow."

"Is that a sarcastic wow?"

She laughed. "Did it *sound* like a sarcastic wow?"

"I wasn't sure."

"Well, it wasn't. She just shot way up in my estimation. I'm impressed—with her helping you, I mean. With this thing with Rick . . . she doesn't really believe there's a supernatural connection here, does she?"

"That I'm not sure about. I haven't had any time alone with her. My recollection is that she didn't go in much for anything except straight ESP powers. Back when I worked with her before, I mean. She said that she thought that the ESP 'gifts,' as she called them, could be explained scientifically. But she pretty much rejected the supernatural and things like that. I remember she said that she felt sorry for the people who got rooked into them."

"She seems to have changed her mind."

"Her sister told me that she now sees all these things as 'of a piece.' "

"I imagine that's a useful way of seeing things when you've got a TV show to do each week," she said. "So tell me more about the shooting."

I did better than that. I put the shell casing on her desk and then drew a description of the cleated boot impression I'd found. I was telling her about the angle the shooter had used when a tall blond man with actor good looks and actor arrogance knocked loudly on the frame of the open door. He wore a white silk shirt, chinos, and had a blue tennis sweater tied jauntily around his neck. He had that easy, smirking, big-lug kind of arrogance that never quite went out of style, not even when most of the men on TV were turning sensitive back in the seventies and eighties. "Excuse my interruption, folks. I'm looking for Laura and Tandy. I'm Noah Chandler. I produce their show."

"There you are!" a female voice said from down the hall.

A stocky woman in uniform khaki appeared, out of breath, next to Chandler. "You were supposed to wait for me to bring you back." She looked at Susan Charles. "I'm sorry, Chief."

"It's all right, Am."

"Sorry," Chandler said, giving us a boyish Hollywood grin. "I saw you on the phone and figured you'd be on there for a while."

"They'll be in the interrogation room," the chief said to Am.

"Well, nice to meet you," Chandler said, giving us a little salute before leaving the room. He stared openly at Susan. Irrationally enough—and to make my ninth-grade crush complete—I got jealous.

"He used to be on a TV show."

"Professional wrestling," I said.

She smiled. "No, some kind of cop show. He was a detective or something." Then, "Well, back to business."

She kept the shell casing and the sketch of the boot sole.

Her phone rang. She listened a moment and said, "Sounds bad. Just a second. Mr. Payne—"

"Please, just Robert."

"Robert, then. There's been a train derailment and I have to see to it. I was going to walk you down to the interrogation room, but I guess you can find it by yourself."

"Sure."

"Straight down to the end of the hall. Then turn left. It's right there."

"Fine."

"Thanks."

"Thank you," I said.

I left her office and started down the hall.

I was about halfway to the end of the corridor when I saw them, two unmistakable impressions made by mud and cleated shoes on the newly polished floor. Three rows of Vs. Just like the ones the shooter had left in the woods. Fresh, too.

The tracks grew faint but they led right to the interrogation room where Mr. Showbiz himself, Noah Chandler, was standing in the doorway.

FOUR

HE HELD THE door for me and I walked in past him. "There's another door," he said, nodding toward the east wall. "That's where they are. I was just thinking about knocking and going in."

We walked over and he knocked. He smelled expensive. He was undoubtedly wearing a cologne whose name was something manly. Mountain Musk. Canyon Connection. Stallion Sweat. You know what I mean. He shouldn't have ogled Susan that way.

Laura said, "Come in."

There were five of them at a long plain folding table, the kind you rent for weddings and funerals. There was an outsize cassette tape recorder on the table. Deputy Fuller sat near us, at this end of the table, by himself, his back to us. Arms folded.

I assumed that the kid with the pimple on the tip of his nose and the green sleep boogers in the corners of his green eyes and the straggly long unclean black hair and the black western shirt with the fancy piping and even fancier fake-pearl buttons was Rick Hennessy. I also noticed the symbol of Satan he'd had tattooed on the top of his right hand. His folks probably got it for him for Christmas.

The short, slender, older man with the Einstein white hair and the searing blue eyes I didn't recognize at all.

"This is Dr. Williams," Laura said.

"Please," the man said. "Aaron will do fine."

"Aaron, then. He's the chief psychiatrist at the Mentor Psychiatric Hospital. He's also been working with Rick for the past two years."

"Almost three years," Williams said, and smiled at Rick.

Rick yawned. "I hope this fucking thing doesn't take much longer."

Williams looked embarrassed, the way you would when your two-year-old just barfed all over the matron's lap. I'm sure the good doctor felt we judged him by the behavior of his patient. And I'm sure he was right.

"I didn't fucking kill her and I'm getting real fucking tired of repeating it," Rick said.

Williams looked up at Mr. Hollywood and me. "He's telling the truth. He really *didn't* kill her. I would stake my entire reputation on that. I want everybody here to understand that before we begin the interview. We don't have a murder trial here. We have a miscarriage of justice."

"How can you be so sure he's innocent, Doctor?" Laura said.

"Because I *know* him. I know him better than anybody's *ever* known him except poor Sandy."

Laura nodded.

"Twenty fucking minutes max," Rick said.

"You mean he didn't kill her because Paul Renard had possessed him," Noah Chandler said.

"No, I mean that Rick feels very guilty about Sandy's death and has convinced himself that he *did* kill her because of Paul Renard's possession. He wants to punish himself for her death," Williams said. "He feels that even if he didn't do it he's somehow responsible. He wasn't a very good boyfriend. If he had been, she'd be alive today. That's his reasoning subconsciously."

"Can we please get the fuck moving with this?" Rick said.

He was a charmer, all right. I hoped they didn't plan to put him on the stand. The jury wouldn't need to take a vote. They'd lynch him on the spot.

☾

THIS WAS THE tale: Nerdy boy meets beautiful girl who, for some inexplicable reason, likes him. Begins going out with him. Begins having sex with him. But nerdy boy is out of control, desperately jealous, possessive. I had a relationship like that myself in high school. I can tell you all about the inclinations of nerdy boys. You're so intimidated by the beautiful princess—you can't believe your luck any more than the other kids can—that you begin to cling. And when you begin to cling—calling too often, starting to suspect she's seeing somebody else on the side, being miserable and dysfunctional when you're apart for even an hour—she begins to withdraw. Comes to her senses, if you will. How did I ever fall in love with *him*? The girl I was in love with did me the favor of moving away. Our friend Rick wasn't able to cut it off clean. Started stalking her, threatening her, harassing the boys she went out with. Grades went to hell; sulked in his dark bedroom; severe weight loss; took up drugs, including crystal meth, which had become a plague upon small, quiet, self-respecting Iowa; and happened upon an article about the infamous Paul Renard and his involvement with voodoo and satanism. Rick starts buying books on voodoo, begins experimenting with hexing people. Drives into Chicago, a mere four hours away, and visits a paranormal shop that sells voodoo dolls and other paraphernalia. Cuts up photos of Sandy and puts faces on dolls and begins sticking them with pins. The meth is becoming a serious problem by this time. Hallucinations. Rages. More weight loss. At this point, two years ago, his parents take him to Dr. Williams's hospital. He sees Rick twice a week for two years. A *People* magazine stringer is in Des Moines covering the national primary and reads an article about Dr. Williams's success with his various patients, most notably

Rick. Voilà. A *People* article about this fab-fab-fabulous doctor and his prize patient Rick. Who has given up stalking his girl-friend. Who has given up his suicide attempts. And, most impor-tant, has given up his use of meth. Dr. Williams's fifteen minutes of fame has arrived. The hospital prospers, as does the doctor. Rick is clean, mentally healthy (though still seeing the good doctor twice a week), and no threat whatsoever to Sandy. Then, four months ago, it all goes to hell. All his reading about Renard floods back to him. The doctor describes these as psychotic episodes; Rick apparently believes that Renard is inside his mind, pup-peteering him. Back to meth. Back to stalking. And then, at least according to the police—Rick himself so swacked on meth he can't remember—he murders Sandy. His trial is about to begin two weeks hence. The national media, especially the tabloids, are rubbing their hands. The only thing more fun than building somebody up is tearing him down. Dr. Williams has become the villain. Rick's parents had begged the doctor to put Rick in the hospital. He was spookier and more violent than ever. They were afraid of what he might do to Sandy or himself—or both of them. They had pleaded with Dr. Williams on four different occasions for their son to be committed. Dr. Williams said that he could continue to see Rick on an outpatient basis and everything would be fine. Rick was just going through a minor setback. Everything would be fine. Very soon now.

"BUT HE'S NOT a killer," Dr. Williams finished. "I know this young man. And he's not a killer."

"You discount his belief that Paul Renard has taken possession of him?" Noah Chandler asked.

"That's why I didn't want you people out here," Dr. Williams said. "Poor Rick has enough problems without some stage magi-cian exploiting him."

"I resent that," Laura said.

"Then resent it," Dr. Williams said. "I'm trying to help this boy. You're just trying to make some money off him."

"You agreed to let Tandy interview him," Noah Chandler said.

"I didn't agree to a damned thing," Dr. Williams said. "His parents did—after you spent an hour lying to them about how much the interview would help Rick's case."

"I consider his parents friends of mine," Chandler said.

"I'll bet you do," Dr. Williams said. "Do you always pay your 'friends' five thousand dollars?"

"Believe it or not," Chandler said, "we just wanted to help them a little bit with their legal expenses. They're not exactly rich people." Then, "That was the agreement," Chandler said to Deputy Fuller. "I've checked this with the chief."

"I know," Fuller said. Then, "Dr. Williams, they have the permission of Rick's parents for Miss West to interview him for half an hour."

"What if I don't want to be fucking interviewed?" Rick said.

"You're finally getting somebody who's willing to talk to you seriously about Paul Renard," Laura said. "And you don't want to talk to her?"

"I don't want to be on TV."

"Don't worry," Laura said. "You won't be." Then, to Deputy Fuller, "His parents said it would be all right if I stayed, too."

Fuller shrugged. Shook his head. To him we were all crazy. You didn't put anything over on Bob Fuller, by God.

"Please, Dr. Williams, we'd really appreciate it if you'd make this as smooth as possible."

He looked at Laura and sighed. "Greed is never becoming— even when it's hidden behind a beautiful mask."

With that, he stood, picked up his briefcase, and left the room without a word.

"Is he always such an asshole?" Chandler asked Fuller.

"I wouldn't know," Fuller said.

Chandler said, "Well, Laura and I will see you back at the motel sometime this afternoon."

"Be sure and call Bailey," Tandy said. "See if the ratings are in."

Chandler looked genuinely sympathetic. He even managed to sound tender. He glanced at Laura before speaking to Tandy—parents keeping bad news from their child. "Don't worry, Tandy. I'm sure we got a bump two weeks ago with that alien abduction show."

Laura smirked. "That's right. How can you go wrong with little green men sticking probes up people's butts?"

Tandy didn't laugh. "They really believe it happened to them, Laura."

Obviously sensing the tension between the sisters, Chandler said, "We'll be leaving now."

"See you in a while," Laura said to me.

"Nice to see you again," Tandy said. "Thanks for coming out here, Robert."

"YOU EVER BEEN in jail?" Chandler said to me as we walked out the front door of the police station.

"No."

"I have. Three weeks drunk and disorderly. After my series got canceled, my life kinda went to shit. Beat up this guy in a North Hollywood bar one night."

"He all right?"

"Oh, yeah." He shrugged. "Eventually."

We walked outside into the fine, clean, small-town air that is almost a religious experience in the autumn.

He said, as we went down the steps, "I stayed there of my own choice."

"In jail?"

"Yeah." He smiled. "How's that for a pisser?"

"Why'd you do that?"

"Because I was sick and tired of all the Hollywood bullshit. Your agents lie to you, your manager lies to you, your lawyer lies to you.

And my wife happened to be lying to me then, too. I knew she was seeing somebody."

"You have her followed?"

"Huh-uh. She couldn't come."

"That's how you knew?"

"She was floodgates, eight years of marriage. Floodgates every time we hopped in the sack. Then all of sudden, no matter what I did, no orgasm."

"Good detective work."

"So all these vampires are surrounding me and I decided screw it, you know?" We were now down on the sidewalk. Grain trucks and a John Deere tractor and a bulk milk truck carrying a shiny aluminum tube for product on the back sat at a red traffic light. "The only thing I was afraid of, in the jail I mean, was if some guy figured if I was an actor I must be gay—a lot of people think *all* actors are gay—and tries to bag me as some sort of trophy. But you know what? I bought 'em off. I told 'em all the inside scandal stories I knew—who's screwing who; who's a cross-dresser; who was suspected of murder by the DA but wasn't indicted; shit like that—and man, they loved me. And I liked them. I really did. They were totally up front. And I listened to their stories, too. They had some great ones, better than mine. I still hear from some of them from time to time. I admit, three weeks, I was ready to leave. But I made some good friends there." Then, "Hey."

"What?"

"How come you keep staring at my feet?"

"I'm not."

"Sure you are."

"I'm staring at your boots."

"Vegas."

"Vegas?"

"That's where I got them. I did a TV movie there and I saw this dude wearing a pair—they look good with chinos—and I asked 'im where he got 'em and he told me. I can dig out the name of the store if you want me to."

"The shooter this morning?"

"Yeah?"

I watched his face. "He wore a pair just like them."

"Oh, bullshit."

"True facts. I was in the woods less than five minutes after he started shooting."

He smiled. "That was me, you dumb shit."

"You were the shooter?"

"No; I was in the woods. Earlier this morning. I drove up to see the gals and the asylum and I went for a walk in the woods. Ever since my wife, the dirty bitch, dumped me, I've really been getting into nature. A friend of mine says I'm compensating. You know, I don't have the bosom of my old lady anymore. So now I've turned to the bosom of nature. Or some crap like that. He's into mystical stuff." He smiled. He looked a lot like Robert Wagner, which I'm sure he was aware of. "So you thought I was the shooter, huh?"

If he was lying, he was good. But then, he was an actor and he was *supposed* to be good. It's what he did for a living.

"You don't believe me, do you, Payne?"

"I'm not sure yet."

"You tell Laura?"

"Not yet."

"She'll laugh her ass off."

"How about Tandy? Will she laugh her ass off?"

He frowned. "Tandy and I don't get along real good."

"How come?"

"She thinks I just took this job because I couldn't find any acting work and was desperate."

"Is that true?"

"Sure. But who cares? I'm a good producer. I stay sober, I show up on time, I'm organized, and I always try to get the talent what they want. Within reason, of course. And that means a lot of back-and-forth with the front office and a lot of headaches when guests don't show up and et cetera. Ask Laura. She'll tell you I'm good. Tandy wanted some pal of hers. Some booga-booga guy. He described my aura to me one time. Gave me the creeps. I think he was a fag." Then, "Tandy also hates me because I keep asking her sister to marry me. I'm hooked, man. I've never been hooked like this. I've got a real jealous, possessive side and I admit it. Tandy thinks I'm going to hurt Laura some drunken night when she tells me she won't marry me."

"How many times you ask her?"

"Couple thousand. I tell you, man, that chick has got my nuts right in the palm of her hand. And you know what? I like it. I like it a lot. Ain't that a bitch? I'm castrated and loving every minute of it." He checked his Seiko. "Hey, I've got an appointment with the kid's parents. Poor fucks. Rick is a crazy bastard."

"You think he did it?"

"Of course he did it. Who else did it?" Then, pointing to his boots, "That's great about me being the shooter. You be sure and tell Laura that."

Then he was gone, basking in the sunshine of showbiz history.

☾

I WAS JUST getting in my car when I saw Susan Charles talking to an older couple on the corner.

I walked over to them.

She smiled. "I was hoping I'd see you again. This is Mr. and Mrs. Giles. They were just telling me that I should throw all you showbiz people out of town."

Mrs. Giles had been pretty at one time. Very pretty. But there was a sense of loss and anxiety about her that made her seem fragile and unpleasant.

Mrs. Giles said, "We've got a petition up is what I was telling the chief here. Us and some others got a petition up to get you folks out of here. *Nobody* wants to start thinking about Renard again."

"Mrs. Giles and her daughter, Claire, were both nurses at the time of the fire," Susan explained. "Her daughter barely got out alive."

"Where's your daughter now?"

"At home," said Mr. Giles. "She never got over it. She stays at home because she's had a couple of breakdowns."

He was the sort of would-be dapper older man you see on the dance floor. The old-fashioned leisure suit. The two pinkie rings. The dyed red hair. The cheap dentures. And a pair of white plastic loafers with gold rings across the top.

"You people been botherin' us since you got here," he said. "First that Laura broad, and then Noah Chandler. Questions about the fire; questions about Renard. Just questions questions questions. Tryin' to make some connection between that mess and this Hennessy kid killing his girlfriend. It's just all crazy bullshit, excuse my French, Chief."

Mrs. Giles said, "You know what McDonald's is like if we get there late. Especially when they're running coupons. We better hurry."

"Sam Masterson's going to see you about that petition," Giles said.

"He's already set up an appointment."

"A lot of us don't want these folks here. No offense, Mr. Payne."

"None taken. I understand."

When they were gone, she said, "They're actually decent people."

"I'm sure they are."

She checked her watch. "Got to drop into the county attorney's office. Nice seeing you again."

FIVE

BACK IN MY motel room, I fired up my computer and started working on my general profile. I inputted the data I had and then started punching up articles about teenagers who were into the occult and satanism.

There seemed to be a consensus that three types of teenagers got involved in such activities:

—the psychopathic delinquent
—the angry misfit
—the pseudo-intellectual

Rick didn't strike me as an intellectual, pseudo or otherwise. While I hadn't seen the psychiatric report of his state-appointed shrink, he seemed, at least superficially, to favor the angry misfit more than the psychopathic delinquent. The background Susan Charles had given me showed no prior arrest record.

He'd also maintained a C+ average throughout high school and hadn't been in any school trouble worth writing down.

As for the satanic movement itself, there was great debate. Those psychologists who tended to believe in repressed memory syndrome spoke confidently of a worldwide movement that "brainwashed" children and frequently sacrificed human life to appease its dark Master. The leading proponent of this theory was a man whose name I recognized. He'd recently been sued by several of his patients, women and men alike, for sexual abuse. An equal-opportunity exploiter. He'd also been sued by two women for planting false memories in their minds through the use of drugs and hypnosis. None of the charges necessarily meant that his satanic theories were wrong, but they didn't inspire confidence, either.

The opposing forces insisted that the so-called satanic movement was, essentially, a bunch of bored perverts and gangsters who wanted an excuse to have group sex, run around naked a lot, and justify any excess or crime with the old joke "The devil made me do it." It insisted that many, many police studies had been done on satanism, and particularly teenage satanism, and that the studies had found the satanism to be largely bogus—something teenagers talked about but rarely practiced in any serious way.

As evidence, they offered up profiles of three teenage "satanic" murderers and demonstrated that none of the murderers, for all their dark bragging about their Master, held any real belief in Lucifer or his alleged "laws." They were just punks taking too many drugs and feeling a deep need—for a variety of domestic reasons—to visit the ultimate violence upon unsuspecting victims.

The most interesting report dealt with a New Hampshire murder trial in which the guilty teenager said that he had been "possessed" by the spirit of a man who had chopped up three teenage girls in a woods one night. His parents testified that two years previously, the local newspaper had run an article about a killer who'd been put to death in the electric chair thirty years earlier. Their son had been so fascinated with the man that he'd begun to read everything he could find about him. He'd even found old photos of the man and begun to imitate him physically. The killer had had a limp; now, so did the teenager. The killer had worn a crew cut; so did the son. The killer had been attached to the jazz music of Dave Brubeck; so was the son. The defense was obviously trying to depict the boy as mentally ill. They cited an earlier fascination—when the boy was eleven—with satanism. Between the "dark magic," as the defense attorney called it, and the influence of the killer on his psyche, no wonder the boy, whose mental health had never been very stable, according to the shrink the defense had hired, had killed the girls. He'd used an ax.

Leaving me with Rick Hennessy.

I used FBI data and I used the reports Susan Charles had given me and I set to serious work on my profile.

"TUNA FISH?"

I looked up. Susan Charles smiled down at me. The café had a counter, six booths, and a jukebox loaded with twang.

"Uh-huh," I said. "I like tuna fish."

"In a red-meat state like Iowa?"

"I'll make up for it later. I'll eat an entire side of beef by myself."

"That's more like it."

"You could always sit down."

"I don't want to bother you."

"I'd like the company."

"Will it bother you if I smoke?"

"Smoking, no. But I have to tell you, I draw the line at chewing tobacco."

Chief Susan Charles smiled and sat down in the booth across from me. "Funny running across you in here."

"Why?"

"You don't look like the type who'd eat in greasy spoons."

"Oh, what do I look like?"

"More upscale."

"I'll take that as a compliment."

"I meant it as a compliment."

"Now, I'll return the favor. You don't look like the type who'd be a police chief in a small town like this."

"I don't?"

"Huh-uh."

"Where *should* I be, then?"

"Big city. Chicago. Homicide detective, maybe."

"Too depressing. There's a small lake in my backyard. And the hills around my place are filled with pine trees. Hard to get that in Chicago." She caught me looking at her scar again. "Knife."

"Knife?"

"College boyfriend. If he couldn't have me, he didn't want *anybody* to have me. I got pregnant. I wanted to keep the baby. He said no. He was on his way to being an important surgeon. Baby would just get in our way. I was enough of a Catholic, I didn't want to have an abortion. But he finally convinced me that was the only way. The funny thing was, I warned him. I said, if I get this abortion I'll never feel the same way about you again. He said I was being stupid. He said that a lot, actually. So I had the abortion and then I broke up with him. I had no feelings left for him. He went berserk like our friend Rick Hennessy. Wouldn't leave me alone for months. Then one night he got me in a parking garage and cut me up."

"God, I'm sorry."

"Maybe it was good for me."

She was about to go on but the waitress came. She ordered a salad and coffee. When the waitress left, she said, "I used to be a real bitch. My father was a judge and we came from a lot of inherited money. And I was always the best-looking girl in the room. I was very arrogant. My scar changed all that. People focus on the scar now, not my looks. And it's taught me humility. I see what a lot of people—people with limps and lisps and lost limbs and things like that—go through. Now when people stare at me it isn't because I'm such a babe. It's the scar." She smiled. "They're always curious how I got it, of course. I'm the same way with other people who have facial scars. I've been thinking about printing up little fliers that give the whole story. Then I could just hand them out and they could read them. I went from a princess to a whole different perspective. So I guess I should thank him for that. I'm a real person now. When I think back to what a spoiled, selfish bitch I was, I shudder. Literally."

"So how did you become a cop?"

"Well, during the trial and everything—my boyfriend came from a wealthy family too, so the trial went on for more than a month—I started getting interested in police work and things like that. I finished up college and went to the police academy in Des Moines. Then I came back here and started out in a patrol car."

"You must like it?"

"Love it."

While we ate, we talked mostly about the disadvantages of small-town life. I told her about my place outside Cedar Rapids, and how the loneliness was good sometimes, and not so good at other times. I told her about my wife.

"You still love her," she said.

"I suppose I do."

"I can hear it in your voice."

"You don't ever forget somebody like her."

"I envy both of you. A relationship like that."

"You're not married?"

"Came close once a few years ago. But it went south, as the saying goes." She paused. "He was a lawyer and he got involved with a woman whose divorce he was handling. A lot of lawsuits and litigation. The woman sued him and so did her husband. I figured if he couldn't be faithful while we were engaged, he'd never make it while we were married. Even when I was a spoiled bitch, I was faithful. Adultery is something I can't abide. My aunt was unfaithful to my uncle, and it destroyed him. I was very young when it happened. It made a terrible impression on me. I never forget it."

"You don't sound like any chief of police I've ever talked to."

She grinned. "More like Oprah, huh?"

"A little. But I like it."

While chewing the last of a forkful of celery, she said, "He's guilty."

"Rick?"

She nodded.

"Not according to Dr. Williams."

"Dr. Williams can't afford to believe he's guilty."

"Why not?"

"All the publicity he got for 'curing' Rick. No drugs. Quits stalking his girlfriend. Becomes the same good little boy he used to be. And then he suddenly starts taking meth again and stalking her and ultimately killing her. Dr. Williams was hoping to get a big book contract. One of his nurses even told me he was speculating who'd play him in the TV movie."

"Wow. A modest man."

"But if Rick's found guilty, all that's gone."

"I take it Dr. Williams isn't your favorite guy."

"I don't have much faith in psychiatry. And I feel the same way about the hired guns who work for the state. They mostly play word games and puff themselves up. My understanding is that most of Freud has been discredited anyway."

"So I hear."

She shrugged. "To be fair, we've all got our angles. I was the one who arrested Rick, so I want to see him convicted. So does Sandy's dad, because *he* knows all the terrible things Rick did to his daughter—even before he killed her. Dr. Williams and Rick's folks don't want to see him convicted because they've convinced themselves he's innocent, and because it will reflect badly on them if he's found guilty. They saw the wild kid he became but they couldn't do anything about it. A lot of people in a town like this always blame the parents."

"You don't see any possibility that it's somebody else?"

"Not really."

"And being a dutiful chief of police, you've considered other possibilities?"

"I know the rap."

"The rap?"

"That we make up our minds who did it and then never investigate anybody else."

"It happens."

"Did Dr. Williams tell you Rick was seen leaving the boathouse where the body was found?"

"No."

"Did he tell you that DNA tests showed Rick had her blood all over his hands?"

"No."

"Did he tell you that her bra—with her blood on it—was found in Rick's car?"

"Wow."

"Wow is right. How'd you like to be the attorney who has to argue against that kind of evidence?"

"Who *is* his attorney, by the way?"

"Woman named Iris Rutledge. Two blocks down and around the corner. Upstairs. She's young and smart and good. But she's not going to win this one."

"More coffee?" the waitress asked. We both said yes, please. She filled our cups.

She said, "Do you bowl?"

I smiled. "Not so's you'd notice."

"Good. How about going bowling with me tonight?"

"Really?"

"I usually go with a friend but she's got a cold. I need somebody to bowl with."

"Boy," I said. "Bowling."

"And afterward we can walk down to the DQ."

"Dairy Queen?"

"Right."

"Life in the fast lane."

"You know you want to go, Payne. You're just trying to be this big-city sophisticate."

"How do you know I want to go?"

"The way you're looking at me."

"Maybe I'm looking at your scar."

"Huh-uh. You're past that point. Now, you're looking at *me*. And I appreciate it. I guess I've still got some vanity left after all. Pathetic as it is." For the first time, I sensed her self-consciousness about the scar. And maybe a little bit of the pain.

I laughed. "My pleasure. You're still a good-looking woman. So do I pick you up or what?"

"I'll just meet you there. It's on the east edge of town. Night Owl Lanes."

"I don't have a bowling shirt."

"They'll probably let you in anyway."

She stood up. Picked up both checks.

"Hey."

"I'm also on the chamber of commerce board, Payne. I'm *supposed* to pick up checks like this." Then, "See you about eight o'clock."

IRIS RUTLEDGE'S OFFICE was on the top floor of what had once been a grocery store. In the first-floor windows, you could still see some of the produce stalls and two of the aisles. Dust to dust. Rats roamed the place now. They left their little turds everywhere. Another era come and gone. It was sad somehow, and scary. Someday my era would come and go, too, my whole generation vanished utterly.

I walked up the outside steps to the second floor. They creaked and wobbled. I wondered if she did personal injury law. The stairs seemed on the verge of collapse. She might end up defending herself someday.

There was a sign that read COURTHOUSE. BACK AT 3.

I went back down the stairs, and that was when I saw him. He hadn't been there before. Heavyset balding guy in a nondescript, forest-green, Ford four-door sedan. Illinois plates. White button-down shirt. Dark glasses. Motor running. He was intently writing something in a small black notebook. Then he abruptly pulled away. The bands in the automatic transmission sounded a little loose for such a new car. Down to the end of the block. Turned right. Gone.

I was just walking back to my own car when a girl pulled up on her racing bicycle. She wore black leather riding gloves, black latex racing shorts, and a white T-shirt inside of which bobbed merry little braless breasts. She was somewhere around eighteen, pretty in a freckled, prairie way. "You Mr. Woodson?"

"Afraid not."

"Oh. You work with Iris?"

"No. But I was looking for her."

"Me, too." She frowned. She had nice, long legs planted on either side of the bike on the cracked sidewalk. "I finally work myself up to telling her the truth and then she isn't even here when I stop by." She held out a gloved hand. We shook. "I'm Emily Cunningham, Sandy's cousin."

"Robert Payne. I am in town trying to find the truth about your cousin's death, though."

"Really?"

"Yes. I'm a psychological profiler."

"Oh. *Silence of the Lambs.*"

"Something like that."

" 'I had an old friend for dinner.' I love that line."

"That's a good one, all right." I wasn't sure if it was exactly ver-batim but it didn't matter.

There was a breeze, carrying on it the heady smell of burning leaves. I thought of high school and football games and sitting in the stands with the girl who'd become my wife. All that sweet fran-tic necking in the backseat of the car later on, and a wolfed-down midnight pizza at Pizza Hut. Then more necking before she finally went in for the night. It was painful to confront my loss this way; and yet it was pain lined with pleasure.

"Are there really cannibals?"

"I'm afraid there are."

"You ever meet one?"

"Once. When I was with the FBI."

"Wow. You were with the FBI?"

I nodded.

"So how many people did he eat, the cannibal, I mean?"

I smiled. "Well, I don't think he ate whole people. Just little bits and pieces of them."

"You ever meet anybody who ate an *entire* person?"

"Not that I can think of."

She was a great kid. Cute and smart and curious, even if her curiosity did take a macabre turn here and there.

I said, "You think he did it?"

"Who?"

"Rick."

"Killed Sandy, you mean?"

"Uh-huh."

She looked at me. "Maybe."

I guess I was surprised she hadn't simply said yes. His history with Sandy. The blood on his hands.

"You think of anybody else who might've done it?"

"That's what Iris wants me to talk about."

"Somebody else you suspect, you mean?"

I could see her tense up. "You were really with the FBI?"

"Yes."

"How long?"

"Eleven years."

She watched me some more. "I still probably shouldn't ought to tell you anything."

"Why not?"

" 'Cause Iris'd get mad. She's got a terrible temper."

"She does, huh?"

"She got kicked out of court one day because she told the judge he was stupid." She checked her watch. "Well, I guess I'll ride over to Wal-Mart. I need to get some stuff. Then I'll stop back here."

"She left a note. She's supposed to be back in half an hour."

"Well, if you see her first, just tell her Emily Cunningham stopped by."

"Any other message?"

She smiled. "You just want to know what I want to tell her, don't you?"

"I sure do."

"We'll have to talk some more about cannibals sometime."

"I can't wait."

She looked at me and said, "Tell her I want to talk to her about Sandy's dad. And that baby picture. She'll know what I mean."

Then she was gone.

I SPENT TWO hours in the library reading about Paul Renard and the asylum fire. The librarian, a sweet-faced woman with a slow sad smile, said that this was the most exciting story in all of Brenner's history. She said she could remember seeing Paul Renard when she was a young girl and that he'd been quite handsome. She then gave me what she referred to as the "Renard File."

Renard had been a local boy of great means. He'd gone east to school and graduated from Princeton, then returned here to run his father's bank. His parties were famous. He'd once brought a string quartet in from Chicago. On another occasion, he got Robert Frost, who'd been doing a reading at the University of Iowa, to have dinner at his estate. Renard was cultured, smart, generous, and a heartbreaker. He flew women in from as far away as Los Angeles and New York for some of his three-day weekends. His manse had a pool, a tennis court, and a beautiful view of the Iowa River, complete with natural dam.

It was believed he killed his first woman when he was thirty-one. This was never proven—or at least, the local police didn't *try* very hard to prove it—and he killed his second when he was thirty-three. Both were hitchhikers. Both took months to identify. He had buried them in deep pits. During all this time, he continued to run his bank and have his parties. There were those who believed he belonged in prison; and there were those who believed he was completely innocent, and that his accusers were merely jealous of his lifestyle. He was an awfully charming man, apparently, and a lot of people liked him. Six months after the discovery of the second body, an assistant county attorney went to the town council—behind his boss's back—and gave a rambling and melodramatic speech, the point of which being that Paul Renard should be indicted on two counts of murder. When his boss *did* find out about it, he fired the young man, who left town shortly thereafter.

The quirk in the story had to do with a third murder. A local waitress was found strangled to death in her house trailer. Paul Renard could not possibly have committed this murder. He was in New Jersey at the Princeton homecoming. But the feeling of the town's three or four most powerful civic leaders was that violence was getting out of hand—three murders in five years in a town that hadn't seen a murder in the previous two decades—and while they were resolving the waitress's murder (her boyfriend, a redneck drifter with ties to the KKK, had already been indicted), they might as well deal with Paul Renard as well.

They gave him his choice. He could face indictment and trial or he could agree to voluntary incarceration in the local psychiatric hospital. He offered a third option. He would go away and never return. They said no. They were decent people; why inflict a sociopath on another community? There was no doubt about his guilt. He'd lost a wristwatch at one of the death scenes. They kept reminding him of this. They kept reminding him that after the second death, the local police had secretly searched his manse and found bloody clothes. The blood on shirt and trousers matched the type of the dead girl.

Paul Renard was incarcerated. The story went that he'd suffered a complete nervous breakdown. Apparently, those parties weren't as easy to stage as they might appear to the untutored eye. They had taken their toll on the poor dear.

One year into his stay at the psychiatric hospital, Renard began to cause trouble. He'd discovered voodoo, a belief system which fascinated him. He had his little cult of followers. He was their absolute master. He began by sacrificing rats and cats and stray dogs. A nurse, in love with him, even allowed herself to have sex with all of the men in the cult as Renard watched. The cult grew. The staff did everything it could to turn his followers against him. They were always pointing out how he abused and degraded them in his "authentic" rituals, and how said rituals were really nothing more than excuses for Renard to have sex. The two hospital administrators in charge were reluctant to call for outside help because the publicity would shut them down. Who wanted to send a troubled loved one to a mental hospital where voodoo was practiced in the patient rooms?

And then the fire.

More than thirty years ago.

Twenty people dead.

And Paul Renard on the run.

It was commonly believed that nobody could survive a fall into the rapids. Not even Renard. Two of the deputies who followed him to the edge of the cliff swore they saw his head being smashed against the jagged rocks in the churning waters. One even said that he saw blood spray from Renard's skull when Renard hit the rapids and then the dam. He assured the press that nobody, however wealthy, however elegant, however cunning, could possibly have escaped those rapids. And then being hurtled over the dam itself.

But still, there were those locals who insisted that he had not only survived but had returned in another guise. This was at least in the realm—however unlikely—of the possible.

The supernatural stories were another matter. Rick Hennessy

wasn't the first person to claim that he had been possessed by the malignant spirit of Renard. At least three others accused of murder had also blamed Renard's hardworking ghost for their troubles.

A sanitized version of Renard's life story (wanton mental-hospital voodoo orgies not included) was told to local students at Halloween. And a Hollywood producer, no less (*Angels and Tramps, Sisters in Sin,* and *My Bed or Yours?*) had visited here twice, both times discussing at length the Paul Renard story. He was especially interested in the "wanton mental-hospital voodoo orgies," a descriptive phrase that he, as a matter of fact, had come up with. So far, the cap was still on the lens.

"FASCINATING, ISN'T IT?" the librarian said when I brought the file back to the front desk. She was a nice-looking woman in a navy blouse and bias-cut print skirt.

"He was a busy boy."

"You think there's any chance he's still alive?"

"He'd be seventy-two years old now."

She gave a little shudder. She was fiftyish and very cute. "I guess I just like scaring myself. I still love ghost stories. And I always watch the horror movies with my two boys." Then, "But you know, a lot of people still believe that he's still here somewhere."

"Just wandering around spooking people?"

She gave me an impish smile. "You picked yourself an interesting case to work on, Mr. Payne."

SIX

I RAISED MY hand and was about to knock when I heard Tandy's voice say, from behind the motel room door, "Just go fuck yourself, Laura."

"Oh, that's nice. I'm holding all this together and you're telling me to go fuck myself."

"Don't play the martyr. If you're holding this together, it's for your own sake. Not mine. You like all this bullshit."

I figured I'd do them a favor by knocking. I knocked.

Tandy opened the door. "I'll bet you heard us screaming."

I smiled. "Just the 'fuck off' part."

"Oh, good," Laura said behind Tandy. "He didn't hear the 'stick it up your ass' part."

"Now, that would've shocked me."

Tandy waved me in. "Our secret is out, I'm afraid. My sister is an arrogant cynical, selfish bitch. Nothing personal, of course."

"This is just like pro wrestling," I said.

"The diva is throwing a diva fit," Laura said. "The cable folks want her to do a couple of teasers about the ghostly spirit of Paul Renard. And she won't do it."

"We don't even know if there *is* a ghostly spirit," Tandy said. "That's why I won't do it. If I honestly believed that Rick was possessed, then I wouldn't *mind* doing it."

"You want me to show you our last Nielsen, babe?" Laura said.

"Don't call me babe."

"Lowest rating we ever got."

"The ratings'll get even lower if I start faking stuff."

"They *can't* get any lower. Babe."

The motel room was identical to mine. Badly scuffed brown outdoor carpeting. Heavily glued but surprisingly spindly desk, a small water-scarred bureau, bed. And paintings of horses done by somebody who didn't know much about anatomy, equine or otherwise. There was a submarinelike darkness and dampness to it, a netherworld atmosphere—with the door closed at least—where salesmen battled loneliness and adulterers battled guilt and drifters battled those stray dangerous impulses that came on with meth or coke.

"You know a teenager named Emily Cunningham?" I said.

"Sandy's cousin," Laura said.

"She was over at Rutledge's office. Says she's going to cooperate. What's that supposed to mean?"

"Sandy supposedly told Emily something right before she died," Tandy said. "But Emily has been reluctant to tell the Rutledge woman what it was."

Tandy looked down at her sister, who sat on the edge of the bed. "I hate you, Laura."

"Well, I hate *you.*"

"Go to hell."

"No, *you* go to hell."

Tandy sat down next to her and they were soon enough entangled in girly white arms, giggling and sort of half-assed crying and saying, "Oh, I'm sorry."

"No, *I'm* sorry."

And I could see them in that moment as little girls, sweet and pretty and smart, making up over some idiotic fight they'd had.

"You think we'll ever be adults?" Tandy asked me.

"Probably not," I said. "And I won't, either. Very few people ever make it."

"I'll be an adult before *she* is," Tandy said.

"Huh-uh," Laura said. And playfully nudged her with an elbow. This was their makeup routine, apparently.

"I think the chief has a crush on you," Tandy said.

"I doubt that," I said.

"Yes, she does," Laura said. "The way she kept looking at you."

"She was setting me up."

"Setting you up for what?" Tandy said, now genuinely interested in the subject of Chief Susan Charles.

"I'm not sure. But she asked me to go bowling tonight."

"Wow," Laura said, "talk about hot dates. And maybe the malt shop afterward?"

"She wants to pick your brain," Tandy said.

"Right," I said. "I just wonder what she's so curious about. The only thing I can think of is that she thinks I have something that takes suspicion away from Rick Hennessy. She's convinced there's no other legitimate suspect."

"Maybe she thinks Tandy can prove that Rick is actually possessed."

I shook my head. "This is a very no-nonsense woman. No room for the occult in that beautiful head of hers."

"Then she really must think we can screw up her case for her," Laura said.

"How did your interview with Rick go, by the way?" I said.

Tandy shook her head. "He wasn't cooperative at all. He keeps denying he murdered Sandy but it's like he does everything he can to look guilty."

A knock. And moments later Noah Chandler graced our lives. "Boy, what a seedy bunch you three are."

Tandy smiled; Laura rolled her eyes.

Chandler said, "Well, Payne, you'd be proud of me."

"I doubt that," I said.

Chandler looked at Tandy. "He hates me. Thinks I'm just a Hollywood glamour boy. Nobody home upstairs. Tell him that I once read nearly a hundred pages of Thomas Wolfe."

"He did," Laura said, "and it took him a year and a half."

He sat on the edge of the overstuffed armchair and lit a cigarette. "I hope nobody minds."

"I think you're supposed to ask that *before* you light up, Noah," Tandy said.

He grinned. He was posing for a publicity shot. "Why stand on formality?" He took a drag, exhaled. "There's a girl named Heather Douglas. Her boyfriend dumped her for Sandy. A guy at the gas station where they're putting on some new tires for me—remember I said something felt funny yesterday, Laura? It was the tires, worn right down to cord—anyway, I told this kid why we were out here, working on the Hennessy case and all, and he told me about this Heather Douglas. Said she'd really gone crazy when her boyfriend dumped her. Said she threatened to kill Sandy quite a few times in front of several witnesses. He said two or three people even went to Chief Charles. Said the chief interviewed Heather a couple of times but decided there wasn't any real point in pursuing it. She had her killer—Rick." Another deep inhale. Exhale. The smoke blue and lazy on the shadowy damp air. "Sounds like I scooped our detective here."

"I know you're still working on your profile, Robert," Laura said, "but is there any chance the killer could be a girl?"

"Sure," I said.

"She might be worth checking out," Laura said.

"Definitely."

"Did I hear somebody say 'Thank you, Noah, for that fine detective work?' " Chandler said.

"Not that I know of," Laura said.

"Very funny," he said.

I stood up. "I'm going down to my room."

"I'll be glad to go with you to check out this Heather chick," Chandler said.

"No, thanks."

"But all Great Detectives have sidekicks," he said. "Holmes and Watson. Nero Wolfe and Archie. Mike Hammer and Velda. I'm a mystery buff."

"He doesn't want you tagging along, for God's sake, Noah," Laura said. "So just give it a rest."

I felt sorry for him. I didn't like him—God only knew how he'd gotten the producer's job—but Laura's contempt was withering.

I said, "You did some good work, Noah. The gas station guy, I mean. Thanks. I appreciate it."

"You hear that, Laura?" Chandler said. "*You hear that?*"

"I heard," she said wearily. "He's just trying to be nice, you moron."

"Well," I said, feeling even sorrier for big dumb Noah Chandler. "I guess I'll be going."

FROM A QUICK look around I'd sensed somebody had been in here. I'd called the desk to talk to Pete, the handyman. He was always around. Maybe he'd seen somebody. Ten minutes later the phone rang.

"Hi. This is the front desk." Friendly female voice.

"Hi."

"Did Pete find you?"

"Nope."

Then, "He's down the hall. Excuse me for a second." She was back within a minute. "He's coming down to your room right away."

As I was talking, I noticed the clasp on my suitcase affixed to the strap. I always belted the strap on the fourth loop. It was now belted to the second loop. And the empty metal waste can next to the desk had been knocked over. I'm enough of a neat freak to notice things like this. You will find no room of mine with a waste can on its side. Somebody had been in here.

"Send him down."

"He's a nice guy."

"I'm sure he is."

"His son, he just got laid off over to this factory in Davenport. Pete's real worried about him."

I had to admire her loyalty. She was going to make me feel sorry for Pete even if I didn't want to.

"So please don't chew him out."

"I'm going to pistol-whip him."

"What?"

"And then I'm going to stick straight pins underneath his fingernails. And then I'm going to douse him with gasoline and set him on fire."

"Smart-ass."

"Pete'll be fine. I just need to talk to him is all."

Pete, when he came, was dressed in bib OskKoshes with a flannel shirt underneath and a black-and-yellow Hawkeye ball cap on top. He was old enough to have wattles and rheumy, faded eyes and a bit of palsy in his left hand. Or maybe he was just scared. He said, "I just want to get one thing clear." He said this before actually stepping inside. "I been working here ten years—after I retired out to the tire company—and I've never stolen one thing in all the time I been here."

"Fine."

"Stuff people leave layin' around, a dishonest fella'd have a hey-day. Wristwatches and diamond necklaces and big fat wads of cash. I admit I've daydreamed about it a few times. But I've never taken anything."

"I believe you."

He smiled. "Good. Helen said she thought you was a nice guy."

The door was open. A breeze came in, smoky with autumn. It made me think of growing up in a small town outside Iowa City. Riding horses through the cornfields of fall, all the way up to the timberland where there were Indian burial mounds and a winding river so clear you could see the fish weaving along its bottom.

"I just wondered if you saw anybody around my room."

"That's what I wanted to tell you, this heavyset guy leaving your room. He got into a green car."

"Balding guy?"

Thought a moment. "Yeah, right. Balding."

"You happen to notice the plates on his car?"

"Sure. They're the first thing I look at. I got kind of a thing about license plates, I guess. Always have had. My dad used to nail all his license plates to the wall of the garage. My the time he died, he had quite a collection."

"I'll bet."

"The garage burned down right after he died. Never did figure out what started the fire."

"How about the plates on the green car?"

"Illinois."

"You're sure?"

"One thing I'm sure about, mister, is license plates."

Not too difficult to figure out what had happened. The heavyset guy, whoever he is, waits till Pete heads back to the office, and then uses some kind of tool to get in my room. Obviously, a pro.

I picked up the phone again. Pete looked nervous. "It's Payne again. You have anybody currently registered here from Illinois?"

She checked. "No." Then, "How's it going with Pete?"

"Just fine. Thanks." I hung up and turned to Pete. "You wouldn't happen to remember the plate numbers, would you?"

" 'Fraid not. For one thing, my memory ain't so hot these days. And for another thing, it never even crossed my mind."

"I'm sure it didn't. Thanks, Pete."

"That's all, huh?"

"That's all. Thanks again."

He latched his thumbs on either side of his bib straps and looked around the room and said, "You'd really be surprised about what people leave right out in plain sight. It's almost like they *want* you to steal it, you know that? Just like they're *beggin'* you, in fact."

THE KNOCK CAME about a half hour later. I was mindlessly channel-surfing. They had a dish antenna. On one of the talk shows a neo-Nazi named Fred goose-stepped up and down the audience aisle until an audience member attacked him. A good-looking Wall Street woman told me how to invest my money. A very young Roy Rogers sang a song to his horse Trigger. A KKK member with a real bad complexion told a talk-show host that "good ordinary white men" were the most discriminated-against minority group in the USA. And a voluptuous woman in a cow-boy hat and snug-fitting and very spangly cowgal shirt assured me that even I of the lead foot could learn all the latest line dance moves right in the shamed darkness of my living room. I just kept surfing. Maybe I was looking for God—as opposed, I mean, to all the TV ministers so eager for my bankbook.

I was grateful for the knock.

I put the surfer stick away and went and answered the door and there stood Tandy West.

"Still a channel surfer, I hear."

The door, apparently, wasn't real thick.

"Yeah. I couldn't decide between wrestling and women who got probed while in the hands of aliens."

"Maybe that's what I need, Robert," and I could see she was only half-kidding. "A little alien probing."

The psychologists and psychiatrists who had examined her over the years trying to determine the authenticity of her "gift" had also noted that she was manic-depressive. Severely so. She had long been a Lithium baby.

"You want to come in?"

"I was hoping you'd take me for a ride."

"Anywhere in particular?"

"Back to the asylum."

"Any particular reason?"

"A couple of particular reasons. I thought I'd explain on the way."

"Long as I'm back to keep my bowling date."

"I still think she's got a crush on you."

"And I still think she just wants to pick my brain."

"How's your love life?"

I looked over at her. "You've really changed."

"I know. I'm not the virgin girl anymore." She looked out at the country road. It was late afternoon. The impending dusk was already casting long shadows and touching all the autumn foliage with dramatic life. The pumpkins in the field, orange and round as merry balloons, looked especially festive. One of nature's little jokes, I suppose, to make the season of death so seductive.

"I'm sorry," she said. "I shouldn't have said that."

"Well, since you asked, not all that good."

"How about that rich woman you were living with?"

"Went back to her ex-husband."

"I thought he was such a bastard."

"He is."

"So you're not involved right now."

"Not by choice, unfortunately."

More staring out the window. "I either have too little sex or too much."

"Right now I think I'd opt for the latter."

"Maybe you'll get lucky with the police chief tonight."

"I doubt it."

Then, "You think I could sleep in your room tonight?"

"Sure. But why?"

She turned back the cuff of her white shirtsleeve. First the left one. Then the right one. She'd done a pretty good job of it. Somebody must have found her in time and gotten her to a hospital. She had pale skinny little-girl wrists, and the razor scars were sad and lurid and ugly.

"What's that all about?" I said.

"I got real depressed a while back."

"Apparently."

"Maybe I won't want to have sex tonight."

"That's all right."

"If it gets real rough for you, I'll give you a hand job."

I smiled. "Boy, you *have* changed." Then, "You going to tell me about your wrists?"

She looked over at me with her sweet little waif face, glassy tears in her eyes, and shook her head.

I didn't push it.

☾

THE SHADOWS, AND the darkening sky, and the chill drop in temperature, lent the land around the burned-out asylum a forlorn quality I hadn't sensed in full daylight. The songbirds in the fading tree light were melancholy, and even the dogs down the hill near the horse meadows sounded lonely. It was true. You could almost hear the screams of those who'd died in the fire.

"You mind if I just walk around a while and not talk?"

"Fine."

"I mean alone."

"No problem."

She walked around alone. No problem. I watched a mother raccoon in a tree try to get one of her babies down from a topmost branch. The baby was swaying back and forth and making fear sounds. The mother moved with great delicacy and picked the kid up by the back of the neck and brought it back to safety. In the midst of all this desolation, it was a life-affirming act.

The moon came up. A half moon, it was, clear and radiant as the finest diamond, its luminosity ancient and brand-new at the same time, a marker of our entire brief span on this world that would never quite be ours. It was fun sometimes to think of what species would eventually replace us; sometimes, it was fun; other times, it was scary.

"Damn," she said, sitting down next to me on a fallen tree.

"What?"

"In other words, how he became 'possessed.' "

She paused. "Yeah, I guess that's it."

"You really think he's possessed?"

"I think it's a possibility."

"That doesn't answer my question."

She sighed. Stared up at the moon again. "I don't have to sleep in your bed tonight. I mean, if you don't want me to."

"Knock off the bullshit and answer my question. You really think this kid is possessed?"

"Probably not."

"But you need me and my background report on him to lend your story credibility."

"That's the plan, I guess."

"It kind of pisses me off, Tandy."

"I told Laura it would."

"My word is all I've got. If I get involved in some stunt like this, who'll want to hire me?"

"So you're saying no?"

"I'm saying no."

"Fuck," she said.

I didn't say anything.

"You're really pissed, huh?"

"Yeah."

"I don't blame you."

I didn't say anything.

She walked up toward the burned ruins. Then turned back to me. "I can't believe what I've become. I blame Laura and Noah all the time. But I'm just as guilty as they are. I don't want to give up the life, either. I'm just as bad as they are."

"Maybe not as bad as Noah."

"I know you don't like him. I admit he's kind of a peacock, but he's not such a bad guy."

"Why'd you bring me out here, Tandy?"

She came back and sat next to me on the toppled tree. "I thought you might bring me luck."

"What kind of luck?"

"I thought with you here, I could walk around the grounds and maybe something would happen. Rick used to come out here all the time. I thought maybe I could make some kind of telepathic contact. See if there really were malevolent spirits out here."

"Then you've really contacted spirits before?"

"Oh, sure. That part I believe in completely. I've contacted spirits several times over the years, in fact. I mean, back when I was holy."

"Holy?"

"I know that's kind of a funny word. But that's how I felt. When I was young and was aware of my power. I was in touch with God and with myself and I felt a great peace, and a kind of wisdom. Like when my dad got cancer that time. I was really able to comfort him. And I think that helped him recover completely. I really believe I played a part in that, a part I don't even understand myself. I would go into church and make the stations of the cross and then kneel in front of the votive candles and look up at Blessed Mother and I felt—holy. That's the only way I can explain it, Robert. Holy."

"And you don't feel holy anymore?"

She shook her head. "Not at all."

"And when you were walking around up here tonight—"

"Nothing. No kind of spiritual contact at all." '

The owl got busy again. This time he didn't sound plaintive; he sounded triumphant. There was something regal now in his cry.

"Thanks for telling me the truth, anyway."

"Laura's going to kill me."

I took her hand. "Maybe you should think about quitting."

"A has-been at twenty-eight."

"Maybe you'll find your powers again."

"I've thought of that, actually."

"You really were helpful to people, Tandy. And you really were holy."

She took my hand and touched it to her cheek. "Tonight? Am I still invited to your room tonight?"

"Absolutely." I tapped my wristwatch. "Now I need to get back."

"Oh, yes," she said, laughing. "I forgot. It's bowling time."

SEVEN

THE TAVERNS WERE all fired up and ready to go. There was a block of them. When we'd left town, there'd been only a few cars parked slantwise in front of them. Now both sides of the block were lined with pickups, vans, and cars. Some of the vans still bore traces of the seventies and eighties in the form of heavy-metal drawings on their sides. In the taverns tonight, as every night, there would be bumper pool and lottery tickets and fistfights and adultery and young love and old weary love and loneliness, lots and lots of loneliness in the neon shadows of beer signs and juke-box glow.

The streets were mostly empty. It was that limbo time when teenagers were actually at home stuffing food in their faces, fortifying themselves for the night ahead. Soon they'd burst forth in a rumble of glass-pak mufflers and rock music and hormones, and ignite the night into an explosion of joy, lust, cosmic ache and cosmic confusion and cosmic arrogance and cosmic terror, and lust lust lust.

As I drove into the parking lot, I saw, at the far end, the green Ford that I'd seen outside Iris Rutledge's office. I drove past it.

Empty. I wondered where the big man was. The motel looked shabby in the soft lights of the parking lot, the prairie sky filled with stars now. I pulled into a parking slot near my room.

"I'm glad I told you," Tandy said.

"I'm glad you did, too."

"I don't blame you for not wanting to be involved."

She slid her arm around me as we stood in front of my door. Hugged me. I seemed to represent a mixture of Daddy, brother, and lover to her, and the combination made me uncomfortable.

"See you," she said, and walked to her own room several doors away. She gave me a tiny wave and inserted her key and went inside.

I went in and got the light on and took care of my bladder and washed my face and hands, and then the phone rang.

"Hey, pal. What exotic place're you in this time?"

Brady. Chicago cop. Friend of mine from my bureau days. I'd called him earlier this afternoon but he'd been busy.

"Brenner, Iowa."

"Wow. They got indoor plumbing?"

"Next year."

"Well, we all have to have our dreams."

"How you been?"

"Other than a teenage son who may be doing drugs, fine."

"Damn. You really think so?"

"His mother says the signs're all there. I wouldn't know. I rarely see him. I was a really shitty father to him when he was growing up—we had joint custody but I rarely took him on weekends—and now he's paying me back. Won't even return my phone calls most of the time. So I'm working on spending a lot of time with the younger kids."

"I'm sorry."

"Hell, even the commander's kid got into the drugs last year. Been in and out of two substance abuse programs already."

"It's everywhere."

"Kill 'em all, anybody who deals that shit."

"We're trying that with mandatory sentencing, Tom. It doesn't seem to be the solution. Maybe it's time we legalize it."

He sighed. "Who the fuck knows?" He was a big man easily given to depression. We needed to change the subject.

"You run a license number for me?"

"Sure," he said.

I gave him the number. It belonged to the green Ford that I'd seen earlier at the lawyer's and again in the parking lot.

"Be tomorrow before I can get to it."

"No problem. I'll send you twenty-five dollars. I appreciate it."

"Aw, hell. Forget the money. Just buy me a spaghetti dinner at Mario's next time you're in the city. We can swap cop stories."

I smiled. He loved cop stories. Not the violent ones so much. The odd ones. The four-year-old kid wearing his bathrobe like a cape and wanting to jump off a three-story roof. The wife who caught her police captain husband whacking off while wearing a pair of her panties. The nun who packed heat. The powerful mobster who took painting lessons in night school, complete with his bodyguard standing right next to him. They were Chicago stories and if they were slightly exaggerated, so what? Why couldn't cops take a little artistic license, too?

"Well, I'd better get ready."

"Heavy date?" he said.

"Yeah. Bowling."

"Nude bowling?"

"Yeah. Right. Nude bowling."

"Hey, you gotta do something out there to liven things up."

"Yeah, and nude bowling sounds just like it."

"You see this new gal the detectives got for a secretary, you'd *want* to see her bowl nude, believe me."

"Spectacular, huh?"

"Spectacular? And you should see them. What a rack."

"You sure they're real?"

"Oh, they're real all right. I got an eye for that. They hang a certain way when they're real." Then, "You know, women with the real thing should maybe start carrying papers."

"Papers?"

"Yeah. You know. Like pedigreed dogs. So you could know for sure they were real."

"I think we should let the United Nations work on that one, Brady."

"Yeah, like the UN can ever solve anything."

On that note, we hung up.

I WENT TO get some ice and a Diet Pepsi. On my way back, I made the mistake of passing by the motel door belonging to Laura West.

She was shrieking at Noah Chandler. "Why would I want to marry some washed-up TV actor? Now get out and leave me alone!" Then, "Let me go or I'll start screaming!"

I paused. I might have to go in there.

"You ever grab me like that again, you bastard, and I'll report you to the police!"

"You bitch! I've done everything I could for you and look what I get out of it!"

Something smashed to the floor.

"Oh, great," she said. "Now you start breaking everything?"

"You'll be sorry you treated me like this, Laura. You damned well will."

I wasn't the only one being treated to this soap opera. Half the motel could hear it.

The door started to open.

I scooted down to my room.

He slammed the door so hard behind him, the entire motel wall shook.

"Fucking bitch," he said, loud enough for me to hear. Then he stalked off to his own room.

I TOOK A quick shower and shave. Dry and naked, I walked out of the bathroom and over to the accordion-fold closet. I opened the door and looked at the two shirts and two pairs of trousers and sport jacket I'd brought. Then I saw him. Or rather, I smelled him before I saw him.

The closet was deep and dark enough to do a pretty good job of hiding him. He looked even bigger than he had in his car. The funny thing was, he still had his aviator shades on. The killer had stabbed him several times in the chest and then cut his throat. For good luck, maybe. He'd filled his pants, which was what I'd smelled. I went through his pockets carefully and found a small key in his shirt pocket. It looked like it belonged to a locker, and lockers were usually found at bus stations.

I went over to the phone. Male voice. "Yes?"

"Would you connect me with the police station please?"

"Sure. Everything all right?"

"Everything's fine. I just need to contact the chief."

"Oh."

A minute lapsed. A voice identified the police station. "My name's Robert Payne. Susan Charles is expecting to see me in about twenty minutes. I wondered if you could give me her home number."

"I can't give out the number," the dispatcher said. "But I can call her at home and have her call you back."

"That'd be fine."

"She had some trouble last year. Somebody making obscene calls to her. Took six months to find the guy. So she's gone unlisted since then."

"Don't blame her." I gave him the phone number of the motel and my room number.

The phone rang a few minutes later. "Chickened out, huh?"

"There's a dead man in my room."

"God," she said, "I'm sorry. You know who he is?"

"No."

"Or how he got there?"

"No."

"Or who might have killed him?"

"No."

"You're just the kind of witness cops dream of."

"I don't know the drill out here, Susan. But we'll need the whole nine yards."

"The SBI, too?" Meaning the State Bureau of Investigation, which could get here from Cedar Rapids quickly, and which would have a van or two loaded with all the appropriate high tech crime tools.

"Absolutely."

"So much for bowling."

"I guess so."

"You didn't by any chance kill him yourself, did you?"

"No."

"Good," she said. Then, "See you in a few minutes."

I dressed quickly.

ONE

THEY CAME IN groups. First the cops. Then the motel staff. Then the motel guests. Then the teenagers. Then the adults.

I've never resented crime scene crowds the way some law enforcement people do. A natural reaction, to be drawn to the scene of death. As the Irish say, when you go to a funeral you're preparing yourself for your own demise, too. Rehearsal, if you will.

This crowd was well behaved. Nobody tried to push through the demarcation lines of yellow tape. Nobody bugged the two deputies or the ambulance attendants or the whiskery little man who turned out to be the coroner. They just stood and watched and talked among themselves on the pleasant autumn night, the rumble and roar of semis on the nearby interstate being the loudest sound. I kept looking for Tandy and Laura, or even Noah Chandler, but they were nowhere around.

I was the guest of honor.

Susan Charles, in crisp white blouse and jeans, led me to an empty motel room, sat me down in a chair, had one of the deputies get us both Diet Pepsis, and proceeded to question me. She wrote things down in a small black notebook.

"So you don't know who he is?"

"Right. And you don't either?"

"Whoever killed him took his wallet. No ID whatsoever."

"Damn."

"And you have no idea how he got in your room?"

"Right."

"And you never saw him before?"

"Wrong."

"You saw him before?"

"Once."

A knock. Our Diet Pepsis. It tasted ridiculously good.

I said, "This afternoon." I told her the circumstances. "Tell your people to start looking at the green Ford with Illinois plates in the parking lot. I noticed it when I pulled in earlier."

"You think he was following you?"

"Possibly."

"Why?"

"Why would he follow me, you mean?"

"Right."

"No idea."

"You have any idea where your friends are?"

"If you mean the West sisters, I was kind of looking around for them myself."

"Or Noah Chandler."

"He's probably with them. But I have no idea where."

"You came out here because of them. If the man in your room was following you, it probably had to do with them."

"That's sort of what I was thinking."

"So he has something to do with the Rick Hennessy case."

"Maybe," I said. "A celebrity like Tandy, there could be a lot of people after her for a lot of different reasons."

"You're probably right. We don't get many celebrities out here."

"Consider yourself lucky."

She sat on the edge of the double bed across from me. She

looked beautiful and sweet in the light from the lamp. The soft light dulled the redness of her scar and made it less noticeable.

The phone rang. She picked it up, said hello, listened. Then held the phone out to me. "For you."

"Me?" I stood up to take the call.

She nodded. "The Chicago Police Department."

Brady. "What's going on? A cop answered your room phone."

"I'll explain later." I smiled at Susan. She didn't smile back.

"Turns out I had to check a license number myself. Some bastard sideswiped my daughter in a supermarket parking lot. Broad daylight. Guy's drunk out of his mind. Luckily, Cindy got his license number. So I checked out your guy while I was at it."

"And?"

"Private investigator name of DeWayne Kibbe."

"How was his record?"

"Was?"

"He's why a cop answered my room phone."

"He's dead?"

"Unless he's awful good at faking, he is."

"You have all the fun, Robert. His record was clean."

"He part of an agency?"

"Freelancer. But most of those boys hire out to the big agencies all the time. The agencies like the setup because they don't have to pay any bennies."

"You got a phone number for the guy?"

He dragged out his yellow pages. Gave me the phone number. "You have an address?"

"You don't want much, do you, Robert?"

"His address'll tell me something about how well his business was doing."

"You should be a detective. It's a lot of fun. We've got a secret handshake and everything."

He gave me the address. It wasn't exactly what you'd call tony.

"How about one more favor?"

"I won't mow your lawn."

"See if he's listed in the residences."

"You should be mowing *my* lawn." There was a pause while he looked it up. "Sorry this is taking so long."

Susan Charles said, "He was a private investigator?"

"Right."

"Here you go, Robert." He gave me the address and phone number. "I've got to haul ass out of here. I've got Cub Scouts with my youngest kid tonight."

After hanging up, I said, "He was a long way from Chicago."

"He certainly was."

This time, I didn't sit down. "I didn't kill him."

"You probably didn't."

"There's a ringing endorsement."

"I can't rule it out."

"No, I suppose you can't."

She stood up. "I'd better get back to your room and see what's going on. The SBI boys will be wondering where I am. They like to write nasty things about local police chiefs whenever possible."

"Sounds like a love affair."

"They're helpful but arrogant."

"That's what city cops used to say about the bureau."

She smiled. "And it was probably true."

"It probably was."

She walked to the window. Peeked out between the curtains. "It's starting to look like the county fair out there." She turned back to me. "This is the second homicide since Rick Hennessy killed Sandy. Before that, we didn't have a homicide for six years."

"I suppose you'll want me to stick around for a day or two?"

She seemed surprised. "I thought you were working with your good friends the witches."

Her tone irritated me. "If you mean Tandy, she's a very serious person. She actually has psychic gifts. I can't explain them and she can't either. But I've seen them work so I believe in them."

"If I didn't know better, I'd say you had a crush on her."

I thought of how infatuated I'd been with Susan this afternoon. There was a divide between us now, and it seemed to widen by the minute.

"No crush," I said. "I just wanted to keep the facts straight."

"I hope you'll defend me like that sometime. I like that kind of loyalty, Robert. I really do." Then, "Sorry if I was nasty."

"It's all right."

"And I'm sorry we didn't get to go bowling."

"Me, too." I liked her again. Just like that. She looked oddly lonely just then, and I wanted to put my hand on her shoulder.

She walked over to the door and looked out. "They're out there."

"Who?"

"Tandy and her sister and the big hunk."

"Chandler?"

She looked back at me. "I remember his cop show on the tube. It was terrible and so was he. There's something about him I don't trust."

"Me, either."

Then she was gone.

I went outside. Scent of burning leaves and diesel fuel from passing trucks. An orange half moon and ranks of cars in the motel lot. Giggles and gawking from the little kids; somber adult eyes peering out from beneath the bills of John Deere caps, men and women alike. Teenage boys found this a fine brave time to put protective and possessive arms around the shoulders of their girls, keeping them safe from the savage randomness of death, while being every bit as dry-mouthed and shaken and baffled as the girls themselves.

Tandy and Laura and Chandler stood off to the right, leaning against the front of a van, watching it all.

I walked over to them. The crowd was six or seven yards to my left. Cars kept pulling into the lot, radios blasting. Rap music sounded strange out here in the boonies, especially on the radios of white farm boys. They wore green John Deere caps just like their fathers, except they wore them backwards in the style of city kids.

"So much for the myth of the small town," Chandler said. He sounded drunk. His words weren't quite enunciated. "I thought it was supposed to be safe out here."

"They said a man was murdered," Laura said.

"Yeah. And they found him in my room."

"What?" Tandy said.

"I was the one who found him. He was pushed back in the closet. I didn't even see him at first."

"Who was it?" said Laura.

"A Chicago PI named Kibbe."

"A private detective?" Tandy said.

Laura said, "And he was from Chicago. I wonder what that's all about?"

"What's the big deal about Chicago?" Tandy said.

"*We're* from Chicago," Chandler said.

"I still don't get it."

"Think about it," Laura said. "The coincidence. What's the likelihood of a Chicago private investigator being here while *we're* here?"

"You mean he's here because of us?" Tandy said.

"*Was* here," Chandler said, not sounding as drunk as he had at first.

Tandy looked at me and said, "Do you think he was here because of us, Robert?"

"Too soon to tell. We need to know a lot more."

"I think it's damned strange," Laura said.

"Me, too," Chandler agreed.

"He could have been here because of me," I said.

"Why you?" Chandler said. He sounded almost disappointed that he might have to give up the spotlight. Kibbe's presence here would be ever so much more interesting if it had to do with *Chandler.*

I told them about my path crossing with Kibbe's today.

"But why would he be following *you?*" Tandy said.

"I have no idea."

"Is there any way we can check on this guy?" Chandler said.

"I have his home phone number. Hopefully, he had a wife and she'll be able to help me. But I need to wait till she's been officially notified by the authorities. That'll be an hour or so yet." I paused. "He could have been following the girl, too."

"What girl?" Chandler said.

"Emily Cunningham. I had the feeling he ran across me by accident when he pulled up at the lawyer's office. I think he might have been following the girl."

"Maybe he was a rapist," Chandler said. "We did this plot on the show once about this small-town guy who went to the city to commit his rapes. Why not the other way around?"

"Wouldn't it be a lot riskier in a small town?" Tandy said. "Easier to get caught?"

"I need to pee," Laura said.

"As a matter of fact," Noah Chandler said, "so do I."

"You think we can get into our rooms?" Tandy said.

The cops had cut off a wide area with yellow crime-scene tape. The area included the rooms of the sisters and Chandler.

"I'm sure they'll let you in," I said.

"They'd better," Laura said. "Or I'm going to tinkle behind that car over there."

"She'd actually do that, too," Tandy said.

"See you later," Noah Chandler said. Then he paused and said, "You should find out if he had a rifle with him. He may have been the one who shot at you folks this morning."

"The first thing I'll check," I said, pointing down to the shoes that had left the clear impressions in the woods this morning, "are his shoes."

I DRIFTED OVER to the crowd. The ranks had increased with the arrival of media from Cedar Rapids. There were two trucks with satellite dishes on them and at least two station wagons with reporters.

"Mr. Payne?"

She was a tall, elegant black woman in a starched pink blouse that looked even pinker against her dark skin. Short hair that fit like a helmet. Her jeans were loose and sloppy, the style of late. She had the graceful, enigmatic features of ancient African womanhood I'd seen on a TV show about African art down the centuries, a kind of stoical, maternal eroticism.

She gave me a long, slender hand, dry and strong to the touch. "I'm Iris Rutledge. Emily Cunningham said you were looking for me this afternoon."

"Oh, right. I wanted to talk to you about Rick Hennessy."

She laughed softly. "You and everybody else."

"I'd invite you into my room but the cops have it closed off."

"Well, if you're up for an adventure," she said, "I can give you a ride down to Wendy's, which is about two blocks away."

SHE HAD AN old-fashioned ten-speed Schwinn. It had a light and a horn and a big red alien-eye reflector on the back of the seat. I'd had a bike just like it in college.

I hadn't been on a bike in a long time. I'd forgotten how bumpy the ride is. But it was enjoyable. A few dozen childhood memories came back, the scents, sights, and sounds available only to bike riders. I sat on the handlebars. She didn't seem to have much trouble steering with me aboard.

Wendy's was empty. Everybody was up at the crime scene. We had coffee and tuna pitas.

"It's a good thing I have the right kind of metabolism," she said.

"This isn't too bad, the tuna. Not much fat or calories."

"No, but when I get home tonight and turn on Letterman, I'll have popcorn and part of a candy bar or something like that."

"You look good to me."

"Thanks. It's pure luck, believe me." Then, "He's innocent." This around a delicate bite of her pita.

"You and Dr. Williams."

"Aaron's a good man."

"Seems to be."

"And he knows what he's doing. You don't get to run a hospital like his without having the right credentials. When he says that the drugs Rick was doing induced a psychotic state, I believe him. I just hope I can convince the jury of that."

"A psychotic state in which he couldn't tell reality from fantasy, right?"

"Exactly. He truly believes that he killed Sandy. But he didn't."

"How do you know?"

Another delicate bite. The face, even in the light of Wendy's, more and more exotically commanding. "You have much faith in hypnotism?"

"Depends on who's doing it."

"Aaron has worked with Rick under deep-hypnosis conditions several times. He's also given him whatever the latest spin on Pentothal is. Rick didn't do it."

"Maybe he's repressed it to the point that he's convinced himself that he didn't do it."

"Pentothal is pretty potent stuff."

"So he didn't do it?"

"He didn't do it."

"Then who did?"

"I've got suspicions, nothing else."

"Is that why Emily Cunningham wanted to see you this afternoon?" She looked irritated that I'd know something like that. "She asked me to give you a message. Said she was willing to talk to you now. About Sandy."

"She actually said that?"

"Yup"

She laughed. "I'll have to tell her about discretion." Then, "I think Sandy's father might have murdered her."

"Her father?"

"He's an amateur photographer. He started taking photos of Sandy when she was very little. Apparently, the wife was upset but wouldn't or couldn't—or *thought* she couldn't—do anything about it. He kept on taking the photos until Sandy herself threatened to turn him in to the authorities."

"How'd you find this out?"

"Sandy. I went to her high school to speak on Law Day and she came up afterwards and asked me if she could come to my office and talk to me. Three days later, she was dead."

"You ever talk to the father?"

"I drove out there once—they live on an acreage—but he wouldn't let me in. He was pretty nasty. He gave me a little speech about how he wouldn't trust a white lawyer, let alone a black one. Except he said nigger." She smiled. "Unfortunately, that isn't proof he's a killer. The terrible thing is, a lot of people are very nice folks as long as you don't get them on the subject of race."

"Any idea what he did with the pictures he took of her?"

She shrugged. "Not really. But I'd like to get in that house sometime when nobody was home."

"Why?"

"See if he's got any other child porn around the house."

"You think he ever molested her?"

"Not from what she said. He was satisfied with just the pictures, I guess. And then she got too old for him. She said he stopped taking photos of her when she turned eleven. Probably about the time she started having noticeable breasts."

"You never went to the county attorney?"

"No point. Sandy said that if I did, she'd just deny everything. Her mother died of heart disease five years ago. He's all she has—had."

We had three cups of coffee. She said, "How'd you get involved with all this?"

I told her about Tandy and the show.

"Oh." Her disappointment was easy to see.

"She's not a fake." I sketched out the two cases I'd worked on.

"I just don't believe in that kind of thing, I guess."

"Then how did she locate the bodies?"

"That's the funny thing. I know stuff like that happens. But I can't believe it. My husband buys it, though. He's a psychologist. He thinks that someday we'll all be in touch with our full mental powers." Then, "He's white, by the way."

I smiled. "Good for him."

"I just meant it's a novelty. You still don't see a lot of black women with white guys. I think that's why people here are so nice to us. If it was the other way around—if it was a black man with a white woman—I think we'd get a lot more grief."

"You're probably right."

We finished up our pitas and started on our last cups of coffee.

"So you going to see him?"

"Who?" I said.

"Sandy's dad."

"I'll try."

"If you learn anything, will you tell me about it?"

"Sure."

"He really is innocent."

"Between you and Dr. Williams, I'm beginning to believe it."

"Really?"

"Well, maybe a little bit, anyway."

A police cruiser swung into the parking lot. I could see Susan in the windshield. She looked serious, serious but beautiful. You couldn't see the scar from this distance.

She got out of the cruiser and strode inside. She came directly to our table.

She nodded to Iris Rutledge. "Hi, Iris. Don't buy anything from this guy."

"Don't worry, Susan. I already had him checked out with the Better Business Bureau. They said buyer beware."

"Everything going all right?" I said.

"I just had a few follow-up questions."

"Well, that works out fine," Iris said. "I need to get back home, anyway."

She stood up. Extended her hand. Then reached in the back of her jeans and took out a thin leather wallet. "Here's my card."

"Thanks."

"Call me."

"I will."

" 'Bye, Susan."

" 'Bye, Iris."

"You want some coffee?" I said to Susan.

"She's a sweetie."

"She sure seems to be."

"Just black'll do. I've got a long night ahead of me."

I got a refill and a cup for her. The place was starting to fill up. The novelty had worn off the crime scene. Yellow crime-scene tape is bedazzling for only so long.

When I got back, she was gone. She reappeared a few minutes later. "Pit stop."

"I could use one of those myself."

The two urinals were busy. Two teenage boys peed and talked about the murder.

"Drug deal," one of them said.

"That what the cops said?"

"No. But I'll bet your ass that's what it was."

"They said he was old. Maybe he was a Mob guy or something."

"If he was, somebody else is gonna die."

"How come?"

"They don't let you run around and kill Mob guys like that."

"Who doesn't?"

"The Mob, you dumb ass. The Mob don't let you."

"He was a mobster," I said, when I got back to my table.

"Who was?"

"The dead guy in my motel room."

"Mafia, you mean?"

I laughed and told her what I'd heard in the john.

"Oh, that'll go on for weeks. Everybody in town'll have his own theory about who did it, and why." Then, "He was a little more interesting than just your run-of-the-mill private eye."

"Oh?"

"I've got a few friends in Chicago, too. I had them run his name through the crime computer."

"Anything interesting?"

"He was arrested for letting his gun permit expire and he was arrested for drunk driving. Found guilty on both counts and both were enough to get his license lifted both times. He had to reapply to get reinstated. Technically, he was out of work for twelve months following each arrest."

"He doesn't exactly sound like a death row kind of guy."

She sipped her coffee. "It's actually cold in here. I've got goose bumps. Look."

"You're wearing short sleeves."

She held her arms out. "Feel them."

She wasn't kidding. Her slender arms were covered with coarse little bumps.

I sat there feeling my groin stir. Now I had a new item to add to my list of turn-ons. Goose bumps.

She withdrew her arms.

"You weren't kidding." I was wearing a windbreaker and a long-sleeved shirt. It was time for gallantry.

I stood up, took my jacket off, slid it around her shoulders. It covered up the small .38 she wore hooked to the side of her jeans. "That's very sweet. Thank you."

I sat down. "So tell me what you came here to tell me."

"I told you about him losing his license."

"Yeah, but you wouldn't drive over here for that."

She laughed. "I thought it was Tandy who read minds. But it's you." More coffee. "Boy, that feels good going down." Then, "The DA there was prepared twice to bring charges against him for extortion."

"Blackmail?"

"Exactly."

"And the charges were dropped?"

"At the last minute, both people asked that the matter be tabled."

"You learn why?"

"Nope. But presumably they decided it wasn't worth dragging their secrets through court."

"So now we have to figure out why he was here."

She nodded. "You don't have any ideas, I suppose?"

"No, afraid I don't."

"Your friends are from Chicago and he was from Chicago."

"Last time I looked, Chicago was only about four and a half hours right down the interstate. I drive in there at least once a month. So do a lot of people."

"True enough. But the river doesn't flow that often in the opposite direction. Not many Chicago people come here. I mean, we have some nice skyscrapers and a big new airport and a lot of Picasso statuary not too far away, but somehow we still don't get many Chicagoites out here."

" 'ans.' "

"Pardon?"

"Chicago*ans*. Not Chicago*ites*."

"Ah."

"And there's a fifty-fifty that the Wests and Kibbe being out here at the same time was a coincidence."

She made a smirk of her lovely lips. "You really believe that?"

"Pretty much."

"That would be some coincidence."

"More coffee?"

"No, thanks. I need to get back and see how things are going."

"If there's anything I can do."

"I know. You'll be glad to help. Here's your jacket back, Robert."

She stopped by a few tables before she left. In small towns, police chiefs are celebrities subject to election. They learn to work a room the way politicians do.

I finished my coffee slowly, staring out the window at the cars streaming past in the night. A kind of lonesomeness came over me then. It didn't tie to anyone or anywhere—no special person or place I missed—and it was certainly a familiar feeling so it didn't startle or scare me. It was a late-night train-whistle loneliness; a sad-barking-dog-at-midnight loneliness; a hobo loneliness that I had first found in the books of Jack London way back in grade school. I used to think this marked me as special, but the older I get I know it's something we all feel sometimes, that sense of melancholy and dislocation we can't explain but can only endure, that inexplicable ache that lets you know you really do have a soul after all, despite what the skeptics say, because the pain is spiritual and not merely mental. The closest approximations are the paintings of Edward Hopper, those lonesome faceless souls in those lonesome midnight cafés in those mysterious midwestern midnight towns of his.

I walked back to the motel.

I WAS GIVEN another room—this time on the second floor. I didn't see Tandy or Laura or Noah Chandler. I went up and tried to watch some TV. The Cedar Rapids stations used Kibbe's death as the lead. Murder, as it should be, is still a big thing out here.

Letterman came on. There was a young actress I fell in love with before the first break. She reminded me of my wife was why. A quiet elegance, and yet a certain quiet smart-ass quality, too. Playful, in a kitten-soft sort of way.

I turned the lights off, stripped out of my clothes, and crawled into bed. The semis moved through the night like dinosaurs. I wondered where they were going. I'd always wanted to drive one of those big rigs. Places with names like Cheyenne and Red Rock and Yuma had sounded exciting as hell when I was in high school. I'd had a stepfather I didn't like much, and a girlfriend who couldn't or wouldn't love me, and an imagination that told me a town called Yuma was exactly what a kid like me was looking for.

I slept. Not a good sleep. A restless, tossing one. Not nightmares. But those lonesome dreams where a girl is rejecting you, or somebody you considered a friend has suddenly turned on you. An extension of that inexplicable lonesomeness, I suppose. The smart answer was probably that when my father died my twelfth year, I felt betrayed and abandoned and never quite recovered from that feeling. He'd been my best friend. But I'm too smart to believe in smart answers. The dreams of desertion were probably inspired by events far more complicated than my father dying. Anyway, I get tired of the modern tendency to blame everything on parents.

The knock woke me quickly. I sat up and reached for the gun I kept on the nightstand. Bureau training is hard to break. I grabbed my pants and tugged them on, managing to stub my toe against the bureau as I did so. I had to swear real, real quietly.

I tiptoed to the curtain and peeked out.

Tandy stood there hugging a bottle of wine. She looked cute and sweet and sexy and scared. The night was mauve and alive with the mercury vapor lights of the parking lot and the blowing dust and cosmic seeds the prairie winds were whipping across the open spaces. I couldn't smell the impending rain in here; but I could feel it.

I went and opened the door.

TWO

"You forget about me, Robert?"

"No. Huh-uh." Yawn.

"God, you did, didn't you? You were asleep, weren't you? I told you I'd sleep in your bed tonight and you *forgot* me?"

I'd forgotten how personally Tandy took everything. I plucked the bottle of wine from her hand. "I really appreciate you delivering the wine, though, young lady."

"Very funny. God."

"I'm sorry. I was tired. I fell asleep."

"It's barely eleven." And pushed past me, inside.

She pulled out the chair and sat down. "Your room doesn't smell as bad as ours."

"I'm sure the management will be glad to hear that."

"It's a good thing you're cute because otherwise I'd be pissed right now. I really would."

"I fell asleep. I'm sorry."

"You have so many women throwing themselves at you that you forget when somebody tries to be tender and affectionate toward you?"

"How about some wine?"

"You could at least say you were sorry."

"I did. Twice."

"Well, then, you could at least say it again."

"I'm sorry I'm sorry I'm sorry I'm sorry. How's that?"

"I even took a shower and put on special panties."

"I'm sorry I'm sorry I'm sorry."

WHICH IS HOW it went for the first fifteen minutes, the banter and her hurt feelings.

By the time I went into the bathroom and came back with two plastic glasses, she'd calmed down. I poured us vino and we drank, sitting up in bed, MTV on real low on the tube.

"Noah was pretty drunk tonight."

"Good for him."

"He got into it with Laura again."

"About getting married?"

"Yeah. In a weird way, I feel sorry for him. He's a jerk but he loves her. He really does."

"I kind of got that impression."

"I wish you loved *me* that much."

"Well, I wish *you* loved *me* that much, too."

"Really?"

"Well, sort of."

"You dipshit."

"Thank you."

"Here I was all ready for some romantic talk. You know, lovey-dovey. It's still hard for me to sleep around. Without *some* sort of lovey-dovey, anyway. But you've probably slept around a lot more than I have and you're used to it."

"I haven't slept around that much."

"You faithful to your wife?"

"Absolutely."

"But you've been sleeping around since she died?"

"Not much. I've had two long relationships."

"That's all?"

"God," I said, "you working on a new Kinsey report? And while we're at it, how many have *you* slept with?"

"I keep strict count."

"How many?"

"Should I count the one who was so drunk he fell asleep inside me?"

"That must've been a nice experience."

"And he was as big as a bear. It took me half an hour to get him off me."

"Don't count him. So how many?"

"Eight."

"Well, that's not bad."

"That's home runs only—"

"Ah. So just getting to first, second, or third—"

"That stuff's just sort of high school, don't you think? I mean, I don't think I should have to count that."

"Yeah, I guess you're right."

She laughed. And put her head on my shoulder. "Some kinds of wines make me really horny."

"Is this one of them?"

"I'll have to see."

THAT'S HOW IT went from roughly eleven-fifteen to eleven forty-five. I'd forgotten how easily she got drunk. Two modest glasses and she was well on her way.

"You want to see my underwear?"

"I thought you'd never ask," I said.

"I'm serious."

"Sure, I want to see your underwear. You want to see mine?"

"But that doesn't mean we'll, you know, *do* anything."

"Understood."

But it would be, I figured, a pretty good start.

So she stood up and dropped trou and showed me her under-wear. They were microbikinis and almost totally transparent. The shape of everything could be seen. They had happy faces all over them. Except these happy faces were red and had tiny devil horns sticking out of them.

"Like 'em?"

"They're great."

"It was kind of embarrassing buying them. The clerk looked kind of superior when I handed them to her."

"She should've been embarrassed for selling them, then."

"That's what I thought." She came over and got back on the bed. "I'm scared to try it."

"Try what?"

"Sex."

"How come?"

"Because I haven't enjoyed it for a long time. Not since I stopped getting those images in my head. I'm not too smart, Robert, as you know. I mean, Laura got the brains. Seeing those images—helping you and the police—that's the only thing I could ever do that mattered. And now I can't even do that anymore. And it's spoiled my whole life for me. Every part of my life. It's even screwed up my periods. Laura says that's impossible. But I know better."

"We'll just sleep if you want to."

"Won't you get horny?"

"Sure."

"Then what?"

"I'll resent you and then I'll probably make a vague pass at talk-ing you into it and then I'll go to sleep."

"I could give you a hand job."

"Well, I could give *you* a hand job, too."

She laughed. "I guess I never thought of it that way. I guess you could, couldn't you?"

So we lay next to each other in the bed. It was still warm. We pushed the blanket to the end of the bed. "You mind if I turn that song up?"

"Huh-uh."

I actually hated the song. An unending string of love-song clichés sung by this sneering white kid with too much hair and too little talent. I seem to remember my parents saying something like that about Alice Cooper. But this kid didn't have mascara and a snake.

We lay like that for twenty minutes. Both of us in our underwear. Not quite touching.

"You have an erection?"

"Yeah."

"I'm sorry."

"You have an erection?"

A giggle. "No, but I am getting kind of horny, actually. Lying like this is kind of sexy. It's like when I was a freshman in college. I was still a virgin. There was this kid I really liked. But the AIDS scare was everywhere. So night after night we'd just lie on my dorm bed."

"Whatever happened to him?"

"I found out later he was gay. Or at least bi."

"See what you did to him? All those nights of bottled-up temptation."

Then her hand was on me. "Yeah, you've got an erection, all right." Then, "I guess we may as well do it, huh?"

"What changed your mind?"

"Hormones."

And she wasn't kidding.

WE HAD TWO goes at it, one quick and frantic, the other, later, slow and tender. Afterward, she said, "I almost came."

"We can keep working on it."

"No, that's OK. I haven't even come close in a long time. That must mean I'm better. You know, sort of working my way back to it."

"You want to tell each other how good we were?"

"You were fabulous."

"You were fabulous, too."

Then she rolled over and clung to me. "We shouldn't make fun."

"I'm sorry."

"I really did enjoy it."

"So did I."

"And it really was good sex."

"Yes, it was."

"And I hope we do it again sometime."

"I hope so, too."

It felt ridiculously good holding her, just as good as the sex. I pulled the covers up on us and we snuggled. She was my wife and she was the last serious woman, too, the crazy and sweet woman who'd recently dumped me for her ex-husband, and she was this night's woman, Tandy West herself, and she was all potential women, one of whom I hoped would help give some shape and meaning to my future.

And she was a snoring woman.

She snored quietly, the way a kitten does. She didn't let go of me. She clung like a kid and I clung right back. I kept stroking her and putting little kisses on her head and forehead and shoulder and it was fucking wonderful.

Eventually, I slept, too.

WAKING UP SO abruptly, I immediately thought of danger. But there was no danger, there was just prairie wind slanting hard prairie autumn rain against the window and the door and the roof, and the kitten mewls and tiny nervous fits of Tandy's nervous limbs, arms and legs thrashing, jerking in response to something terrible that was stalking the corridors of her mind.

I had to pee and pee I did, closing the door against the steady noise of the yellow stream.

When I got back to the bed, the mewl had become nightmare cries. I rushed to her, held her, rocked her the way I would a child.

Then she was awake. Wide startled eyes. No recognition at first. Who was I? Bad guy or good guy? Then recognition, followed by her pushing away from me, heels of hands hurting my chest as they pushed. Then she was up, naked, pacing, screaming, "Don't say anything! Don't say anything!"

I had no idea what was going on. It was scary. All I could think of was a seizure of some kind. Or madness.

She just kept pacing, naked, arms flailing wildly as if she was being attacked, and then she'd abruptly put her hands to her head as if a headache were splitting her skull in half. And then she was sobbing. Fell to the floor. And sobbed. And sobbed.

I was scared to approach her. Scared not to approach her.

Two naked people in a shabby little prairie hotel room, her wailing louder than the wind, and me without a clue of what to do.

I approached her. Knelt next to her. She came to me instantly. Enveloped me, warm tear-wet face against mine, soft tender breasts to my chest, arms desperately tight around me.

"An image came to me, Robert. An image."

There was joy and fear in her voice, maybe even a real edge of lunacy.

"What kind of image?"

"An old railroad trestle bridge."

"Any idea where?"

"No."

"Any idea of what it means?"

"There's a body there. Buried. Long ago."

"Are you all right?"

"I don't know." Then, "Can we get in bed and you just hold me?"

"Sure."

So we got in bed and I just held her.

"What if I'm wrong?"

"We'll look for the bridge."

"But what if I'm wrong?"

"Then you're wrong. It's not a big deal."

"I don't want people laughing at me."

"This is how it happened before, right? In your sleep?"

"Yes."

"And they were just images. Disconnected."

"Yes."

"Then why wouldn't this one be right?"

"Because it's been so long. I thought I'd—lost my power. You remember our conversation."

"Yes."

"Cheated on it. Sold out. And it went away."

"We won't tell anybody about it. We'll work on it together."

Then, after a time, "You think we could ever fall in love, Robert?"

"Maybe."

"You're as lonely as I am."

She needed me to say something strong. Even if it was only momentarily truthful.

"Yeah. I probably am."

"Then it could happen for us?"

"Sure. It could."

"God, things can get so fucked up, can't they?"

I thought back to the restaurant tonight, and that attack of the lonesomes. This was nice. Maybe it wasn't love—hell, it *wasn't* love—but it was two people who liked and trusted each other having a little fleshly fun and connecting, however briefly, however superficially, with each other's soul. That was a lot better than the lonesomes any day, and not fucked up at all.

WHEN I WOKE up in the morning, we were totally entangled, so complicatedly, in fact, that my first act of the day was to smile. God only knew how we'd ever gotten pretzeled-up this way.

She said, "Oh, man, my breath is so bad. I eat so much garlic these days."

"Mine isn't any better."

"I didn't fart last night, did I?"

"Not that I noticed."

"I eat a lot of beans, too. I'm a vegetarian. I take stuff that's supposed to help vegetarians with flatulence but it doesn't always work."

"You're just fine, relax."

"I'm sure I look like shit, too."

"Bad breath. Farts. Looks like shit. You're just the girl I've been waiting for."

She laughed and jumped out of bed. "I'm doing it again, aren't I? Running myself down?"

"Yeah. You are."

She said, "I get the bathroom first."

THREE

BACK IN THE first days of the prairie, the government had trouble rounding up soldiers to fight the various Indian wars. This was particularly true of the Black Hawk Wars in 1832 and the Civil War.

That's when they got a very bright idea. In addition to wages, the soldiers would be given land. In Iowa. All the way up to 120 acres. This served two purposes. The army got soldiers (or cannon fodder, depending on your point of view), and Iowa, not exactly teeming with new arrivals, got new voters and taxpayers.

The land back then was about $1.25 an acre. A hundred dollars could buy you a very nice farm. You'd stack rocks as a fence meant to define the dimensions of your land, and then you'd build yourself a soddy—a house made of sod—and then you'd move in. If disease, flood, or prairie fire didn't get you, you could have yourself a nice, ass-busting life for you and your family.

On my drive up to see Dr. Williams, I looked at prairie land that had undoubtedly been the site of soddies. Nearby creek. Plenty of timberland for firewood. Rich black earth for planting. Of course, the Big Mac billboard probably hadn't been there in the distance.

Nor the small airport to the east, a small plane just now landing in some turbulent air. Nor the TV tower beaming forth mediocrity twenty-four hours a day. There was always something to spoil the idyllic vision I had of pioneer days. I wanted to crawl into one of those pulpy old book covers of the brave musket-carrying mountain man and his flaxen-haired immigrant woman surveying a beautiful valley just at gorgeous sunset.

The hospital was located on a hill overlooking a valley, all right. But the valley was filled with two strip malls, a high school football stadium, and a truck depot. To make things even worse, I didn't have a flaxen-haired immigrant woman with me.

If you faced away from the valley, you had a very different sense of the area. A much nicer one. Oaks and hardwoods surrounded three large brick buildings. A swimming pool, tennis courts, and a picnic area lay to the west of the buildings. Nurses in crisp white uniforms watched over a variety of adults engaged in various quiet endeavors such as checkers, chess, badminton, and volleyball. Oddly, nobody was in the pool—the temperature was in the seventies—nor was anybody playing tennis.

A sign, black letters on white, read ADMINISTRATION. I parked in the visitors' area and went inside. It had that smell, that feel, that aura of all bureaucracies. Busy busy. Even people with the brightest souls would be blanched to an administrative gray after a few months of working here. Each little office group would have its gossip, its victim, its slacker. Each group head would have his or her secret, a drinking problem, an adultery problem, a money problem, a son or daughter with a law problem. Some of the nurses would be sleeping with some of the doctors. And some of the lesser staffers would be sleeping with some of the other lesser staffers, hoping someday to be sleeping with some of the doctors, thereby enjoying a new status. Every year at the Christmas party somebody would jump up on a desk and announce that this wonderful group of folks was the best fucking wonderful group of folks in the wide world—pardon my French, ladies—and he was goddamned proud to be a goddamned part of it. The more emotional would cry; the more sensible would want to fill a barf bag. But Christmas was three months away, this was still Indian summer, and a workday, and so busy busy was what was going on here, busy busy the computer keyboards, the ranks of phone consoles, the clack of high heels on polished floors.

While I was waiting for Dr. Williams—I'd called half an hour ahead for an appointment and was told I could have fifteen minutes—I read up on psychology magazines. The current obsession in psychiatric circles seemed to be the growing reaction to "recovered memory" cases. I hadn't paid all that much attention to the subject until a California jury put a man in prison for a murder of twenty-five years earlier, a murder his eight-year-old daughter claimed to suddenly remember eleven months before the trial started. Her father had, she said, murdered her best little friend. There was no physical evidence; there were no witnesses. Simply the woman saying that yes, after several visits to a "recovered memory" psychologist, she suddenly recalled what her father had done. The verdict scared the hell out of me. The judiciary has enough trouble ascertaining the truth—thanks to things like new DNA testing that helped free eleven men on Illinois's death row, proving that the system is hardly infallible—we certainly don't need "recovered memory" cases making things even worse. Under the guidance of a clever shrink, you can "remember" virtually anything he wants you to.

Dr. Williams looked much as he had yesterday, a short, stout man who vaguely resembled Albert Einstein. Good, firm grip. Nice, quick smile. Then he led me inside.

The walls were a testimonial to his brains, pluck, and talent. Scroll after scroll, plaque after plaque, degree after degree—all arranged imposingly on the same wall—attested to his magnificence. The furnishings were cherry wood and in such good taste you almost wanted something vulgar—a screaming orange canvas chair—to liven them up.

"I'm sorry I'm in such a hurry today. We have six new patients arriving and that's always our busiest time."

Busy busy.

"That's fine. All I really want to know is if you saw Sandy when she was alive."

"Saw her in what sense?"

"I'm sorry. I mean 'saw' her in a professional sense."

He nodded. "Yes. Twice. I asked her to come once with Rick and once without him."

"Did she open up to you?"

He shrugged. "To some degree, I suppose. She was very nervous. Her father was angry that she was here. She said he hated the whole notion of her being here."

"I'm told that her father used to take nude photos of her."

He half smiled. "You really are a cop, aren't you, Mr. Payne?"

"I used to be. Now I'm just sort of a glorified field investigator."

He leaned forward. He had stubby arms. He pulled his chair flush against his desk. "You know I can't discuss what my clients told me."

"The shrinks I knew at Quantico did. In fact, they never shut up. They were always swapping stories about who had the weirder patients."

He frowned. "Very unprofessional. I know it goes on. But I certainly don't approve. I'm from the old school—when it meant something to be a so-called shrink. Now anybody who can finish a few night school courses can go into the counseling business."

"Did you ever talk with the father?"

"No. He called once and was vaguely threatening, said he'd sue me if I saw his daughter again. I have to admit, he did seem like a man who had a secret."

"Afraid his daughter might tell you something about him, you mean?'

"Exactly. I understand that there are people who don't believe in psychiatry, and people whose religion forbids them from seeing a shrink, and people who think it doesn't work and costs too much money—all the familiar objections. But he was too strident. So the only thing I could think of was that he had something to hide." He smiled. "Shrinks have very suspicious natures, I'm afraid."

"I'm going to go see him."

"I'm told he's a very violent man. I know he was arrested a while back for public intoxication. And he managed to knock out two policemen before they could restrain him."

"Great. Just what I want. A fistfight."

The intercom buzzed. "Mr. Alexander has arrived," his secretary said. "You asked me to tell you."

"Thank you, Beverly." He tapped his Seiko. "I guess I'm even busier than I thought. We didn't expect Alexander until late this afternoon."

He stood up and came around his desk and shook my hand. "Rick's parents aren't wealthy by any means. In fact, they're almost poor. I have a lot of faith in Iris Rutledge, but she can't afford to hire any outside help. I'm giving her all the money I can, but my resources are limited, too. Some people are very skeptical of Tandy West trying to build a show around this. But I guess I should be grateful she is because we're getting a very good investigator in the bargain—and we don't have to pay for him." Then, a little dramatically, he said, "My only concern is Rick. He's innocent."

Rick, and your reputation, I thought. *It won't look real good if the kid you "saved" is convicted of murder.* Like the time Norman Mailer, among others, helped free a convicted murderer who then killed some poor young man who was working as a waiter. There were good reasons ordinary people distrusted the psychiatric profession.

I walked out with him.

In the reception area, he said, "Excuse me, Mr. Payne. I need to hurry down the hall."

"That's fine."

I was just leaving the building when a voice behind me said, "Mr. Payne."

She was a pleasant-looking gray-haired woman in a blue suit and a frilly white blouse. "I just wanted to tell you something I forgot to tell the detectives." When she reached me, she said, "My name's Myrna Haines. Dr. Williams has two offices—the administrative office and his personal office. He oversees a lot of the electroshock and things like that, so he needs an office close by. Anyway, I'm the secretary for his personal office."

"I see."

"Are you headed out?"

"Yes."

"Good. I could use some fresh air."

We stood on the front steps. The day made me feel twenty and immortal.

"The man they found in your room, Mr. Kibbe?"

"Yes?"

"One afternoon I found him going through my desk. He'd been in to see Dr. Williams earlier in the day, so I recognized him, of course."

"Did he take anything?"

She nodded. "I saw him stick two envelopes and a very small paperweight and a couple of pieces of paper in a briefcase. What would he want with things like that?"

"Did you confront him?"

"Yes. He pretended not to know what I was talking about. Then he just pushed past me and left."

"You told Dr. Williams?'

"Of course. He called Chief Charles right away. She came out and talked to us and then said she'd try and find Kibbe. But she called later and said he wasn't registered at any of the motels in town."

"Did you ever figure out which envelopes and papers he took?"

"Yes. And they were nothing important at all. Just routine correspondence I'd typed up to two different HMOs. They're always trying to talk us into accepting less of a payment." She smiled bitterly. "I can remember when we thought HMOs would save the entire medical profession."

"When was this?"

"Two days ago. I know you're trying to help Rick. He can be pretty obnoxious, but I agree with Dr. Williams. I don't think he killed that girl."

"You have any suspicions about who might have?"

"Not really."

"Well, thanks for telling me about the papers and the envelope."

"And the paperweight. About the size of a poker chip, with Dr. Williams's initials on it."

"That *is* strange."

She inhaled deeply. "God, I hate to go back inside. I wish a butterfly would just carry me off."

It was a nice little Ray Bradbury image, and it stayed with me for most of the afternoon.

FOUR

NOAH CHANDLER WAS waiting for me.

I wasn't supposed to *know* he was waiting for me, of course. But as I came down the steep hill leading away from the hospital, I had a wide view of the road below. His TV private-eye profile was hard to mistake.

I turned left, toward town, pretending not to see him. He came right after me. He kept a proper distance, but on an empty county gravel road, he wasn't real difficult to spot. A couple of times he talked on his cell phone. I was naturally curious about who he was talking to, and what about.

As soon as we hit the town limits sign, he fell away, turned left into a strip mall.

I HAD AN address for Frank Caine, Sandy's father, so I drove out there. He collected cars. Or rather, parts of cars. The front lawn of the small white bungalow was strewn with transmissions, radiators, steering columns, windshields, doors, and bumpers. A sign, red letters on white, announced: FRANK T. CAINE, AUTOMOTIVE. A loud portable radio playing heavy metal blasted from a sagging white barn.

I pulled into a rutted dirt driveway covered by chickens. They paced like cartoon fathers in maternity wards. I'd read that slaughter animals know when their time comes. For no reason apparent to scientists, the blood pressure and brain waves become agitated. Somehow, they know. And these birds looked as if they knew, too, the frantic way they moved up and down the rutted drive.

Frank Caine turned out to be a tall, balding man in a white oil-stained T-shirt. The way his long arm muscles moved, he had to spend some frequent time with weights. He stood with unmistakable insolence in front of an ancient white barn where he'd apparently been working on a red Plymouth with the hood raised. He held a long greasy wrench in one hand and kept slapping it against the open palm of the other. Frank planned to be a gangsta when he grew up.

The barn-garage looked interesting, actually. Inside there would probably be yellowing newspapers going back to the forties or maybe even the thirties (Iowa farmers are savers, which is why so many antiquers ask farmers if they can look through their attics and barns and garages). There would be the odd cheap child's toy (my wife being an antiquer, I'd learned what some of that species is constantly looking for: a Captain Midnight Big Little Book about fighting the Japanese during WW II; a Davy Crockett figure from the midfifties, maybe; a Frank Sinatra album; a Monkees lunch box even; and magazines, rat-nibbled and time-faded, depicting an era when the sexiest thing in prim Mom's life was her new appliance or dressing up for hubby when he got home for dinner).

I parked and got out of my car and immediately saw the largest canine God had ever created.

Dogs have replaced guns as the preferred macho toy. I'm not talking about man's best friend, the sloppy, sweet, faithful clown of a family dog we grew up loving and will remember to the end of our days. No, I'm not talking about the killing machines that the macho boys keep telling us are necessary in such a violent society. Tell that to the two-year-old ripped and killed by such a beast, or the mailman whose leg was shredded and ultimately amputated.

They aren't dogs, they're monsters. And while it isn't their fault—and objectively I feel a real sorrow for them—I take no chances. The Roman legions used such dogs, and there are many historians of antiquity who wrote about watching the savage canines turn first on the enemy, and then on their masters. The dogs are the same today. Their owners have the dogs so over-wrought, they can't even control them. So what chance would *I* have of controlling them?

This one was a patchwork gray mutant combination of Saint Bernard and greyhound. It came trotting out of the barn with an insolence equal to that of its master. It crouched next to him. Even from here I could smell it, an animal that gorged on other animals during the night. No Puppy Chow for this one. It had been cursed with mindless, relentless fury, a miserable life for an animal that could have been a loving and valued part of a family, or a guide for a little blind girl.

Frank Caine smirked and stroked the dog's head. He was proud of his work.

The dog growled at me and the earth rumbled.

"I do believe Henry here doesn't like you," Frank Caine said.

"Gee, and I was hoping he'd go to the prom with me."

"Henry doesn't like sarcasm."

"Henry is awfully sensitive. For a dog, I mean."

"Henry's a lot more than a dog, mister." Slapping the long wrench into his palm. "Some people around here think he's some sort of supernatural being."

That, I didn't have any trouble believing.

"We got him from this priest. Not that I'm a Catholic. I'm Lutheran. Anyway, we got him from this here priest. He said he found this strange little puppy in the church one night. It was about midnight and the priest was asleep and he heard all this noise in the church. So he rushed over there and there was this here puppy. He said the puppy really spooked him. The eyes, he said, at night they kind of glow. And they still do. Give me goose bumps myself sometimes, they way they kind of have this amber light inside them. Anyway, this here puppy had destroyed the altar. Knocked everything over and smashed it. The priest said that there was a good chance that the puppy was evil. He said he didn't usually believe in stuff like that. But he just felt this dog was really dangerous."

"So he gave it to you?"

"Well, I'd heard about it, of course, how it'd knocked over everything on the altar. I just thought an animal like that sounded kinda interesting. And if he gave it to the animal shelter, they'd just put it to sleep. By then, everybody who saw the puppy was kinda spooked by it. So I took it."

The throat rumble again. Henry's back arching slightly, preparing to spring.

"He don't like you."

"Well, I'm not crazy about him, either."

"In fact, *I* don't like you, either."

"You don't even know me."

"Nope. But know who you are and why you're here. You're some kind of detective fella and you're working with that scam-artist lady from that TV show and you want to prove that that sonofabitch Rick Hennessy didn't kill my Sandy."

"A lot of people don't think he did."

"Not the chief of police. Not the county attorney. And not the jury they end up pickin', either. He sure as hell *did* kill her, mister. And he admits it himself."

"Dr. Williams says he's delusional."

"Dr. Williams." He sounded as if he wanted to spit. He went back to slapping the wrench against the palm of his hand. "I'd like to get Dr. Williams in a room with this here wrench sometime."

"What've you got against him?"

"That don't matter anymore. She's dead."

"Sandy?"

"Of course Sandy. Who the hell else would I be talkin' about?" Then, "Fucker tried to turn my own daughter against me."

The wrench slapping harder and harder now.

The photos, of course. Sandy had told Rick about the photos and Rick had told Dr. Williams and Dr. Williams had talked to Sandy about it the few times she'd come to visit.

"He's a fucking liar is what he is. I'll bet he's a fucking Jew."

"I don't think so."

"Well, then he ought to be. He'd fit right in."

Gosh, who wouldn't want this guy for their dad? Between being a bully, a child pornographer, and an anti-Semite, he'd be a delight every night around the hearth. At Home with Hermann Goering.

"I know about the photos you took of your daughter."

He didn't say anything. He just looked at me. I'm sure he was wondering if I was Jewish.

"You cocksucker."

"I'm just giving you a chance to prove *you* didn't kill her."

"Rick Hennessy killed her."

Henry and Frank were telepathically linked. The beast was picking up on his master's shift of mood. He moved slightly away from Caine, going into a crouch. And I'll be damned if there *weren't* tiny amber lights showing in the irises of the mad dark canine eyes.

"Henry's going to tear your nuts off, mister." Then he snapped his finger behind his back. It was quiet enough for me to hear.

"Then he's going to die for the privilege."

You get a lot of arguments in both directions about shoulder rigs. I've always preferred them myself, even if they are a tad more awkward than the holster on the belt.

I had my .38 out and aimed directly at Henry's face. "I'll put one right between his eyes."

"You sonofabitch." But angry as he was, he bent down and took Henry's collar and gave it an almost imperceptible tug. Cool it, Henry.

But Henry wasn't having any.

He leapt at me with perfect grace and timing. He was in midarc when I shot him. I wasn't lucky enough to get him between the eyes. I had to settle for two bullets in the throat.

Henry seemed to freeze in midair. I had a perfect slow-motion portrait of his face—silver spittle flying from his mouth, mad eyes madder than ever, teeth startlingly white, startlingly sharp. And then he flung himself to the ground. That was how it looked, anyway. A hundred and fifty pounds of dog hurling itself to the sandy back driveway. Blood started firing from his right ear. It was ugly to see and I half wished I hadn't killed him. He started choking and gasping.

The wailing, it took me a moment to realize, didn't belong to Henry but to Frank Caine.

He dropped the wrench, then dropped to his knees next to the dog. He was sobbing and wailing and rocking back and forth and touching the throat wound gingerly. And then sobbing all the more.

I wanted to feel sorry for him. I couldn't. Henry was the victim here. He hadn't asked to be raised this way.

"You fucker!" Caine screamed at me suddenly. "You fucking sonofabitch!" He was now as crazy as Henry had been. He stood up. He started walking toward me.

I kept my gun drawn. I aimed it right at his chest. "Don't be stupid, Frank. I'm going to get in my car and drive out of here."

"You fucking sonofabitch!"

"You said that already. You shouldn't have sicced him on me."

"I didn't give him a command. I didn't say jack shit to him."

"No, but you snapped your fingers, and that was the signal for him to jump me."

"You sonofabitch."

I walked backwards to my car.

He bolted towards me without warning. Ran up to my car and spit on the windshield. And then started pounding with his fists on the windshield. "You fucker!"

I got the motor going in the rental and backed away. For a few yards, he followed me back up the drive, just as Henry would have. But I gave it more gas and he soon fell away.

He turned slowly back to Henry. Then he was on his knees next to the dog, and sobbing again. I tried hard not to feel sorry for him. But I guess, despite myself, I did. He'd destroyed all hope for the dog to have a good life. But in some perverse way, Frank probably loved the big snarling mutant animal. Love is a strange thing sometimes.

☾

TANDY WAS AT the pop machine. Her blue-jeaned bottom was nicely rounded as she bent over to retrieve the Diet Pepsi can.

She tangled her head to see me. "Want one?"

"Please." I dug in my pocket and produced the right change.

The machine was located at the end of the first-floor corridor. Early afternoon, the motel lot was pretty deserted. A fifteen-year-old Pontiac covered with NRA and BUCHANAN stickers had collapsed in front of one of the rooms. The only other cars belonged to us.

She handed me the can and said, "Guess what I did this morning?"

"What?"

"Went over to the railroad roundhouse and found out where all the trestle bridges are in and around town. There are four of them."

"Good idea."

We started strolling down the corridor toward her room. A cleaning cart stood in front of an open door. An aged Mexican woman smiled at us.

"Noah wants to come along."

"Well, he played a detective on TV. He should know what he's doing."

She laughed. "Right." Then, "I told him he didn't need to because *you* were going with me."

"I bet he loved that."

"He told me you were a jerk."

"You tell him what I thought of him?"

"I think he already knows." Then, "So will you go with me?"

"Sure. When?"

"About an hour."

"Just walk upstairs and knock on my door."

When we reached the stairs, she said, "You know this morning when you kissed me good-bye?"

"Uh-huh."

"You didn't kiss me very long."

"I'm sorry."

"It was my breath, wasn't it? I used Binaca and everything."

"Your breath was fine. God, kid, relax, OK?" I pulled her to me and held her.

"I know I'm crazy."

"No, you're not. You're just insecure. *Real* insecure."

"You would be, too, if you'd grown up around Laura." Then, "I can feel you." We were pressed pretty tight.

"Merely an errant afternoon erection."

"I like it."

"So do I, actually. It's sort of a teenage thing. Holding a girl in a public place in the afternoon. Makes me feel young."

"Maybe *you're* the one who's crazy, Robert."

I kissed her sweet little mouth. "That's a distinct possibility."

I CALLED CHIEF Susan Charles.

"You're going to be hearing about me."

"I already have. You killed Frank Caine's dog."

"I feel like hell about it. Caine is the one who should have been shot. He was the one who raised the dog that way."

"He wants to press charges."

"Fine."

"I told him to forget it. I told him that a *lot* of people wanted to kill his dog. Even the folks at the pound. Henry attacked a couple of teenagers who were hunting in a field last fall. He nearly killed them."

"I sure could see that guy killing his daughter."

"So could I," she said, "if we didn't already have a confession from Rick Hennessy."

I sighed. "You find out anything new about our private-detective friend Kibbe?"

"He'd been here eight days, from everything we've been able to piece together."

"You find out who he was working for?"

"Got hold of his wife. She said she wasn't sure. Said he rarely talked about business because it always upset her. Said her brother has an Amway distributorship and was always trying to get Kibbe to join up."

"I have new respect for Kibbe. Resisting Amway folks isn't easy."

"He gave his wife the phone number of the motel here where he was staying and said he'd probably be back in a week, week and a half. He called her four or five times while he was here. Then for three days, she didn't hear anything at all. Until I called her and told her what had happened to him."

"You find a notebook on him?"

"Notebook?"

"You know. A list of people he saw or anything. They usually have to keep detailed records of where they went and who they saw. They copy it and send it along with the invoice to the client."

"No notebook, sorry."

"Now what?"

"There was an autopsy. No surprises. So now we ship the body to Chicago."

"You shipping his effects back, too?"

"Such as they are. There wasn't much."

I thought of what the nurse at Dr. Williams's hospital had told me. "You find a paperweight with the effects?"

"A paperweight? Why would he have carried a paperweight around with him?"

"Just curious."

And now, being a good cop, she was curious about *my* curiosity. "Why'd you ask me about a paperweight?"

"Oh, damn."

"What?"

"Just realized what time it is. Got an appointment."

"Tell me about the paperweight."

"I'll call you when I get a chance."

I hung up quickly.

I PROBABLY WOULDN'T have thought of it if I hadn't seen the cleaning cart in front of Noah Chandler's open door.

I knocked on the metal doorframe and said, "Noah?"

The cleaning woman came out of the bathroom. "Mr. Chandler is gone for a couple hours, he said." Barely an accent. If she was an illegal immigrant—illegals finding Iowa a haven in recent years— she'd been here assimilating for a long time. More likely, she was a legitimate citizen and maybe she could help me.

"I was having a couple of drinks here last night. This morning I realized I'd lost my watch. I've looked several places. But I just now thought of Noah's room. Mind if I look around?"

"Fine."

"You didn't happen to see a watch around here, did you?"

"Sorry, I didn't."

I realized now, her English was so good that my first reaction to her had been racist. A Mexican maid? She had to be an illegal. Father Hesberg at Notre Dame once noted that all white people are racists, and that what matters is to recognize that fact and fight against it within ourselves. I think he's right. Whenever I hear a white person say "I don't have a prejudiced bone in my body," I try real hard not to laugh.

I spent five minutes looking. Nothing very interesting turned up. She kept busy in the john.

Since I didn't like Chandler, I was pleased to find that he kept a stack of autographed glossies of himself in one of his bureau drawers. Probably went to strip malls and handed them out, even if you didn't know who he was and didn't want to take one. Take one or I'll kill ya.

There was a small multicolored pad next to the phone. He'd scribbled on several pages. I flipped through them. Most of the notes pertained to the TV show. But there was one interesting one.

Then there was Kibbe's name with a 312 area code next to it. Chicago. How and why would Chandler have Kibbe's phone number?

I tore the page off and stuffed it into my pocket.

I spent a few more minutes looking around but found nothing. I poked my head in the bathroom. She was bent over the toilet bowl with a brush. I felt sorry for her. This was probably going to be the rest of her life.

"No luck," I said.

"I'll say a prayer for you."

"Thank you. Very much."

A tough life like hers and she was praying for me. That's why I have such a difficult time being a cynic. For all the nastiness of the human soul there always seems to be a counterbalancing amount of goodness.

She was going to say a prayer for me.

LAURA WEST WAS polishing her silken sun-blessed legs. Her regal blond head was bent down, carefully eyeing every square millimeter of her gams. They were well worth polishing. She sat in an armchair with her feet stretched out on the bed while she worked.

She said, "Tandy's in the john getting ready."

"Fine."

She said, "I'd appreciate it if you'd knock off the bullshit with Noah."

"What bullshit?"

"What bullshit? Right. Innocent Robert. Everybody's favorite good guy. Well, Noah may look like a Hollywood cream puff, but he isn't. He's bright and he's sensitive and he doesn't appreciate your attitude."

"Is that why you won't marry him? Because he's so bright and sensitive and you want a caveman type?"

"For your information, I love Noah at least half as much as he loves me. I just wanted to wait a few years before we get married. But he's the possessive type."

She polished her legs some more. She wore only a T-shirt and panties. Her full breasts dared me to look at them. I couldn't help myself. Even as she was chewing me out, I was occasionally looking at her breasts.

"He wants what I want, Robert. And that's to save the show. We've got a book deal and a big European tour riding on the fact that the show continues. Without it, we have nothing."

"To be honest, I'm more concerned with her losing her powers than losing the show."

She looked up at me angrily. "What good are her fucking powers if she can't use them for anything?"

"Well, she helped me find a couple of bodies and solve a couple of murders."

"Yeah, right. And you know how much money she made on the deal? Exactly nothing. Zip."

"I don't think she looks at her powers that way."

"Well, that's how *I* look at them. And you can think whatever you want. I could give a shit, Robert. You and I have never liked each other and we never will. My job is to protect and guide my little sister commercially. Noah's trying to help me. Yes, we're making money off her—and yes, I've become very accustomed to the life the show has given us—but I genuinely want Tandy to have some money, too. The people who have these gifts usually lose them after age thirty-five or so. The Russians are right about that. I want Tandy to have enough money to live reasonably well the rest of her life."

I was about to say something but Tandy came out. She had changed clothes. Wore a black sweater and black slacks. Her rust-colored hair looked rustier than ever. She looked crisp and sexy.

She sensed the mood instantly.

"Maybe I should get you two a fight promoter," she said. "Maybe you could slug it out on TV."

"Robert was just telling me how he doesn't give a damn if you end up broke."

"And Laura was just telling me," I said, "how she doesn't mind exploiting you and your gift at all."

"It's kind of funny," Tandy said. "Having a good friend and my sister absolutely despise each other." She slid her hand in mine. "We'll probably be back around dinnertime."

Then she led me to the door.

Behind us, Laura said, "Just remember, Robert. I expect you to be nice to Noah from now on."

IN THE CAR, as we drove to the first of the trestle bridges, I said, "I can't believe Chandler's all that touchy-feely. He just looks like this big, slow, dumb guy who happened to look like everybody's misconception of a private eye."

"Oh, yeah. Very sensitive. He's been through it all. EST. Primal scream therapy. Back-to-the-womb therapy. He's 'in touch' with himself."

"He and Laura seem an unlikely pair."

She looked out at the afternoon shadows. Another furiously beautiful autumn afternoon, tractors working in the fiery autumn cornfields, a scarecrow with flung-wide arms embracing the very essence of this time of year, sleek mahogany-colored colts running in the hills, and over everything that melancholy smoky scent of fall, the one that conjures up nights by the fire and winter pajamas and hot chocolate with tiny marshmallows bobbing on the surface.

"He's nice to her."

"When he's not screaming at her," I said.

"Believe me. She's no picnic. She's cheated on him a few times and he knows it."

"Ah, love."

"I'm scared, Robert."

"I know."

"And that's why you're talking so much. Because if we stop talking about other stuff then we'll have to talk about this, won't we?"

"Yeah."

"What if we don't find anything?"

"Then we don't find anything."

"Then the image I had was wrong. Or just a dream of some kind. That didn't mean anything."

"You'll find something."

"But if I don't, then my powers won't have come back, will they?"

I took her hand. "We're going to find something."

"Oh, God, I hope you're right." Then, "Am I wearing too much perfume?"

Tandy, the walking bundle of insecurities.

"No. Not at all."

"I just wondered because you opened the window a ways."

"I just wanted to smell the autumn afternoon."

"Honest?"

"Honest. Now, please, Tandy. Just relax, all right?"

"You don't think I'm crazy, do you?"

I looked over at her and laughed. "No, but you're driving *me* crazy."

FIVE

IF YOU GREW up in small-town Iowa, a trestle bridge likely played some part in your life. The adventurous, who sometimes included me, liked to stand on the top span while the train hurtled through below. Or you could take a stopwatch and see if you could best your previous time scrambling up the brace. Kids can come up with some pretty neat games. Or, when the bridge wasn't shaking with a train, you could sit on the top chord, dangle your legs, and fish in the river or creek below. I used to do this on sunny Saturday mornings back in the sixties when I was struggling toward teenhood. I had my pole, my night crawlers, my sack lunch of Ritz crackers and Kraft cheese slices, three cans of Pepsi, and my Ray Bradbury paperback. I went through a period when I wouldn't read *anybody* but Bradbury.

Anyway, the trestle bridge.

I became a half-assed expert on trestles simply because I parked my ass on so many of their top chords. You have your timber deck truss and your straining-beam pony truss and what they call your simple truss. And many others types as well.

The bridges we saw today were all of the lattice-truss design, the first one being in a field behind a manufacturing plant.

When I pulled up and killed the engine, Tandy said, "God, I want to puke. I really do. My stomach's a mess."

"C'mon. You'll be fine."

"I won't pick up any vibes, Robert. I know it."

"Then you want to go back?"

She frowned. "I'm being a pain in the ass, aren't I?"

"Yeah."

"I'm sorry."

I sighed. "How about we make a deal?"

"A deal?"

"Uh-huh. Every time you apologize for yourself from now on, you pay me five dollars."

"Five dollars is a lot of money."

"That's the point of it." Then, "I know why you're apprehensive. That makes sense. But I also know that on at least two occasions in the past, you were able to locate bodies the police couldn't—and that you found them through sleep images. Last night, you had another image like that. At least relax enough to give it a good try. Maybe you'll turn up something."

"Can I hold your hand and just sit here for a minute, Robert?"

"I'm afraid I'll have to charge you."

"How much?"

"At least a dollar thirty-seven."

"How about a dollar three?"

"How about a dollar twenty-two?"

"You know, Robert, you're almost as much of a dipshit as I am."

" 'Almost' being the operative word there."

We sat in the car holding hands for five minutes. I got two frustrating little erections but spoke to them in nice gentle paternal terms and they went away. I was here on business.

Then we got out of the car, still holding hands, and drifted down through a dusty field toward the bridge. The creek beneath the bridge was shallow and dirty. The trees on either side ran to willows and birches. The narrow shoreline was a city dump of pop cans, beer cans, fast-food wrappers, and the occasional spent condom. I walked over on the railroad tracks and looked a long quarter mile down to where the tracks curved out of sight. The tracks sparkled silver in the waning sunlight. As a boy, I'd always wanted to be one of those old men who sat in the swaying red caboose with one arm cocked out the open window. They always wore OshKosh work caps and smoked pipes. I'd add one thing to that when I got to be one of them: I'd be reading a Ray Bradbury paperback.

I decided the best way to handle this was to leave her alone unless she asked me to be with her. She'd be less self-conscious that way. I was starting to get this crush on her; it was starting to feel funny without her small, fine-boned hand in mine. But I spent a few minutes just walking the tracks. A squirrel looked me over pretty good and didn't seem impressed. A garter snake slithered beneath an oily railroad tie. A number of flies were picnicking on some dog turds. I thought of Henry and felt like hell. Maybe I really *should* have killed his master instead of him.

Finally, I drifted back toward her. I stayed out of sight, off at an angle and hidden by some white birches.

She walked the shoreline. Facing me. Her eyes were closed and she lightly touched her fingers to her temples. She was mouthing something. Prayers, I imagined.

She walked up and down the shoreline several more times. Birds sang and cried; in the distance a dog barked and yipped. At one point, she sat down on a log and raised her face to the sky.

I wanted to help her. But of course there was nothing I could do.

This went on for a half hour, her sitting there on the log. Then she got up abruptly and looked around and saw me and climbed the angled shoreline to the field.

"Nothing," she said.

"We've got three more to go."

"Nothing," she said again. Then, "Maybe I need to start smoking again."

"What's smoking got to do with it?"

"I was a cigarette fiend during the time I was helping you and the other cops."

"You were also wearing your hair long."

"I guess I didn't think of that."

"And you weighed a hundred and twenty pounds more."

She gave me a sarcastic look. "I take back what I said, Robert. You're *more* of a dipshit than I am."

"And that takes some doing."

Without warning, she slid her arms around me and started crying softly. "I just can't do it anymore, Robert. I just can't do it."

WE DIDN'T SPEND much time at the next two bridges.

The first one was over a leg of river that twisted westward. It was a long span bridge whose construction marked it as built in the thirties. We tried both ends of the bridge. No vibes whatsoever.

The second was what they call a king-post trestle bridge. It was wood and at least eighty years old and spanned an old section of a highway that had fallen into disrepair since the coming of Interstate 80.

For a moment, she got excited. Her eyes rolled back. She appeared to go into a brief convulsion, shaking. But it passed quickly. Her eyes came open and she said, "Shit."

"Nothing, huh?"

"I was just starting to *feel* something. Not see it. But feel it. And then—" She shrugged her frail shoulders. "You hungry?"

"I could stand to eat something. Eight, nine thousand calories maybe. But not any more than that."

"How do you say 'dipshit' in Spanish?" Then, "We passed a Perkins on the way here."

"My stomach and I noticed that."

"Why didn't you say something?"

"I was waiting for you to start apologizing for yourself. I figured you do that three, four times, I could afford to buy dinner."

PERKINS WAS CROWDED at dinnertime. A diverse group. Moms and pops, our time's version of Ozzie and Harriet, with their vans, credit cards, and little plastic cards that instructed them how much 15 percent of their bill was. Truckers. Bikers. Native Americans from a nearby reservation. Young people who looked to be in love; young people who looked to be breaking up. Old isolated people eating alone and staring out the window at the past.

"Actually, breakfast sounds good."

"Good. Then have breakfast."

"I shall."

"Nice word, shall."

"Yeah," she said, "I heard Myrna Loy use it in one of the *Thin Man* movies and I've been working it into the conversation every chance I get."

While we were waiting for our food, and enjoying our coffee, and both reveling in the fact that she seemed inexplicably happy for the moment, they came over. Two of them. Mom with a camera, son with a grin.

Son said, when they arrived, "See, I tol' ya."

"Oh, God, it is you!" Mom said.

Tandy had been getting a lot of glances. A lot of people here recognized her right away. They'd whisper to their mate and mate would turn and look over here and a little explosion of recognition could be seen in his eyes.

"Tandy! I love your show!"

Tandy blushed. It was a real true little-girl blush, too. Sweet. "Thanks," she said.

"My husband isn't going to believe this. He loves your show, too!"

"Well, tell him thank-you for me."

People were watching us now. I was self-conscious suddenly, embarrassed. I hate being the center of attention, or even anywhere near it.

"In fact, a friend of his was abducted last summer and was going to call your show to see if you'd like to do a bit on him. He said the inside of the mother ship was different from what he'd expected. He said it looked more like the inside of this big huge tavern than anything else."

"Well, you can just call the eight-hundred number at the end of the show and talk to one of our scheduling staff about it."

The woman leaned forward. She was prairie stock, hardworking skin-and-bones at fifty sharp angles, and mad lonely eyes. Whatever she'd spent her life looking for, she hadn't been able to find. Religion had likely failed her, so now she turned to UFOs. She wore a faded western shirt and faded Levi's. The camera was a small ancient Polaroid. Son, who was tubby in his western getup, said, "Could I get my pitcher taken with you so I can bring it to fourth grade show-and-tell?"

"Sure, honey," Tandy said. "We'll take one with you and your mom and me and then one with just you and me. How's that?"

I took the pictures.

People watched, whispered, pointed, smiled, smirked.

This was my one and only brush with celebrity and I hated it.

I snapped the photos Tandy told me to and then finally Mom and Son were gone, after belatedly cadging an autograph on a napkin.

"I'm sorry," she said. "God, you looked mortified."

"I hate having people stare at me."

Then, in light of the fact that her first reaction to the fans had been to blush, she said, "I actually like it, Robert. I always feel a little funny at first, but then I really get into it."

The food came. We ate. It was good. I had breakfast, the best-tasting meal of the day. Pancakes and eggs and hash-browns. You can't go wrong with such a meal. Ever.

She said, "You know what this is all about?"

"What what's all about?"

"My powers and the show and everything? So I won't feel so inadequate around Laura. She got the beauty *and* the brains."

"I think you're going to owe me five bucks. I think you're trying to sneak an apology for yourself past me."

"It's true, Robert. God, look at her. Listen to her. She's gorgeous and she's brilliant."

"This one may cost you *ten* bucks."

"So my power and my celebrity—when I have those things I don't feel so inadequate around her. And I can appreciate the fact that she's always taken care of me. Loved me and protected me and tried to help me. Which she has."

"And maybe exploited you a little, too."

"Yes, true. But if she hadn't, I'd never have gotten my own television show."

Or lost your power, I thought.

But I sure wasn't going to say that. I sure as hell wasn't.

SIX

THE LAST TRESTLE was deep in the woods and spanned a dry creek bed. A coyote on the rim of a small hill watched us approach, its scrawny and patchy body aglow with moonlight. I'd cadged a small shovel from the motel office and brought it along.

The woods were heavy, thick, noisy with night.

Steep clay and shale cliffs rose sharply in the air, lending the area an isolated sense. Fir and pine stretched deep to the west. To the east was the grassy barren hill where the coyote crouched.

"My last hope," she said. And gave my hand a squeeze.

"I'll leave you alone. In fact, I think I'll climb the trestle."

"Second childhood?"

"Exactly."

So I climbed the trestle. Which was not as easy as it sounds. The brace I used was at a seventy-degree angle. Tandy watched me for a time. "God, be careful."

"You're talking to Tarzan."

"Yeah, right. I can see that. The way you slipped just a minute ago."

I didn't know she'd noticed. So much for my Tarzan image.

I reached the chord, stood up, dusted my hands off on my pants, and took my first good look out at the night. King of the hill. Untouchable. Impregnable. Velvet dark blue sky. Crisp silver moon. A big commercial jet far away, probably heading for Cedar Rapids. The autumn air, cool and melancholy and erotically inspiring. I hoped she'd be beneath my covers tonight, snuggling against the jack-o'-lantern chill, all warm and silky and sexy and still a little sad-faced even in sleep, our bodies entangled and her sweet little mouth against my shoulder, lover and daughter and friend and mystery.

She went about her business and I went about mine.

I'd been up on the chord ten, fifteen minutes, walking back and forth like the ten-year-old I'd always be, when I felt the train coming.

Didn't see it. Didn't hear it. *Felt* it.

There's a story about Genghis Khan that has always stayed with me. How villages miles from his thundering horseback army, sometimes numbering in the thousands, would literally feel the ground shake with his approach.

And this would give them time to flee before his terrible horsemen reached them.

The train was sort of like that. I had a straight look down maybe a half mile of shining silver track in the vast prairie shadows . . . and I still couldn't see it. Or hear it.

But feel it, yes.

There was still plenty of time for me to climb down, and I just assumed that's what I'd do as soon as the train came into sight.

As for Tandy, she had suddenly vanished. That didn't trouble me. She might be forming images, and the images leading her somewhere down the creek bed. I sure didn't have to worry about her drowning.

Then the train was sliding around the distant bend, and it was an imposing ghostly figure in the Iowa night, a long freight of jerking rumbling boxcars and tanker cars and lumber cars, and one big golden boogeyman eye scanning the countryside for any-thing that displeased it. Roaring, rushing toward me.

There were all kinds of stories about people who stood on tres-tles when the heavy trains came through. How they fell to their deaths and were ground to bloody fatty hamburger after several train cars had passed over them. So the sensible man would quickly work his way down the brace and stand in the dry creek bed and watch the train go by.

But as Tandy had hinted, I was having a second childhood experience. So I decided to stay right where I was.

You could *smell* the train coming. The hot oily engine. The fric-tion of steel wheel and steel track. The taint of the various prod-ucts the train was carrying.

And the whistle. I always thought of Jack London and Jack Ker-ouac when I heard train whistles like that, so lonely and longing in the midwestern night those whistles, both men rushing their whole lives to a haven they never lived long enough to find, and probably wouldn't have found anyway no matter how long they'd lived.

And then the train was crashing through the tunnel the trestle had created. And the steel bridge jerked and swayed and bobbled as the roaring train seemed to explode beneath my feet. The noise of engine and steel and speed obliterated everything else.

I stuck my arms out for balance, the way I would on a surf-board. But it didn't help much.

I was being tipped off the chord.

The creek bed was sandy, true. But the fall was a good twenty-five feet. Far enough to break more than a few bones, no matter how gentle the landing.

The noise was starting to spook me now. I was inside it. There was no escape. I had one of those paranoid flashes that I'd some-how crossed over into another realm. And I was in this realm for-ever.

I did the only thing I could. I dropped to the chord, straddling it like a horse bent over and hung on.

I forgot about Tandy. I just clung to the steel.

It was a rough ride, so rough that a couple of times I wished I was wearing a jock.

The train was one of those spectral mythic unending ones you see only on the prairies, long as a country mile, and even rolling at eighty, ninety miles an hour, taking forever to pass by.

The whistle again. And the cold dead air created by the cars as they charged through the night. And the different shapes of the cars—boxlike, cylindrical, open and flat. I even glimpsed a hobo sleeping in a gondola, though God only knew how you could sleep in the belly of such a beast as this one.

I glanced up once and saw the moon and a kind of awe gripped me momentarily, all the things that had happened on this little nowhere planet beneath the moon, before the Ice Age when this prairie didn't even exist, and then water eventually becoming landmass, and since that time so many, many epochs and eras for the moon to indifferently note, culminating in this era of screech-ing train and girl with psychic power. The moon didn't give any more of a damn about us than it had the Vikings or the Indians or the pioneers from New Hampshire and Rhode Island, or the hairy, forlorn, utterly baffled creatures who'd trod these lands so many millions of years ago we don't even know what to call them.

And then it was gone. And there was this strange quality in the air called silence. And my first reaction was not to recognize it for what it was. My entire body had been shaken by the thunder of the train.

After a time, I heard the night birds and the coyotes and the horses in the hills. And feeling, human feeling, came back to my limbs and my crotch, and into my mind, too.

I looked for Tandy and didn't see her.

THE CREEK BED was pale and shadowy in the moonlight. I fol-lowed her footprints westward. You could smell mud and wet dead leaves from the recent rains.

I listened for her, too. Light as she was, she had to make at least minimal noise as she moved.

I didn't want to call out for her. She might be in a trance. My voice could destroy whatever she was learning.

The creek narrowed at one point and became little more than a path. I had to duck beneath low-hanging branches. Moonlight glinted off beer cans and pop cans angled out from the sandy creek bed. A possum switched its lengthy tail, watching me.

In the tree-broken silver glow of the moon, standing perfectly still on a hill, fingers touching her temples, eyes crazed and raised skyward, she stood like some piece of mad statuary, a benign prairie Medusa, slight as a child, frail as an autumn flower, a song of some kind coming from her lips, or what I mistook as a song, at first, anyway. It was really a moan, I realized, as I climbed the bank and started up the small hill toward her. In the sudden wind, the trees around her bent branches toward her, as if in supplication. Her crazed gaze was unwavering, and the moan grew only deeper and more disturbing.

I stopped several feet from her. I didn't want to scare her. She was completely unaware of me.

And then she started moving. There was a moment where her movement was almost comic, melodramatic and stagy as a zombie sequence in a bad old late-night TV movie. Her arms weren't outstretched before her and she didn't plod as she walked, but still there was something overwrought about her, and I even wondered guiltily if she might not be faking all this for my benefit.

She answered my question by pausing halfway down the hill and throwing up.

Moaning ended. Eyes became real and focused again.

And the throwing up was all too real.

She sank to her knees to do it, and I rushed to her and knelt next to her and held her as she finished her work.

And then I recalled another night. The first murder case we'd worked on together. Near the time when the image came clear to her and she was able to lead us to the buried body. Vomiting, then. Inexplicably. Me holding her.

Now she said, "I didn't get it."

"Get what?"

"The location."

"A body?"

"Yes. A child. An infant."

"Oh, shit." A child, let alone an infant, is always the worst to find. It changes you. You can never quite look at the human heart the same way again. In a very real way, you're no longer a virgin. In my FBI years, I'd lost my cherry early on. I'd worked a case in which a child had been mutilated and then burned. But Tandy still had her virginity. Until tonight, anyway. "Anything I can do?"

"No. Just please don't talk. In fact, how about walking back to the car? I'll come back when I'm through. Maybe—maybe something will come to me yet."

I touched her arm. "You've already accomplished something, Tandy. You've located a body."

"No, I've *seen* a body. In the old days—before I ruined my gift—I would have known where it is by now." Then, frowning, "Listen to me, Robert. There's a dead child somewhere out here and all I can talk about is losing my gift. Me me me. Laura's right. I'm not better than she is. I just hide it better." Shaking her head. "And anyway, maybe this is all just fantasy. Maybe I'm just feeding myself images. Maybe there's no body of *any* kind around a trestle bridge."

I knew there was nothing I could say.

She was right. She needed to be left alone.

I WALKED BACK to the car. I saw a doe on the way, standing at the edge of a shallow woods. A couple more weeks, the hunters would be out here blasting away. Maybe I'd seen *Bambi* too many times when I was a kid, but somehow hunting with guns has always struck me as singularly unfair. Maybe we need to teach the deer how to shoot back. Even things up a little.

I sat in my car listening to a National Public Radio story about the state of tabloid journalism in England. Impossible as it sounded, the Brits were even sleazier at the tab game than we were.

The cell phone rang. I once saw a cartoon where a man was out in the woods in walking shorts and backpack taking a pee in some bushes and talking to his cell phone at the same time.

I picked up.

"Laura gave me your number."

"Who is this?"

"It's Noah Chandler. Who the hell do you think it is?"

"You sound different."

Pause. "We need to talk."

I realized why I hadn't recognized the voice at first. He was so upset, his voice had gone up half an octave. "What about?"

"You know yesterday when you accused me of being the one doing the shooting out at the old asylum?"

"Yes."

"Well, you were right. It *was* me."

"Why the hell were you shooting at us?"

"Publicity, of course."

Of course.

Pause. "It's getting out of hand."

"What's getting out of hand?"

"The whole thing—the plan."

"I wish I knew what the hell you were talking about, Chandler."

"When're you getting back to the motel?"

"I'm not sure. Hour, hour and a half maybe. Why?"

"I'll watch for you. I'll come to your room."

"So I don't even get a hint?"

Pause. "Paul Renard? The guy that Rick Hennessy claims to be possessed by?"

"Yeah."

"That's what Kibbe the private eye was working on."

"So you knew Kibbe?"

"Yeah," Chandler said. "Pretty well, in fact."

"So he was out here because of you?"

"Because of me *and* Paul Renard."

"Paul Renard's dead."

"Maybe not."

"What the hell're you talking about? He jumped off a cliff into rapids. According to the locals, nobody could have survived those rapids."

"Well, Kibbe and I were working on evidence that Renard is still alive and that he's come back to town here." Then, "I've got to go. Somebody's coming. Like I said, Payne, I'll watch for you."

SEVEN

MOST HOMICIDES ARE cut-and-dried. No big surprises along the way. You do the legwork, you interview enough friends of the deceased, you get a clear picture of the deceased's life and thus a pretty good sense of who killed him and why. And then you keep eliminating suspects until your best bet comes along.

What you don't get very often is the possibility that a man long thought dead turns about to be alive.

I.e., the one and only voodoo child, Paul Renard.

I was still thinking about Renard when I saw Tandy come up on top of the field from the bank below. She was moving slowly, her shoulders slumped. The news obviously wasn't good.

When she reached the car, she opened the door and dropped into the seat. "It's all my own fault."

"What is?"

"That I lost my gift. I pissed it away trying to be rich and famous."

"No more images?"

"Of the infant, yes. Of where the infant was, no."

"We can come back tomorrow."

"No, I'm done."

I touched the back of her head gently, cupping it in my palm. She said, "You're such a gentle lover. I really appreciate that."

"Yeah. Like the time I knocked us out of bed and you cut your head on the end table."

"You were just a little horned up that night. But most of the time you're really nice." She shook her head and stared down at her hands. "Shit. Shit." Then, "Shit."

"You need a meal and a few glasses of wine."

"I need a lot more than that."

I decided not to tell her about Chandler's call. Information that she didn't need right now. But I did ask, "How did you find out about the Rick Hennessy case, anyway?"

"Rick Hennessy's lawyer."

"Oh."

She looked up at me. "How come you want to know?"

"I'm just trying to find out all about Kibbe."

"Oh. I guess that makes sense. I mean, Noah did what he usually does to check out a prospective case. He called the editor of the local newspaper and the editor told him everything. Faxed him a bunch of stuff, too. At first, I wasn't very interested. I thought it sounded like bullshit. All the stuff about Renard and possession. I'm very leery of that sort of thing. But after I read the faxes, I got interested. How Rick started dressing like him and getting into voodoo and supernatural things. I thought it'd be an interesting story from a legal standpoint."

"So Noah came out here?"

"Noah and Laura. They used it as kind of a makeup vacation. They'd broken up again. You know, the marriage thing as usual. They're always breaking up. Noah has been a pretty boy all his life. He isn't used to women turning him down. Plus, emotionally, he's a very hungry guy. He's kind of a vampire. He wants to take her whole life over. Doesn't want her to think or do anything that he doesn't approve of in advance. I can see why he was married three times. And that's why he and Laura always get into it."

"Because she wouldn't marry him?"

"Right. And he was getting violent again. He even hit her a couple of times. He'd go on a binge, smashing things, ransacking rooms. He's got a terrible temper. She really does love him. But her first marriage just spooked her. The way Bob drank and everything. She doesn't want to go through that again. I know she's arrogant and cold, but she's a true-blue type. She's always faithful to her men, even when they treat her badly. She intimidates them, I think. They're afraid they're going to lose all that beauty." She smiled sadly. "It's like having your fortune taken away from you, I suppose."

"But they patched things up and came out here?"

"Right. And sort of laid out how the show would go. The production company really started getting cheap with travel when the ratings started to fall. They said they wanted me to come out here and shoot a little 'test footage,' as they called it. And when they saw it, they'd decide how much money they wanted to spend on covering the trial."

"You didn't know Kibbe?"

"No. I never even heard of him until he was killed." Then, "Oh. Damn."

"What?"

"Headache."

"Just came on?"

"Just like that." She put her head back against the seat.

We drove several miles in silence. She'd groan every once in a while was all. A couple of times, I reached over and held her hand briefly. She gave me a brief squeeze to let me know she appreciated it.

I was thinking about Noah Chandler. So he'd been the one who'd shot at us. So he'd been the one who'd arranged for Kibbe. So he was one of the ones pushing the notion that somehow Paul Renard was alive.

I assumed Laura knew everything Chandler wanted to talk about. He didn't seem bright or ambitious enough to do any of this on his own. He wanted Laura and Laura wanted the show. To get Laura, he'd had to help her save the show. And that, for some reason I still didn't understand, had involved Kibbe.

THE CRY WAS almost sexual.

In fact, when I turned to look across the seat at her, the way she was writhing in the moonlight, all sharp sensuous angles, I thought she might be having a sexual experience of some kind.

"Are you all right?"

She didn't answer.

Another moan and then a spasm of some kind and then a loud cry that carried a sense of finality. And then she slumped in the seat.

"Are you all right?" I said.

"We need to go back there."

"Where?"

"The trestle."

"Why?"

"Now I know where the body is."

I GRABBED THE shovel from the trunk and followed her across the moonlit field, down the bank, and onto the sandy dry creek bed.

She rushed on ahead of me, stumbling sometimes, hurrying, hurrying. A frantic air about her now.

I could imagine what she was going through. She wanted her power back. For a woman who thought so little of herself, her power was her whole identity, her sole reason to ever take pride in herself and her skills.

I was afraid for her. What if this was another false alarm? There were only so many reassurances I could whisper; only so many hours I could hold her.

I knew how badly she needed for this to be real. I said a silent prayer that she'd find what her mind had told her she'd find.

She hastened on ahead of me.

It was four or five degrees cooler now. An autumn chill upon the land.

Sounds of frogs and snapping twigs and feet stomping into damp silty sand.

Smells of night air and stands of jack pines and dirty polluted water, the trickle of creek carrying with it the stench of the factories it passed to the east, where industry was burgeoning and the creek was wide, deep, and fast.

Sights of deep shadow from the canopy-forming trees, then a burst of treeless moonlight suddenly, and then the angling shadow of soaring clay cliffs on our left.

And then, momentarily lost in the shadows, she cried, "Here!"

I caught up with her.

I clipped on the flashlight I'd brought along and shone it on a sandy area beneath an overhang of the embankment.

"In there?"

"Yes. Hurry. Please."

"You hold the flashlight."

She took it from me. Shone the beam on the exact spot.

I jammed the shovel into the wall just beneath the overhang and got to work.

THE SANDY EXTERIOR was only a half-inch deep or so. Behind it was good true Iowa soil. With plenty of tree roots, rocks, and tight-packed earth.

At one point, she said, "Oh, God, Robert. What if I'm wrong?"

"I'll just keep digging."

"What if nothing's there?"

I looked back at her. "You just hold the light steady."

"I'm sorry I'm so hysterical."

"You're not hysterical. Now just hold the light steady."

She held the light steady just fine. I dug another fifteen minutes. It was still tough going. I began having the same doubts she did.

The night was no longer cold. I was hot and sweaty.

Once, I thought I found something. She got excited and so did I. It turned out to be the edge of a piece of rather porous rock.

I kept digging.

"We should've brought some pop or something for you."

"I'm fine."

"Aren't you getting discouraged?"

"No."

"You're just saying that."

"I'm going to give it another few feet. Then if we don't find anything, I'll get discouraged."

The flashlight blinked and went off.

"Great," she said.

"Give it here."

I did what mankind has always done with unreliable flashlights. Plan A, if you will. I pounded it hard against the palm of my hand. You need to show flashlights who's in command. That not working, I pounded it even harder. And *that* not working, I pounded it harder still.

"Let me try it," she said.

She went to mankind's flashlight plan B.

Opened it up, dumped the batteries out, hefted them a few times in her hand, and slid them back into the flashlight tube.

She clicked the button on. Nothing.

"Screw it," I said. "There's enough moonlight."

And went back to digging.

I WAS ABOUT to give up when I found it.

At first, I wasn't even sure what it was. I held it up to the moonlight. Then I was all *too* sure of what it was.

A finger. Or the skeleton of one. An infant's finger.

The flesh had long ago decayed. The skeleton had been buried many years ago.

I scraped around in the burial site and found another piece of bone. This looked to be a piece of long bone. From a forearm perhaps.

I held it up to the moonlight again.

I said, "You were right."

"Now I'm not sure I *want* to be right." Then, "It's going to be a baby, isn't it?"

"Probably."

"I heard it crying. In my sleep, I mean. I saw this site and heard it crying. It must have been the night it was killed and buried here. And now here I am, happy that I found it and that my career is saved."

I took her arm. "You have to listen to me."

"All right." But she was still distracted with her guilt.

"I'm going to do a little more digging. Find another bone or two. Make sure there's more evidence here."

"Then what?"

"I'll call Susan Charles. Tell her to call the state crime lab right away. There's a very strict protocol for working with remains like this. The crime lab'll know what to do."

"What should I do?"

"Just give yourself a break, Tandy," I said. "You're a good woman. You really are. This may save your career. But it's also going to help solve a crime. Remember that. Whoever the child was who was buried here deserves a proper burial. And it wouldn't get it without you."

She stood on tiptoes and kissed me. "God, I'm lucky I know you."

DEPUTY FULLER DIDN'T look any friendlier than he had when he'd chaperoned our meeting with Rick Hennessy in the police station the other day.

He arrived shortly after the first squad car. Even if I didn't like him, I had to admit he was a competent cop. He set up the crime scene efficiently and quickly.

I walked over to him as he was carrying fistfuls of evidence bags from the trunk of his car.

"Where's Chief Charles?"

"She's in Marshalltown."

"Oh? What's she doing there?"

He glared at me. "Speaking to a library group about modern law enforcement. Does that meet with your approval?"

There was no point in being friendly. Fuller and I probably wouldn't be prom dates anytime soon.

He started walking away, then stopped. "You're really going to push that load of shit on us?"

"Which particular load of shit are you talking about?"

"The spook gal."

"Tandy?"

"Yeah, Tandy. It just happened to come to her that there were some bones buried out here?"

"You want her bona fides, I can give you the names of several law enforcement people she's worked with."

"Some people'll believe anything. Even cops."

"Then how else could she have known about the burial site?"

He went back to glaring at me. "That's what I plan to find out."

OVER THE NEXT half and a half, the crime lab arrived, and so did Susan Charles.

The crime lab came in two vans, one for agents, the other for laboratory personnel.

Excavating the bones would be a delicate and painstaking process. In addition to the skeletal remains, they'd also be looking for any other ancillary evidence. The person who'd buried the body might well have dropped something in the process. I'd left the shovel and all the dirt I'd extracted right near the point where I'd dug.

Susan said, "Your friend is a celebrity."

Press was already here from Des Moines and Cedar Rapids, and several smaller towns. Unearthing bones wouldn't ordinarily have been treated like breaking news. But this involved not only a celebrity but also a so-called psychic.

Even the sky was suddenly busy. Helicopters from two local stations crisscrossed the crime scene. Every once in a while, a Highway Patrol chopper also appeared.

Susan looked great. White turtleneck. Dark brown suede car coat. Brown suede slacks. That intriguing ambivalence—arrogant beauty and disfiguring scar—was riveting as always.

"Fuller's a good man."

"Yes," she said, "except when it comes to public relations."

I smiled. "I guess I noticed that."

She looked around. There was a crowd now. Thirty, forty onlookers. Several cop cars. State. Highway Patrol. Local. And the press.

"Any idea who this might be?" I said. "Any infant missing in recent times? Kidnapping, anything like that?"

"Nope. I was thinking of that myself. Most likely—if I had to bet, I mean—it's probably a high school girl burying her illegitimate infant out here."

"Most likely."

"I'm glad my mother didn't do that to me."

"Yeah."

"That's the only thing I can't figure out about all the abortions in this country," she said. "I'm not a big pro-lifer. But why can't they just adopt their babies out? There are plenty of places that'd take them."

"They're young," I said. "They panic. I'm sure they think about what they did the rest of their lives." Then, "Anything more on Kibbe?"

"To tell you the truth, I got the call on this while I was still on the highway. I came right here. Didn't have time to stop at the office. When I get down there, I'll check the phone and the fax. If there's anything that looks like anything, I'll let you know."

"Thanks."

"Well," she said, "I'd better get back over there and start acting like a chief of police."

"Nice to see you, Susan."

She touched my elbow affectionately. "We've still got some bowling to do sometime, Mr. Payne."

I STAYED ANOTHER half hour, hoping to snag Tandy and take her back to town.

But by now she was more than a mere celebrity. She was a full-fledged shaman. In addition to the press, everyday people were surrounding her now, too. I heard the word "holy" mentioned by a very old woman. Some would still be convinced that Tandy was a fraud and had used a variation on stage magic to find the bones (or perhaps that she'd even planted the bones herself); others would credit her ESP powers, about which they'd been informed many times on her show; and a few would see her gift as divinely inspired (which it probably could be, this not being mutually exclusive to paranormal powers, as Tandy frequently pointed out).

Her crowd grew wider, deeper. They wanted her autograph. They wanted to know if she'd be doing a segment of her show from town here. One woman wanted Tandy to touch her leg-crippled daughter. Tandy gently declined. She looked embarrassed, even a tad frantic.

I could understand them. They wanted something to believe in. Since you could no longer believe in government, business, movie stars, sports stars, or even many religions . . . that left you exploring the fringes for people to believe in. That explains Pat

Robertson and all the other pseudo-religious con artists; and that also explains our obsession with things extraterrestrial, even though there's no hard evidence yet that we've ever actually had a close encounter.

So when a fragile young woman through mental powers alone unearths long-buried bones . . . that's remarkable.

So why not push your crippled son toward her? Or your blind daughter? Or your cancer-dying husband? If any of these folks were my kin or beloved, I'd probably do the same thing.

Where's the harm?

At least Tandy wouldn't ask you to send her "prayer messages" in the form of twenty- and fifty-dollar bills and "reward" you with little pamphlets of inspirational bilge. And she wouldn't get involved in far-right politics, pushing their message of hate.

So where's the harm?

Maybe on the off-chance Tandy *can* do something miraculous for you . . .

It was all a little frantic and desperate and sad, the yearning way they surrounded her, but there was a human sweetness about it, too.

By now, it was full-fledged football weather, the chill almost tart but fresh and invigorating. Somebody started a small fire. A woman showed up with a small van loaded with coffee and doughnuts and Danish. As the crowd seemed to be increasing steadily, she'd probably turn a nice profit.

I watched the lab people work under their big lights. Extracting the bones was laborious work. We'd taken a course at Quantico in such excavations. Hard, important work.

Somebody tipped the press to who I was, so I had my turn, too. I said very little. Their excitement was based on the fact that I was formerly an FBI profiler, and that Tandy and I had successfully worked together on two murder cases.

I was assaulted in all media—audiotaped for radio, videotaped for TV, and fed live as a special bulletin interrupting whatever network show was on locally at the moment.

No, I had no idea how Tandy had gotten her special power. No, I had no idea whose bones we'd found. No, I had no idea who the private eye Kibbe was, but I doubted that his presence and subsequent death had anything to do with the bones that Tandy had found.

They were disappointed in my responses, of course. They wanted a sound bite that'd be good at the top of the ten o'clock news, which was coming up fast.

They wanted me to link Kibbe and the bones and say that Tandy was having visions of Kibbe's killer and would soon identify him for the police.

They wanted me to say that, in fact, the real killer was already stalking Tandy, fearing that she'd expose him.

The stuff of TV movies—that's what they wanted for the TV news.

And as I said, they didn't get it. Not from me, anyway.

A lot of the time, I thought about Noah Chandler's phone call. Paul Renard still alive? I liked a good urban legend as much as anybody. But the prospect of the tale being true seemed remote.

I was actually more interested in his admission that he'd fired the shots at us at the asylum the other day. What the hell was that all about? Even then, under the anxiety of the moment, I'd felt that the shooter was missing us on purpose.

I wondered if Laura knew about Chandler. Or was maybe even his accomplice.

I tried once more to get close to Tandy. Impossible.

I also tried to say good-bye to Susan Charles. She was busy, too. The press had just discovered her as their next target.

The line at the doughnut van was longer than ever. The coffee was steaming hot and the pastry glistened with sugary coating. If the line hadn't been so long, I'd have indulged myself.

EIGHT

LONESOME PRAIRIE NIGHT. That was the feeling I had when I saw the plastic lights of Brenner, the reds and blues and yellows of all the chain fast-food places and the video stores and convenience stores with the six-deep gas pumps and all the Harleys parked slantwise along the front of the walks.

Kids would be in bed all warm and dream-thrilled and parents would be in front of TVs or in bed early for a quick tumble with their mates and teenagers would be humping in cars or on park benches and cats would be dozing wherever it was warm, and dogs would be doggy-prowling through the night.

Somehow, I didn't feel as if I belonged to any of it, and I desperately wanted to. I wanted to be in the house where I'd lived with my wife and still lived in sometimes; or at the least in my apartment in Cedar Rapids, anywhere where I felt a sense of community, not a fucking motel room and a fucking motel room bed and Tandy all gone from me now with her power back and celebrity dazzling her eyes sure as jewels.

I would have settled for an animal to ride with, dog, cat, raccoon; hell, night crawler if I had to.

I was pulling into Brenner with a full load of dislocation and self-pity. I was not ready for prime time.

☾

"Evening."

"Evening," I said.

"Help you?"

I hadn't seen him before. He looked like a retired gent, earning a little spare cash working the motel desk at night. He wore a ratty cardigan, thin flannel-style cotton shirt, and had some kind of serious-looking wart on the bottom of his lower lip. His HMO had probably convinced him it was nothing to worry about. His dentures clicked when he spoke. He was reading a *Collector's* magazine. BIG MONEY FOR "JUNK"! cried one headline.

"I went to Noah Chandler's room," I said, "but he didn't seem to be around. Just wondered if he'd told you where he was going?"

"They don't usually do that. Tell me anything, I mean. Ho-tels, they tell you where they went sometimes. But not mo-tels. Not usually, anyway."

"Well, thanks."

The trucks on the highway, the trains on the prairie, provided the usual amount of roaring rumbling background noise. The night smelled of cigarettes and cold and exhaust fumes from a truck that had just pulled in. Half the lights above the various motel doors had burned out, lending the place a seedy quality it had plenty of already.

I decided to try Laura and Tandy's room. Maybe Noah was there. I hadn't checked because I didn't know if Laura knew what Noah wanted to tell me. Maybe, given her feelings about me, she wouldn't want him dealing with me.

I knocked and the door creaked open. Nice crisp horror-movie sound effect, that creaking.

Dark room. Tart smells.

I pushed the door open with a single finger.

I knew instinctively that this door would soon enough be dusted for prints. I didn't want to hinder the lab people any more than I had to.

I went back to my car and got the small penlight I use for reading maps.

I didn't go any deeper into the room than I had to. The lab would comb the carpet for prints, too.

She was naked and her throat had been cut. She had a very nice body. Her wild red-blond pubic hair gave me an erotic little charge. And, as you can imagine, I felt very proud of myself.

He'd died from a bullet to the left temple. The side of his head was a salad of blood and bone fragment and puslike brain matter. Presumably, the damage had been done by the heavily blued .45 dangling from the tips of his fingers. The tabs were going to love it. He'd been too unimportant to cover since his cop drama had been canceled. Now he was back in the good graces of vampires everywhere.

I backed out of the room, leaving the door ajar, and pulled my cell phone from my back pocket.

I called the police station first and they patched me through to Susan Charles. I told her what had happened and she said, "Has this whole town gone crazy?"

"Sure seems like it," I said.

ONE

TANDY WAS OUT of Susan Charles's personal Buick before the wheels had quite stopped rotating.

The same crowd of folks who had gathered here to watch Kibbe be carried out were back again. I recognized several of them. Maybe they were part of this portable crowd that got dropped off at all crime scenes.

As she struggled her way toward me—small against the taller, wider, heavier crowd—she looked young and frantic and scared.

She started to go around me, head for the open door where police officers and various other officials came and went.

But I stopped her, pulled her to me. "You don't want to go in there."

She tried to jerk herself free of me. "She was my sister, Robert. Now let me go."

"You don't want this to be your last memory of her."

Her struggling stopped. "Oh, God, is it that bad?"

"Pretty much. I'm sorry."

"But who did it?"

"Looks to be a murder-suicide." Then, "I was thinking about all the arguments they had over getting married."

"But Noah wouldn't—"

"I heard some of their arguments when I passed their door. He got pretty angry. And you told me yourself that he struck her a couple of times."

"But striking her—"

"Striking her means you're into violence. And the fact that she put up with it just made it worse. She showed him that there wouldn't be any serious consequences."

"She wouldn't talk to him for two or three days at a time."

"But she always took him back. And that was all he cared about. He could handle a few days of not having her as long as he knew that he'd get her back eventually. Which he did. Plus, he was a very possessive guy. And he drank a lot."

She'd calmed down. Tears gleamed in her eyes. "I just keep thinking of Laura. How—how did he do it?"

"Knife."

"Oh, God."

I decided to spare her any more details for now.

"Was it fast?"

"Her dying?"

She nodded.

"Probably very fast."

Which wasn't necessarily true. She'd put up some kind of fight. And if this was typical of most throat-slashings, her last minutes had been hell. But Tandy didn't need to know that. At least not now.

"I'm going to be sick."

I got her up to my room and into the bathroom. She vomited twice. I hadn't unpacked everything since I'd been moved. I turned on a nearby lamp, dug out toothpaste, mouthwash, and an unwrapped toothbrush for her. She thanked me between a half-inch of door and frame.

She spent twenty minutes washing up. I sat in the shadows on the other side of the room. Listened to all the activity downstairs.

When she came back, she sat down in the overstuffed chair and said, "He cut her throat, didn't he?"

"Yeah."

"That can be a terrible way to die, can't it?"

"There are a lot of terrible ways to die."

"You didn't answer my question, Robert."

"Yeah. It can be a terrible way to die."

"You think it took her a long time to die?"

"Probably not a long time."

"How long would you estimate?"

"I'm not a medical examiner, Tandy."

"You're evading my question again, Robert."

"I suppose a couple of minutes."

"A couple of minutes after he cut her throat?"

"Yes."

"God, when you're bleeding like that, and gasping for air, and all panicked and angry—a couple of minutes can be a long time."

"It probably can."

"I hope I don't see it."

At first, I wasn't sure what she meant.

Then she said, "Some psychics 'see' their loved ones dying. They can re-create the whole death scene. They live it over and over again."

"I hope you don't see it, either."

"It was starting to go well for us. I'm getting those funny feelings in my arms again. And all the time. Ever since we went out to where we found the bones."

She'd once told me that when her powers were operating at maximum efficiency, she'd get these tingles that raced up and down her arms.

"The tingles."

"Yeah," she said. "The tingles."

She put her face in her hands. "She would've been so happy about it. This whole night. Finding the bones and everything. The cable people would've been ecstatic."

Then she was weeping. More than simply crying but not yet sobbing. Weeping.

I went over and knelt next to the chair and started giving her a shoulder rub.

"That feels good," she said tearfully.

"That's all the encouragement I need."

I lifted her up and carried her over to the bed, where I set her gently on top of the spread. I rolled her over and started working not only on her shoulders but her back as well.

"You're getting a woodie," she said.

"Sorry."

"I really don't want to do anything."

"I know. I'm sorry. This was something it did entirely on its own."

And isn't that always the way? Some nights when you need them, they're nowhere to be found. Other nights, they keep popping up at inopportune times.

I unstraddled her bottom, knelt next to her in such a way that the only part of my body touching hers was my hands.

"You really think he killed her?" She was done weeping. For now, anyway.

"Sure looks like it."

"Couldn't have been faked?"

"Could have. But it's tough to fake."

"She should've dumped him. I don't know what she saw in him, anyway."

"I guess she loved him."

"He was so unfaithful. I'm not sure why she put up with all the bad stuff Noah did to her. She must have really thought she loved him."

"I'm sure she did."

"God, I wish I could get my hands on him."

The calming effect of my massage was starting to lose its charm, apparently.

The knock was curt. "Hello," a female voice said. The uncertainty in her voice suggested that she wasn't sure that anybody was even in here.

Police Chief Susan Charles.

I eased off the bed and opened the door for her.

"I'll turn on another light," I said.

The light revealed Tandy sitting on the edge of the bed, combing through her short hair with her fingers.

Susan said, "I was actually looking for Tandy. There are two detectives here from the state, and they were asking if we could all talk to Tandy at the same time."

"Fine," Tandy said. "I need to go to the bathroom first."

She went in and closed the door.

Susan stepped closer. "You get a good look at Laura West?"

I nodded.

"He must've really been angry."

"There's one thing that's strange, though." I told her about his phone call and wanting to see me.

"Did he say about what?"

"He seemed to think Paul Renard is still alive."

She smiled. Obviously couldn't help herself. "Are you serious?"

"That's what he said."

"God, I knew he wanted ratings but—"

"That's what I thought. But I wanted to hear his story, anyway."

"I'll let you go through his effects with me if you want. See if we can turn anything up. I need to talk to you anyway. About the crime scene when you saw it. We'll go through his things afterwards."

"I'd appreciate that."

Tandy came back. "Do you have any Tums or anything like that? My stomach is a mess."

"I'm afraid I don't," I said.

"I've got some in my car," Susan said.

"Thanks."

She looked around the room. "Forgive me for saying so, but this is kind of depressing."

"Gee," I said. "I hadn't noticed."

She smirked at me. "Uh-huh." Then, "You ready, Tandy?"

Tandy nodded. Then, "Robert says that maybe she died pretty quickly."

Susan knew she was being put on the spot. She avoided glancing at me to tip her hand. "Sometimes, it can be very fast."

"Did you see her?"

"Yes."

"You think it was fast?"

This time, Susan did glance at me. "I think there's a good possibility it was fast."

"She should have dumped him," Tandy said. "I told her to." She wasn't talking to us. She was talking to Laura. "Big TV star. I think she actually went for that somehow. She was so smart. I don't know why she'd fall for that. Do you?"

This time, she directed her question at me.

"No," I said gently. "I don't know why she'd fall for that, either."

Susan led her quietly out the door.

THE RETIRED MAN was still at the desk. He looked, if possible, even worse than I felt, in his old cardigan, old flannel-type shirt, and old tired eyes.

"This here is town is becomin' quite a place."

"It sure is."

"And both of 'em'll make the national news."

"Probably will."

I had two questions for him. But he wasn't going to make it easy for me.

"There was a senator out here once. State senator by the name of Gibbons. Found out his mistress was bein' unfaithful so he killed her. Shot her eight times. Right out on the highway. Couldn't even wait for her to get out of the car, he was so pissed. Shot her eight times inside the car, then took her body and threw it in the ditch. Now, that's pissed."

"That's pissed, all right."

"Then, when they caught him, he hanged himself in jail. And then you know what?"

"What?"

"Three weeks after that, his wife got in a car wreck. Killed her and the oldest boy."

I didn't need any more depressing stories. "Right at the point where tragedy becomes absurdity" has always been one of my favorite phrases. When things get *so* bad you have to start seeing the ridiculous nature of them.

But tonight, because of Tandy, pale frail fucked-up Tandy, I wasn't able to find anything humorous, let alone absurd, about any of it.

"Well, that's quite a story," I said.

"Ain't done yet."

"You ain't?"

"Oh, no. So the youngest boy of the family?"

"Yes."

"Guess what happens to him?"

"I don't think I want to hear."

"He starts stickin' up banks when he's sixteen."

"God."

"And so they catch him one day down to the Missouri border— same place Jesse James was always workin'—and they kill him."

"Well," I said. "I'm sure glad you shared that with me."

He grinned with his shining store-boughts. "And I ain't done yet."

"You ain't?"

"No, sir. Seems the bank-robbin' kid had a girlfriend and she was just about due to have a baby—this here girl couldn't have been more than fourteen; jailbait, we used to call little gals like her—when she finds out that the bank-robbin' kid has been shot to death by Highway Patrol cops."

"Lord Almighty."

"Then *she* tries to kill herself."

"She does?"

"Yep. But she don't make it. They save her life. So she can have the kid. So she has the kid, except she dies when he's ten—overdose, she was a junkie—and the kid is raised by his aunt and uncle. And guess where I seen him the other night?"

"The kid?"

"Yeah. The one the jailbait delivered. He was on TV, and it was last Tuesday. 'Cept he ain't a kid no more. He's twenty years old. And guess what show he was on?"

"You got me."

"*America's Most Wanted.* Armed robbery and two murders in Florida. And guess what?"

"I don't want to guess."

"He's got this sixteen-year-old gal travelin' with him and *she's* pregnant. Ain't that a pisser?"

"Oh, that's a pisser all right."

"The little gal he's travelin' with is knocked up. Who-ee!" And he slapped the countertop.

I said, wanting to change the subject quickly, "Kibbe get any calls the night he died?"

"Cops already asked me that. And you ain't a cop. At least Noah Chandler played one on TV. You didn't even do that."

"I used to be with the FBI."

He looked at me in a new way. "No shit?"

"No shit."

"Well, I'll be damned. The bureau, huh? That's what you folks call it, ain't it? The bureau?"

So I laid some fanciful FBI tales on him. People like him always like the helicopter-to-helicopter shoot-out story. I saw it one night on a TV movie and decided to put it in my repertoire.

"God, so you were just hanging on with one hand?"

"One hand."

"Over the Atlantic Ocean?"

"Over the dark and brooding Atlantic Ocean?"

"You kill him?"

"Two bullets in the heart."

"Wow."

"He hung on to the strut as long as he could, but then he finally fell into the ocean."

"Wow. They ever find the diamonds?"

"I found 'em next day. I used to be a frogman, so I insisted on diving myself. Took me twenty minutes but I had some luck."

"That Atlantic Ocean is big. You were sure lucky."

"Very lucky," I said. "Frogmen don't usually *have* that kind of luck."

"Say, you want a beer?"

"That sounds great."

While he went back and got us beers, I watched the show in the parking lot.

Everything had started to resemble a movie set. The crowd, the cops, the boxy white ambulance, the flashing, whipping emergency lights. I thought again of a portable scene moved whenever needed. You had a suspicious death, the entire menagerie would show up in only a matter of moments.

Mrs. Giles was the only surprise. I hadn't noticed her before. She wore a dark winter coat wrapped tight about her. She'd been there when Kibbe had been murdered. Now here she was again.

He brought the beers and we drank. I gunned mine. I wanted to ask Mrs. Giles something.

"You ever shoot anybody?"

"Once."

"Bet that was fun, wasn't it?"

"Not really."

He looked stunned. "Shoot a guy and get away with it 'cause you're law? And that ain't fun?"

"I felt kind of sorry for him, actually."

"How come?"

"Oh, he'd lost his job and his wife and his little boy was sick.

And he just sort of went crazy one day and held some people in a bank for hostage."

"You kill him?"

"Yeah. But not because I was trying. He slipped at exactly the moment I fired the gun, and that put his chest in direct line of the bullet. Got him in the heart."

The made-up stories were always filled with macho swagger; the true ones were less imposing but a hell of a lot sadder.

I could see I'd disappointed him. He didn't want stories that talked about the human condition. He wanted tales that *distracted* him from the human story. No time to worry about misery or disease or heartbreak when you're caught up in an adventure story.

So I told him the whopper about the time I caught an assassin on the scaffolding of a building, thirty-eight floors up it was (the number of stories increased every time I told the story), and how he almost flung me to my death as I tried to wrestle his gun away. I think, though I'm not sure, that this story had its origin in one of the early James Bond movies.

"Wow," he said, impressed.

The phone rang and he took it.

I strayed to the window. She was still there, Mrs. Giles, shabby and cold and angry in the chill night.

When he got off the phone, I said, "You know, you'd be helping me out quite a bit if you told me about Kibbe's calls."

He looked at me, assessing. My stories had changed his attitude. "There's a doc in this town name of Williams. A head doc. You know, for nuts."

"Right."

"He called a couple of times the night Kibbe bought it."

"He leave any messages?"

"Just that Kibbe was supposed to call him back ASAP."

"Did you give Kibbe the message?"

"No. When I came on, Janice told me she hadn't been able to find him. And now he's dead."

I was the one who supposedly had the interesting stories. But here was one far more engaging than any I could concoct.

Dr. Williams calling Kibbe after Kibbe had stolen certain items from Dr. Williams's office. I wondered if Kibbe had found something. Or knew something. He must have. I doubted Dr. Williams had been placing a simple social call.

"Anything else?"

"Just that little copying joint down on Main."

"Copying joint?"

"Yeah. You know, they make Xeroxes and stuff. Said his order was ready."

"They say what kind of order it was?"

"Huh-uh."

"When was this?"

"Last night. Right at nine. Lady said she was just closing up and that he could pick up his order in the morning."

"I see." Then, "You happen to notice Dr. Williams around here the last couple of nights?"

"Not really. For one thing, we been kinda busy. And for another, when we *ain't* busy, I read them supermarket papers. They're always a lot of fun."

"But you'd recognize Dr. Williams if you saw him?"

"Oh, sure. They always have him on the tube whenever it's Mental Health Day or somethin' like that."

"I appreciate your help."

"Hell, no. I appreciate the stories. Not often you get to hear an actual FBI agent tell actual stories like that."

"Former FBI man."

He shrugged. "Still and all."

SHE ANGLED HER head away from me when she saw me.

She probably would have run but reasoned that would attract even more attention.

I went up to her and said, "Terrible thing, Mrs. Giles."

The faded prettiness, the animal fear of the eyes, the nervous, awkward movements of the mouth. Mrs. Giles hadn't changed much.

"You know the man who died last night?"

She looked at me as if I were speaking in a foreign language.

"Man named Kibbe. Private detective, actually. He ever stop out your way and ask you questions?"

"I didn't know him." Curt, quick.

"And I don't suppose you knew Noah Chandler, either."

"I told you he asked us questions."

"Or Laura West?"

"Her, too. I didn't like the way my husband kept lookin' her over." Then, "Why are you asking me these questions?"

"Just want to know everybody's relationship. By the way, how's your petition going?"

She made no secret of what she was doing. Took a pint bottle from her coat pocket. Took a nice long swig.

"It's goin' all right. But the way you people keep dyin', we won't need no petition drive."

I changed the subject. "I'd like to see Claire tomorrow."

She looked as if I'd slapped her. "Can't be done."

"Why?"

"She's not feeling well."

She was lying and she didn't care that I knew. "What you're saying is that I can't see her."

"What I'm saying is that she's sick."

I stayed on her, the interrogator. "I'm told she used to see Dr. Williams."

"So what if she did? She don't any longer, anyway."

"I don't suppose you'd tell me why."

For just a moment there, her alcoholic features morphed themselves into the grinning, belligerent face of a gargoyle. "I don't suppose I would. You're right about that, Mr. Payne."

One of the bodies was being brought out now. We watched in silence. It was still a waste, all this death, of brisk and bracing football weather. We should have been in the bleachers at some high school game, cheering on the Rough Riders and spiking our coffee with a little bourbon.

The body was on a gurney. They fit it inside the ambulance and then closed the doors again and went back to the motel room.

"I'd better get back. Fred's expecting me."

With that, she turned and started away. I took the sleeve of her winter coat. "Something happened to Claire, didn't it?"

"Nothing happened to her. Not that it's your business even if it did."

"I'd like to talk to her."

"Impossible."

"For just a few minutes."

"If you even try, I'll call Chief Charles and raise so much hell, you'll be in trouble. And don't think I can't, Mr. Payne. Don't think I can't. I may not be important, but I do know the law and I have a cousin here who's a lawyer. He can make your life hell, believe me."

I believed her.

"Now let go of my sleeve."

I let go. She walked away.

Susan Charles came up. "Looks like you two may never be fast friends."

"You may be hearing from her."

"About what?"

"Me. She thinks I'm harassing her." Then, "You know anything about Claire, her daughter?"

"Not much. She's supposedly autistic, although she didn't have any problems until after the fire at the asylum. She almost died in it. Now she lives up in the attic and only the people who watch her when her parents have to go somewhere see her. She got lost a few times when I was younger. There were big searches for her, I remember that. Now they keep her locked up."

"They're sure she's autistic?"

"Meaning what?"

I shrugged. "Meaning, I'm not sure. But certain kinds of trauma can pass for autism. To the untutored eye, anyway."

"You're suggesting what?"

"I'm suggesting that I'd like to get in and see her for myself."

She smiled. "No wonder Mrs. Giles doesn't like you. She doesn't let anybody see Claire, ever."

"No one?"

She nodded. "Oh, a country social worker comes to see her, once a month or six weeks for fifteen, twenty minutes a visit. Nothing in any depth. Just makes sure she's being treated well and things like that."

"Ever been any complaints?'

"None that I know of."

A uniformed cop came over. "They'd like to see you inside, Chief."

"Thanks, Merle. I need to get back, Robert. I wouldn't push Mrs. Giles. She can really raise a lot of hell when she wants to."

"Yeah," I said. "I got that impression."

TWO

READING THE LOCAL newspaper in the john. Feeling superior to some of the stories. Big-city boy like me. Then remembering how many small towns I've lived in in my life. Towns far smaller than this one. Properly humbled.

Washing the day off me with a soapy washrag. Scrubbing my teeth. A final pee.

In bed. Leno or Letterman? Leno so bland. Letterman such an arrogant asshole. What a choice. Settle for *Nightline*. Famine. Genocide. Mass graves. Just the kind of thing I want to put in my mind right before I drift off to sleep.

Try a book. One of the A. A. Fairs of Erle Stanley Gardner. *Gold Comes in Bricks*. Very funny scene with Donald Lam learning martial arts. Finally start to relax. The forties will always be my favorite era, and the Fair books evoke them nicely. Read forty pages. The Fairs rarely fail. Errant erection. Reason with it to give me a break. Please give me a break. What is the use of an erection when you're alone at this time of night? And masturbation at the moment is just too much work. And anyway, don't you need your rest?

So tired suddenly can barely swing over to turn off the light. Sleep, then, immediate, deep.

☾

THE KNOCK DISORIENTS me.

Part of a dream?

What time is it?

Darkness. Where am I? And then it comes back. Brenner. The murders. And according to the digital clock on the desk, 2:39 A.M. Been asleep about two hours.

Exhausted.

Drag myself from bed. Knocking is light, timid somehow.

Open the door and there she is.

Night smells: cold air, cigarette smoke, perfume. Hers.

Leaning against the door frame. Girly grin on her face. "I'm kinda drunk, Robert." Ready to fall down and pass out.

"Gee, no fooling."

"You know what my limit ish? My limit ish two drinks a night. Sshpread out. Guessh how many I've had?"

"Ninety-three."

"You smart-ass." Then she hiccuped to complete the stereotype of the drunk. "Sixsh. I've had sixsh."

She reeled away from the door and almost went over backwards. I grabbed her. "Why don't you come in?"

"All right if I barf in your bathroom?"

"What're friends for?"

"I haven't had very mush to eat so it won't be too bad."

I got her inside. Got a light on. Got her in a chair.

"How'd you get so loaded?"

Her chin was touching her chest. She had started to snore. And then her head whipped up and she said, "Huh?"

"Where've you been?"

"Thish little tavern with thish cute jukebox."

"Boy, there's a novelty. A tavern with a jukebox."

Closing one eye so she could see me better. "My sister died tonight."

"I know."

"How'd *you* know?" she said suspiciously, as if I might have had something to do with it.

"I found the bodies, remember?"

Her head wobbled again and she stared at the floor. "Fucking Noah Chandler. Ish jesh like 'im to kill hisshelf. Take the easy way out."

Her head wobbled in my direction again. "You shoulda been there, Robert."

"Been where?"

"This tavern."

"Oh. Who all was there?"

She grinned. " 'Who all?' What're you, *southern*'r something all of a sudden?" Then she giggled. "Who all? You all? See the connection, Robert?"

"I see it. So who was at this tavern?"

"Oh, lessheee. Susan. You know, the police chief. And a couple of her deputies. And—oh, yeah—Dr. Williams."

"Dr. Williams? What was he doing there?"

She shrugged. Shook her head.

"How'd you get back here?"

"This deputy."

"Fuller?"

"Yeah. 'R somethin' like that, Fuller." Giggled again. "I thought he was gonna put the moves on me. He had to help me up into his van. And talk about 'Russian hands and Roman fingers.' God!" Then, abruptly, "Oh, God, Robert, I wasn't kiddin' about usin' your bathroom."

I followed her to the john.

Frantically.

She vomited.

Twice, actually.

I held her both times.

Then I got the water running in the shower and her clothes off and gave her a good scrubbing down. The shower helped. Alternately hot and cold water. By the time she was ready for the towel, she was self-sufficient again.

Not only did she dry herself off, she partook of my toothpaste tube. She asked if I had a hair dryer. I smiled and pointed to my thinning hair. No dryer required except a towel.

I used the bathroom after her and when I came out, she was propped up in bed with the remote in her hand. The light was on.

"I've never liked Bette Davis," she said.

"Well, from what I hear, Bette never thought much of you, either."

She laughed. But it wasn't the casual laugh I was used to. It was pushed a little too hard.

"She's just so mean. And the men around her are always such wimps."

She went around the dial once and then started crying. No warning.

I crawled into bed and held her. I turned the light out but left the TV on very low.

I must've held her fifteen minutes that way. My erection came back and I felt guilty as hell. Here was I trying to offer my mere and baffled solace to a woman I thought a lot of, and here all my dick could think about was sex.

Then she took my hand and slid it inside her pajama top. And then she slid her own hand inside my pajama bottom.

"I guess we should do something about that penis of yours," she said.

And so we did.

It was not the transforming sex she needed. She didn't have an orgasm. "You go ahead and finish. I'm just not in the mood for it right now."

She did a couple of wonderful little things to make sure my finish came along reasonably soon.

And afterward, we lay in the darkness, and the way she talked, I realized that she'd used sex as a bridge to conversation. Making love creates an intimacy you can't ever quite duplicate in the living room or breakfast nook.

"I want to go to confession."

"I didn't know you were Catholic," I said.

"No. But you are. Don't they have like a citizen's confession deal?"

"What's a citizen's confession deal?"

"You know, where under certain circumstances you can hear confession just the way a priest would?"

"Sort of like a citizen's arrest, only this has to do with confession?"

"Exactly."

"Well, I guess I've never heard of that."

"Well, maybe you should suggest it to the pope or something."

"I'll bring it up the next time we're having lunch."

She lay against my arm. We were silent for a few minutes. The trucks sounded lonesome on the highway. Omaha and Denver and Cheyenne coming up down the pike in the sprawling prairie darkness.

She said, "I should be thinking of her."

"Laura?"

"Yeah. But you know who I'm thinking of?"

"Who?"

"Me. I mean, I feel terrible about her. I loved her. We fought a lot but I loved her."

"I know you did."

"And that's why I got so drunk tonight. So I could hide out and the pain couldn't find me. You know what I mean?"

I remember how my drinking had soared following the death of my wife. "I sure do."

"But as shitty as I feel about her, I feel great about me. I found those bones tonight. *I* did. The girl nobody ever took seriously. The girl everybody said was stupid and not nearly as pretty as her sister and not nearly as much fun to be around as other girls and the girl nobody ever wanted to choose for sports or any of the important clubs or anything like that. I can do something none of those girls can ever do. You know that?"

"Yes, I do."

"I'm somebody again, Robert. I should be thinking of Laura. But half the time—better than half the time—I'm thinking of me and how it's all going to come around for me again. The cable folks are going to be so happy. And the book deal will go through for sure now. And the European tour. And I'll be rich. Really and truly rich. And my ratings will soar again, too."

I took her hand. The anger, the bitterness had never been so clearly expressed before. Almost as if she'd been afraid to confront them because they might overwhelm her. But she faced them squarely now because the power was back. She was right, the power made her somebody indeed. Who else could claim such abilities? But I didn't see her as arrogant.

The ugly duckling, the always-dismissed little girl, the girl who babysat on her prom night, she was finally getting some of the pie. And who could resent her for that?

"You're doing just fine."

"She was my sister, Robert. I loved her. And now all I'm thinking about is me."

"You'll think about her the rest of your life, Tandy. Six, seven times a day, she'll come into your mind. And you'll talk to her. Maybe not out loud. But you'll communicate with her. And you'll use her for strength and guidance."

"You talk to your wife?"

"All the time."

She hugged me. "I just wish—there are just many things I should've said."

I hugged her back. "You'll say them. But not right now. When the time is right."

She went to sleep a few minutes before I did. But I couldn't hold out much longer. I clung to sleep the way I'd clung to her.

THREE

THE PRESS WAS there at seven-fifteen that morning.

At their knock, Tandy started groaning, still asleep.

I crept from bed on tiptoes and went to the curtained window and peeked out.

Two of them. Ken and Barbie. Knocking on the door. Behind them, sweeping over half the parking lot, was an array of vans and trucks and dish antennas. Our story had gone national.

Barbie I recognized as a CBS reporter. Not first-string. But with enough airtime to be taken seriously.

Bright, lovely day. Early sun burning off late fog in the piney hills. Curious small-town dogs already prowling sniff-nosed the parking lot. Who were all these interesting new folks and what was all this odd, bulky equipment? Gee, sometimes it was just so much fun to be a dog. The rewards were so unexpected. And wonderful.

"Tandy." Barbie. Then, "Tandy, it's CBS."

"And NBC," Ken said.

"We'd like to buy you breakfast."

There had to be twenty reporters and twice as many techs in the parking lot.

"Tandy. Please. We know you're in there."

"Don't you want to send some kind of message to your fans?" Ken.

"We talked to your boss, Mr. Kaplan. He said it was fine if you talked to us."

"What bullshit artists," Tandy said from bed. "Kaplan died three months ago in a car accident. They just got his name from some book."

"You'll probably have to face them," I said as I walked back to the bed.

Wan smile. "I was thinking that this'd all make Laura very happy."

"I was thinking that myself."

"CBS and NBC pounding on the door. Begging for an interview."

"This is a national story now. You finding the bones. The murder-suicide."

She swung her slender legs out of bed. Ragamuffin hair. Sleep-scarred right cheek. Tiny yawn. Tight quick stretch of tight quick arms.

"I should take a shower first."

"Probably a good idea."

"Look good, I mean."

"Right."

She looked at me seriously for the first time this morning. "You all right with this?"

"Sure."

"I'm not being cynical? My sister's dead and I'm doing promo?"

"Well, it isn't promo exactly. You're grieving for your sister and you'll convey that. Whatever the show gets in publicity is extra."

She padded over, stood on tiptoes, and kissed me. "I'll bet my breath is bad, isn't it?"

"Tandy, everybody has bad breath in the morning."

"Yeah. But mine is *really* bad. And I probably smell, too, don't I?"

"Something terrible." Then, "You took a shower about six hours ago. How bad could you smell?"

"I got up to tinkle in the middle of the night. I'm starting my period. I smell when I start my period."

"Not to me, you don't."

"Really?"

"Really." And she really didn't.

She started to the bathroom door. "So I'm not being cynical, talking to the press?"

"You're not being cynical."

"I really loved her, Robert."

"I know you did."

She smiled. "I just keep thinking how happy she'd be with all this promo."

"Take your shower."

I tugged on my clothes and went to the door. "Tandy'll meet you at the coffee shop in forty-five minutes."

"Are you a friend of hers?"

A group of ten other reporters now encircled Barbie and Ken. Bobbing up and down like apples in a barrel.

I said, "Something like that."

"Had Laura and Noah Chandler been arguing before last night?"

"Tandy will answer all of your questions. And that's about it for now. See you in forty-five minutes."

WHILE TANDY DRESSED, I took a quick shower. Her old clothes looked better than my old clothes. I changed into a white button-down shirt and chinos. The clean clothes felt good.

She looked sweet. I led her down to the coffee shop, escorted her inside. Her celebrity had doubled in the last few hours. Yesterday, she wouldn't have fetched a half-dozen stares. Today, virtually everybody in the crowded coffee shop glanced and stared at her.

Her sister was killed. Last night. Right over to the motel.

That handsome guy who used to play a cop on TV, he killed her. Noah Chandler, his name was. Remember?

I saw an attractive woman with the word MANAGER on her plastic ID tag. I told her the circumstances and asked if there was a small party room where we could set up. She said there was.

There was a small banquet table. They set their mikes up on it and stashed Tandy in the middle.

There was only room for a half-dozen camera people.

The manager personally brought Tandy a large breakfast, two eggs over easy, hash browns, toast, orange juice, coffee, Diet Pepsi.

When she finished breakfast, the questions started. And that's when I slipped out.

AM LED ME to Susan Charles's office.

Susan said, "Thanks, Am." Then, "Coffee, Robert?"

"Thanks."

She walked over to the Mr. Coffee, poured us each a cup.

"You owe me one," she said, serving me.

"Oh?"

"The press wanted to start knocking on your door at five-thirty. But I insisted they hold off for another hour or so."

"I'll send you a yacht."

"I'd appreciate that."

I sipped the coffee. It was actually not too terribly bad.

I said, "You still thinking it was murder-suicide?"

She seemed surprised. "Yes. Aren't you?"

"I guess not."

She sat back in her chair. "This should be interesting. Why not?"

"I'm not sure."

"There's a convincing argument."

I shrugged. "Why *now*? They'd been having this argument—

whether she'd marry him or not—for months. Why would he suddenly decide to kill her?"

"I doubt he 'decided' to kill her, Robert."

"No?"

Shook her head. "Argument starts. Heat of the moment. Kills her accidentally. Or in such a blind rage that it's *almost* accidental. Sees what he's done and feels so much remorse that he kills himself, too. Happens all the time."

"That's true. But I still don't buy it. Just my gut is all."

Intercom. Am. "City council meeting in ten minutes, Chief."

"Thanks." Susan Charles shrugged. "Maybe you're right, Robert. But we really won't know anything until we get the lab stuff back."

I stood up. "I'll walk you to your car."

The Greyhound station was as worn out as the people it served, shadowy, chilly, vaguely ominous. Bus travel used to be respectable. Not any more. There were still just the good plain folks who took the short rides from one small town to another but there were also the kind of sad and crazed felons who were either just out or just headed to prison—small-time con-artists, would-be political radicals, men expert with knives, gun, burglary tools, and how to move an amazing amount of drugs in a short time. Last year, something like eight Greyhound drivers were killed by their passengers. The old days were long gone.

The lockers were four wide, six deep. Several of them looked as if somebody had taken a crowbar to them from time to time. The lock gave me some trouble. It was just a plain Yale but it wouldn't open without a lot of wiggling and waggling. I picked up what was inside, shut the door, and took off.

All this was watched by a lean, pale man who could have, in the right light, passed for an albino. He wore a cheap Cubs jacket and a shirt opened to his sternum. He inhaled his cigarette so deeply you suspected he was trying to get lung cancer. He grinned at me with bad teeth and said, "Enjoy it, man. Wish I had a stash like that."

They're everywhere these days, even in small towns, the shadow people, all crazed vaguely threatening grins and obscure words and that terrible burden of sorrow in the soft insanity of their eyes. I got away from him as quickly as I could.

☾

THERE WERE MAYBE two dozen sheets of paper in the package. It'd been a long fax. The logo on the cover said ST. JUDITH'S PSYCHI-ATRIC HOSPITAL.

I was sitting on a park bench in the town square. Two squirrels in front of the Civil War memorial were busy digging up nuts. The angling sunlight was warm as only autumn sunlight can be warm. Not burning hot, but nourishing, preparing us for the winter soon to come.

I was just getting a start on the faxed pages inside when I saw her across the street. On her trusty bicycle. She was sliding a letter beneath the driver's-side windshield wiper on my rental car.

Emily Cunningham. The cousin of the girl Rick Hennessy had supposedly killed.

I just watched her. She didn't see me. Didn't even look around, really. Just shoved the letter between blade and windshield and took off pedaling fast. As if moving fast and not looking around at all somehow made her invisible.

I gave her a few minutes and then got up and walked over to the rental car and picked up the envelope.

It was business-sized, white, a number ten.

PAYNE was written on the front of it in blue ballpoint.

It was not only sealed, it was also Scotch-taped.

I carried the envelope back to the park bench where I'd been sitting. The two squirrels were still busy digging up what proved to be acorns.

I was just about to slit open the envelope when somebody said, "Hello, Robert. I snuck out the back door."

Tandy, looking young and revitalized in a way I would have thought impossible a few hours before, sat down next to me.

"Wow. All these papers. Studying for a big test?"

She was jaunty, as she could sometimes be. The media attention had been good for her.

"Kibbe left these behind at a copy shop."

"You looked through them yet?'

"Just started."

"You take half, I'll take half."

They divided ten, ten evenly.

The faxes I had dealt with one Dr. Wayne DeVries. His medical degree had come from the University of Washington, he'd interned in New York City, and he'd spent his first thirteen working years at St. Judith's, on whose letterhead this was written. In 1981, while on a fishing vacation, he drowned. There were no witnesses to the drowning. The body was found washed up downriver three days later. An autopsy confirmed drowning as the cause of death. There were several bruises on the doctor's throat, face, and upper arms, but the meaning of these was inconclusive.

There were other letters citing his brilliant psychiatric career. He'd twice received special awards from the American Medical Association. And once received a presidential citation for his work in dealing with posttraumatic disorders, notably those of Vietnam veterans.

"How you doing?" I said.

"I don't understand why all this stuff about this Dr. Williams is here."

"Neither do I. Not yet." I took several pages from Tandy to compare with my pages.

Three pages later, I began to see the connection between DeVries and Mentor, the psychiatric hospital here in Brenner.

When you put the records of Dr. DeVries and Dr. Aaron Williams side by side, you saw remarkable similarities. They'd had virtually identical careers, right down to receiving presidential citations for their work in posttraumatic stress disorders.

In fact, with only a few minor derivations, DeVries could have been a clone of Williams. Or, more properly, Williams could have been a clone of DeVries.

"Look at this," I said, and handed her the pages I'd been examining.

She looked them over. "Wow."

"No kidding."

"How could two people have the same identical record like this?"

"The short answer is, they couldn't. Not this close, anyway."

"So what does it mean?"

I told her Noah Chandler's theory about Paul Renard still being alive.

"Then Dr. Williams is Renard?"

"It's possible. Plastic surgery. Faked credentials, using this DeVries history as his own."

She smiled. "The inmates running the asylum."

"The most psychotic inmate of them all. The cannibal."

"And now he's in charge of the whole hospital."

The sunlight seemed to dim suddenly, the way it does when a cloud passes chilly and gray across a summer afternoon. A portent, a symbol. I kept remembering the journals Renard had left behind. The prospect of his being alive—and even worse, disguising himself as Williams—both amused and sickened me. All the degrading filth he'd subjected others to. And he was still alive.

"So now what?"

"I drive out and see Williams."

"Just confront him?"

"At least make him explain the similarities."

"But how would that prove that he was Renard?"

And then Kibbe's approach finally made sense to me. The papers and the paperweights he'd stolen from Williams's desk.

"Renard had been in the army briefly."

"So?"

"So his fingerprints would be on record somewhere."

"I'm still not following you."

"Remember when I told you that Kibbe snuck into Williams's office one day and took some stuff?"

"Right."

"That's what he was doing. Looking for something with Williams's fingerprints on it. Then he could send the things in and have them checked. He could tell right away if Williams was Renard."

"Can't we do that?"

"We can. But it'll take longer than we have. And anyway, I want to see how Williams responds to this in person. That'll tell me a lot right there."

"He can always refuse to talk to you."

"He can. But I don't think he will when I tell him what I've got. At the very least, he'll be curious and want to know everything I know."

She touched her head. Her entire body spasmed.

"You all right?"

She didn't say anything for a moment. Another spasm. A couple walking by looked at her. Junkie, they probably thought.

I slid closer, put my arm around her.

"What's going on?"

Still silent. A final body jerk then.

A deep sigh. A whimper caught in her throat. She touched fingers to her head again.

"It started right after breakfast."

"What did?"

"You know how I used to make drawings sometimes?"

"Sure. That's how we found where the second body was buried."

"There's a face—a shape of a face, actually. Ever since breakfast. It's kind of spooky. Like a ghost, I mean. I can see it but I can't see it. It needs to come clearer."

"You think it's the killer."

"I honestly don't know, Robert." She took my hand in hers and then raised it to her cheek. "I'm sure glad you're here."

"You want to give me your sorority pin?"

She laughed. "Asshole."

She sat back on the park bench. Looked around. "Norman Rockwell. You remember his paintings?"

"Sure."

"He was before my time, but my folks had this big book of his cover paintings for the *Saturday Evening Post*. And that's what this park is like. 1948. Everything's just so peaceful and laid back. Not all the city bullshit. I'd love to live in a town like this again."

"Then why don't you?"

She laughed again, but this laugh was a sad one. "Because for right now I'd rather have the fast lane. I'm really starting to enjoy it. The cable people have called me three times this morning. They wanted me to know that they're picking up fifteen more episodes and increasing the production budget at least twenty-five percent. I can't resist that, Robert."

"Sure you can. What you're saying is you don't *want* to resist that."

"Yeah, I guess you're right. I don't want to resist it."

I stood up. "I'd better go see about setting up an appointment with Dr. Williams."

"You're not scared?"

"Of what?"

"Of just confronting him, I guess."

"No. Not really. I'm more curious than anything. I want to find out if Paul Renard is alive."

"God, if he is," she said, "this is going to be some show."

I tried hard not to notice that she hadn't mentioned Laura as yet today. Maybe she was temporarily cried out. We all get that way around death. But she had changed. Subtly, true. But unmistakably.

She was going away. And I guess I understood it, how the celebrity had hooked her and all, but I felt lonely nonetheless. I missed the troubled but relatively simple young woman she'd once been. Maybe I wanted her to remain part child so I could remain part child, too, the oddly protective but youthful part of me—the silly part—she'd always brought out in me in our first affair. Maybe she was growing up and I resented it.

She stopped talking abruptly, putting her hands to her face and then shaking her head as if something had just shocked her. "My God, will you listen to me? My sister's dead and all I can do is blather on about myself." She looked at me and said, "I loved her."

"I know you did."

"Oh, God, Robert, look what I've become."

"People don't always go into hysterics when somebody dies. Maybe you're just in denial."

"You'd think I could at least mention her fucking name once in a while."

"You're doing fine."

She was pacing in little circles. Frantic. Crazed. So many thoughts and feelings bombarding her. "Don't you think I should at least cry?"

"You'll cry later. There's no timetable."

"Or scream? Or throw things?"

"Maybe a drink would be better."

"And you know the worst thing?"

"What?"

"I keep worrying about the show. Here my sister's dead—my sister who raised me—and I'm worrying about the show. Isn't that incredible? I can't fucking believe myself sometimes."

F. Scott Fitzgerald said that when he went to visit his father for the last time, he was deeply moved by the man's suffering—and yet a part of Fitzgerald's brain, he later admitted in his notebooks, was wondering how he was going to write this scene in a novel.

I suppose we're all capable of being distracted that way. Maybe it's just another form of denial. One more wall to put up against the terrible truth.

She said, "I'm such a cold-hearted bitch, Robert. I really am."

My role here was to agree with her. Being a gallant kind of guy, I said, "No, you're not. You're a warm, loving woman and you know it."

"Oh, God," she said, and now the tears came full and hard as she flung herself rather dramatically into my arms, "Oh, God, I hope you're right, Robert!"

But I had to wonder who the tears were for—her sister or herself and the realization that she really had lost something valuable in her rush to become a star.

I SAT IN the car reading the note Emily Cunningham had affixed to my windshield.

You need to talk to Claire in the attic. Ask her to get you the baby picture. She'll know what you mean. Sandy told me about this.

There was no signature.

And just how was I supposed to get to Claire-in-the-attic? It was unlikely her parents would let me go upstairs and visit their daughter.

I took out my cell phone and called the number on the card Iris Rutledge gave me earlier. Iris answered the phone herself.

"I got a strange note from Sandy's friend Emily Cunningham."

"I'm happy for you, Mr. Payne."

"You talk to her?"

"Yes, I did."

"I don't suppose you'd tell me what you talked *about*?"

"I certainly wouldn't."

"She tell you about the baby picture?"

Pause. "What do *you* make of it?"

"I don't know."

"Neither do I, actually." Pause. "She said that Sandy used to watch Claire when her parents would drive over to Cedar Rapids for the day. She said Sandy told her she'd seen something very weird one day."

"The baby picture?"

"Right."

"What was so weird about it?"

"All Sandy said was, 'I've seen that before.' "

"That same picture?"

"I guess so. Emily wasn't sure. She said she was over at Sandy's and her dad came along to pick her up and take her home. She said Sandy never talked to her about it again."

" 'The same baby picture.' I don't understand."

"That's all Emily knows, Mr. Payne."

"But she did say that Claire would understand?"

"Yes."

"So Claire does speak sometimes?"

"That's my understanding."

"I got the impression that she never speaks."

"Her parents are strange people. Especially her stepfather. And those snakes of his. I hate snakes."

"Me, too."

"I've got to get ready for a client, Mr. Payne. Good luck to you."

I got in my car and drove out to Claire's house.

FOUR

IT WAS A two-story frame corner house with the kind of junky garage behind that seemed common in this area. Isolated from its neighbors by half a block on both sides. The garage doors hung awkwardly, seeming about ready to fall off. The backyard was littered with pop cans and beer cans and paper scraps, as well as some gray clumps that might have been boxes that had collapsed when they were left out in the rain. A defeated-looking dog dragged himself from one end of his cage to the other. He barked once but it was a pathetic performance. You could see where somebody had tried to scrape dog poop off the front sidewalk. Maybe they were going to have a party.

The garage was empty.

So their car was gone and I had to make a decision. Should I risk trying to get inside, upstairs to where Claire rocked back and forth and sat silhouetted in the attic window?

The baby picture.

Claire might be the only one who could help me with that.

I got out of the car and started across the sidewalk. Three kids on the tricycles sat two doors down, watching me and whispering to each other. I waved to them. They didn't wave back. I didn't blame them. Earthmen should never humble themselves by waving at Martians.

No sounds from inside as I mounted the three paint-shorn steps. I walked across the age-slanted porch and knocked on the screen door. I angled my ear to the door. No sounds from inside, either.

The shellacked pine door behind the screen door was relatively new. As was the lock mechanism. It was a cheap one.

"Hey," somebody said, and I spun around, scared. I'd been so involved in appraising the lock—seeing how much trouble it represented—that the voice had startled me.

"Hey," I said back.

The mailman was chunky and gray-sideburned and suntanned. His near-empty bag said he was near the end of his route.

"Nice day," he said. "Sure hope this keeps up. Maybe we can slide by until December."

"Wouldn't that be nice?"

He jammed the mail into the rusted black box on the pillar connecting porch floor with porch ceiling.

Then, "Be even nicer if the Hawks'd have a good season."

"Sure would."

He was suspicious of me, of course. The babble was meant to cover his suspicion.

I said, "Doesn't look like they're home."

"I had to drop an overnight package off here this morning. Said they were going to look at a new car this afternoon. Their other one's falling apart."

Still looking at me. Judging me. Still very suspicious.

I faced him and walked to the front of the porch. "Guess I'll stop back later."

We both heard it. Claire's cry. The exotic call of a forlorn night bird.

"Poor gal," he said. "I went to high school with her."

"You did, huh?"

He smiled. "Had a crush on her then—and even after she came back from nursing school. She sure was pretty back in those days. But of course Paul Renard took her away from me."

"You knew Renard pretty well?"

"Hell, no. He wouldn't spend any time with somebody like *me*."

"But you knew Claire?" I wasn't sure why that was especially interesting. But it was.

"Almost everybody knows everybody else in a town like this. And Claire was a real beauty."

I had to finish the charade.

I came down off the steps and walked with him to the sidewalk.

"She went to nursing school?"

"Yep. Worked with her mom out there. The bughouse, I mean." Another cry.

He looked up at the attic window. "You'd think they'd be used to it by now."

"Who?"

"The people on the route. The neighbors around here."

"Oh."

"They say her voice still gives them shivers. All the little kids think she's a witch." He nodded to the tricycle trio down the block. "Those kids think she's a Martian."

I laughed. "Well, they're a little more creative than other kids their age." Then, "Well, see you," I said.

I walked back to my car and drove off.

I PARKED TWO blocks away and came back up the alley.

The garages in the neighborhood, like the houses, were old, sagging. The alley floor was gravel.

A woman hanging out her wash on a clothesline waved, apparently mistaking me for somebody else. A pigtailed little girl jumping rope stopped abruptly to watch me. And a young sweet-faced collie growled proudly at me as I passed her backyard.

When I reached the backyard of the Giles house, I moved quickly to the screened-in back porch.

Amazingly tidy, given everything that surrounded it. Twelve packs of empty Pepsi cans stacked neatly in one corner; an old divan tucked in another; even a small, thrumming refrigerator for cold beer and pop.

The back-door lock wasn't any more troublesome than the front-door lock would have been.

I carry a number of Burglar's Helpers. That's what this cop I knew used to call them. Open most any kind of lock, most anytime I care to. Superman should have such power.

I got inside. The cat stench was an acid physical presence. Two litter boxes sat next to an ancient white stove. The boxes hadn't been emptied in some time. A small cat with pinkeye looked up at me, lost and heartbreaking. Even from here, I could see the fleas.

I had to move quickly.

Kitchen. Dining room. Living room. Cramped and junky, each. Stairway.

I went up the enclosed stairs between the swollen slabbed walls that were still rough and unpainted long years after being plastered into place.

I came to a landing.

The second floor was a junk room. Sort of what the attic probably *should* have been.

Dusty boxes, the dust already playing hell with my sinuses; coat trees; three table-model TVs that apparently hadn't worked for a long time; two large steamer trunks, neither with gay travel stickers on it; a set of twenty-year-old supermarket encyclopedias; and little girls' things—dolls that wet, dolls that talked, dolls that sang, dolls that went at least number one and maybe even number two, two single beds, a giant Mickey Mouse, a Schwinn ten-speed, high school pennants, and an array of framed photos of a very beautiful young woman at various ages. Claire, I was sure.

No wonder the mailman had had a crush on her. She wasn't the obvious sexpot or the shy honor-roll beauty. Instead, there was a simple and clean beauty to her face and slender body that grew more imposing and fetching the longer you studied them. And there was the sorrow, too.

From the youngest shots to the oldest—which I marked at about age twenty—there was a somber quality to the blue eyes and small but erotic mouth. The older she got, the more pronounced the sorrow became. In the later shots, the inherent grief of her eyes belied her sensual charm, made her look older and more severe than she should have.

I sneezed. And felt for a moment like my dear friend Inspector Clouseau, as played by the late Peter Sellers. Certainly, sneezing should be a part of everybody's stealth equipment.

There was a short staircase at the far end of the second floor. This no doubt led to the attic.

The boards creaked even though I walked on tiptoe. Given my sneeze and the squeaking boards, all I needed was a trombone to announce my presence.

The interior of the enclosed stairs held four steps.

I stood at the base of them, listening.

A fey song, an off-key ballad of some kind, sad and sweet at the same time. The voice singing it was barely a whisper, so fragile it was heartbreaking and more than a little unnerving with its hint of madness. The Ophelia scene every actress longs to play.

I crept up the steps one at a time, pushing out at both walls for balance.

The door was padlocked. Big-ass Yale lock.

I tried very hard not to sneeze. I managed to swallow it down.

I put my ear to the small and dusty door. Claustrophobia was starting to fill my chest, increase my heartbeat. The enclosure was small. Buried alive. The day was suddenly sunless.

I listened.

Chains. Singing. And then, without warning, weeping.

And then the rocking chair squawking back and forth.

No more singing.

Rocking chair now. And violent weeping. But all of it done quietly, warped somehow, like a soundtrack played in slow motion.

Drugs. That was what I was hearing. She'd been sedated. She wanted to scream at full voice but couldn't. Didn't have the energy or quite the focus. Drugs took care of that.

I knocked gently. "Let me help you, Claire." Not much more than a whisper.

Rocking. Weeping. As if she hadn't heard me whisper at all.

"Claire. Please let me help you."

Rocking and weeping suddenly stopped.

"Is that you?"

I had no idea who she was talking about, but I had nothing to lose playing along. "Yes."

"You're really back?" Getting excited now. Happy.

"I'm really back. So I can help you."

"Oh, Lord, thank you so much for answering my prayers."

The rocking chair squeaking as she stood up. A long and ragged sigh. "Oh, I don't want you to see me this way. After all these years."

"I want to help you, Claire. I don't care what you look like. I really don't."

She started rattling the door. Uselessly. No way she was going to open the Yale lock from the other side.

Nor any way I could open it from *this* side. I had the proper pick, but I didn't have the proper experience. It would probably take me hours.

Rattling the doorknob with insane fury. "We've got to get this open! We've got to!"

Screaming now. She had hurtled over the drugs. Full voice.

And then pounding her fists on the other side of the door. Hammering. And kicking with her foot.

"Please! Please! You've got to get me out of here! You've got to get me out of here!"

And then, "If you move, I'll kill you, Mr. Payne. Right where you stand. And there's no jury in the world that would convict me, either."

I turned to face Giles. Bottom of the stairs. Formidable Remington pump-action shotgun in his hands. Dressed like someone who hadn't been clothes shopping for thirty years. Out buying a car, trying hard not to look like a yokel.

He said, "Now, you come right down those stairs and right now."

"No! No!" Claire screamed behind the door, pounding and hammering again. The sobs starting to submerge her speaking voice. "No! No!"

"You get your ass down here, Mr. Payne. Or I'll blow it off."

The hell of it was, I believed him.

HE MARCHED ME downstairs.

His wife went up to the attic.

I could hear her opening the Yale lock.

Hear Claire screaming.

Hear Betty Giles slapping her once, twice, three times.

Hear Claire collapsing in her rocking chair.

And then the door slamming.

He marched me out to the kitchen. I'd been a bad boy and he was going to punish me.

"You sit right there while I call the police."

"You sure you want to do that, Mr. Giles?"

"Yeah, I'm sure. Why wouldn't I be?"

To make his point, he walked over to the brown wall phone and lifted the receiver. He wore his leisure suit again. The blue one. The long-pointed collar of his white polyester disco shirt worn outside. His gold neck chain still looked strangling-tight. His face was blotchy from booze. His dyed red hair was a hairdresser's nightmare. The wife obviously did it for him. Or maybe he did it himself.

He started to punch in some numbers.

"All I came here for was the baby picture. Up in Claire's room."

He stopped punching numbers. "Is that supposed to mean something to me?"

But it obviously did mean something. His whole lumpy body froze suddenly, and his mouth was tight as a dead man's. There was true fear in the dark blue eyes.

"You'd better hang up."

"You go to hell. I want to call the cops, I'll *call* the cops."

"Be my guest."

"You sonofabitch."

He stared at his hand on the receiver.

"You think I'm afraid to call them?"

I shrugged.

"And I don't know anything about no baby picture."

I just watched him.

He slammed the receiver down. Lifted his shotgun from where he'd leaned it against the wall. He pulled a chair out from the Formica kitchen table and sat down.

"I need to talk to the missus."

I said nothing.

"You forget how to talk or something?"

"Nothin' to say, Giles. You're the one with the gun. You're the one who makes all the decisions."

"Breakin' into my house like this."

I said, "Who's in the picture, Giles? The baby picture?"

"I don't know what you're talking about."

"What's a child got to do with any of this? Maybe it was something that Kibbe turned up."

"Kibbe. That fat piece of shit. I got tired of him nosin' around here."

"You kill him?"

He smiled. His dentures looked pretty good today. "Yeah, I killed him all right. I shot him. Then I cut him up. Then I set him on fire. Then I fed him to some wild dogs. I just wanted to make sure he was dead."

"Kibbe knew who was in the baby picture, didn't he?"

"Just lay off that baby picture. You don't know what you're talkin' about."

"Maybe your wife does, Giles. Maybe that's why she's upstairs slapping the hell out of Claire right now. Maybe Claire wanted to tell me who's in the baby picture but your wife doesn't want her to. She's going to load Claire up on drugs now, isn't she? You're going to kill her someday, you know that, keeping her that dosed up? Just because your wife worked at the asylum doesn't make her an expert, Giles."

"She knows what she's doin'. She won't kill Claire. Claire's our daughter. I adopted her when I married her mother, because Claire was sick by then. We love her."

Mrs. Giles came into the kitchen. She didn't say anything. She walked to the sink and washed her hands. I noticed how she washed. Like a doc. Good soapy scrubbing halfway up the forearms. And held under the hot water for at least ten seconds. The minimum is eight. Your better class of docs shoot for ten. She dried off on a new square of paper towel. She turned around and looked at me and said, "You get the hell off our property." She wore a tan suit, wrinkled now, with a frilly white blouse and a pair of brown one-inch heels. She was a little squatty now, but it wasn't difficult to imagine that many years ago the fleshy face had been sharp with classic bone lines and the body sleek and inviting. The ghost of those days still somehow hung around her. Maybe it was the sullen mouth. There's a female petulance that can be sexy. Hers would have been, anyway.

"I'd like to talk to Claire," I said to her.

"No way."

"I'm working on a murder case."

"No, you're not. You're working for that TV show. You just want to dig up dirt on people in this town so that it'll make your show better."

"I should've called the law," Giles said.

"Why didn't you?" she said.

"Because I asked him about the baby picture. The one up in Claire's room."

Her reaction was the same as her husband's. Her mouth said no, her eyes said yes. "What baby picture?"

I sighed. "I don't want to go through it all again." I stood up. "I can always get Chief Charles to come out here."

"On what grounds?"

"Abusing your daughter."

"The county people are here once a month inspecting."

"Her social worker, you mean?"

She nodded. "You can check it out if you want."

Implicit in her answer was that I trusted the opinion of social workers. I don't. I don't see them as devils, as the right wing does; but I do see them as incompetents, as most judges and cops do.

I walked over to the back door. "If she's as bad off as you say, you should put her in a hospital."

"She's our daughter," Betty Giles said.

"All the more reason to see she's treated well."

"That's our business," Giles said. The shotgun lay across the table now. He seemed to have forgotten about it. Then, "And next time, I'll blow your head off, you come trespassin' in here."

In a moment of silence, we all heard it. And looked up, as if to the heavens. But it was really the attic we were looking at. Because of the noise. The soft steady thrum of the rocker going back and forth, forth and back; and the wan Irish voice of her sad song.

"She recovers pretty fast," I said.

"Recovers from what?" Betty Giles said.

Her husband said, "He thinks we keep her drugged up all the time."

"Only when she needs it," Betty Giles snapped.

I pushed open the screen door. It was a good day for yard work. The clear sky. The smoky smell. The warm clean prairie air.

"You get going," Giles said.

I smiled at them and left.

I ducked under clothesline and walked back to the alley, where I loitered for a few minutes looking at the rear of the frame house. I wanted to see how far it was from the roof of the garage to the roof of the back porch.

☾

SHE HAD DRAWN six lines under the letters *NBC!* And then written: *Down at coffee shop for interview!!!!!!* Six exclamation points.

And then I noticed the lined legal-sized yellow pad she'd left on the bed.

At least twenty pages had sketches of partial faces on them. A few of the sketches—a portion of forehead, eye, nose; a portion of chin, mouth, jawline; and so on—resembled a male; others resembled a female.

This was how she'd worked on our previous murder case. She'd drawn sketches of possible burial sites for four days before finally settling on one. And then that sketch was enough to lead us right to the body.

Could she really find the killer this way, through the process of sketching? But why not? The pattern was the same.

Half-realized images in her mind. Blinding headaches, each one of which brought her a little closer to a definitive view of what she was searching for, and finally a fully realized sketch.

Why?

The motel room was dark and cold. I went in and washed up with hot water. And then I went to see Dr. Williams.

FIVE

YOU COULD SEE faces in the windows. Some of the windows were barred. Not that they needed to be barred. A lot of the people in the psychiatric hospital carried their own prisons with them wherever they went.

Late afternoon. A lazy feeling, the kind you got at a magnificent country club, which Mentor Psychiatric strove to emulate, long shadows beginning to stalk the golf greens, the lonely *thwop* of a tennis ball echoing off the piney hills, the outdoor swimming pool blue-green and empty, that melancholy time just before dinner, a loneliness and yearning different not only in degree but quality from nighttime. Not quite so frantic; more reflective. But there was at least one difference between country club and asylum. You didn't see clean-cut young men in white T-shirts and white jeans strolling country club grounds, ready, with their beepers and their muscles, for any kind of trouble.

I parked and walked up the front steps. Two female patients were playing chess.

"You look like an old boyfriend of mine," one said winsomely. "He was a lucky guy."

She giggled. "He was flirty just like you, too." She was fortyish, overweight, and emanated a sweetness that played on her Cupid's-bow mouth and in her gentle brown eyes.

"His name was Rick, and I wish she'd shut up about him," the other one said. Then she giggled. "Especially about his buns." She made a goofy face. "He probably weighs three hundred pounds now and belongs to the KKK."

"He couldn't belong to the KKK." Her friend laughed.

"Why not?"

"He wouldn't be smart enough to spell it."

I laughed at that one, too, and then went on inside to the professional marble and shadow and starched white decorum of the place. Nurses' shoes squeaked; phones rang; faxes clattered.

The reception desk was built into a corner. The receptionist wore a smart gray suit and a smart bland smile.

"I have an appointment with Dr. Williams."

"May I have your name please?"

"Sure." I gave her my name.

"If you'll just take a seat, I'll phone Dr. Williams's secretary."

"Thank you."

I sat. The *Time* magazine was current and the Eames chair was more than relaxing. I thought of Claire. If she was truly mad, this was the kind of place she belonged in.

A few minutes later, she said, "Mr. Payne?"

"Yes."

"I'm afraid the doctor has gone for the day."

"We had a four-thirty appointment."

"I'm sorry. I'm afraid he had to leave early. His secretary said that she was very sorry and that you should call tomorrow and that she'd reschedule you."

No sense arguing. He obviously hadn't wanted to see me.

I said good-bye and walked out of the building. The chess players were gone. The sky was bruising to the east, yellow-mauve bruise heralding dusk and all those pinpoints of distant and indifferent stars. The night chill in the knee with the rheumatism, a family curse along with arthritis and bad sinuses.

From my car I called information and asked for Dr. Williams's home phone number. Not surprisingly, the operator told me it was unlisted. I didn't even bother to ask for the home address. I knew better.

There was a lane leading from the back parking lot. A dark blue Lincoln Town Car shot down that lane now, reaching the road. I got only a glimpse of the Einstein-mussy white hair, but it was enough to recognize the good doctor.

Most obliging of him.

I followed him for the next twenty-five minutes.

HIS HOUSE WAS a modernistic glass-and-stone environmental marvel, with three different wings, an imposing atrium, and a picture window big enough to stage a Broadway musical in. All this in the densest part of the woods. À la Frank Lloyd Wright, it was difficult to know for sure where forest ended and house began, they were so deftly entwined here in the center of a Brothers Grimm–like woods.

A narrow unpaved road wound all the way to his double garage door beneath a wing of the house.

He put his car in the garage. The garage door went down instantly.

I wondered if he knew I was behind him.

I pulled my car off the road and went a wide way to his house. A possum sat in the middle of a pile of fallen autumn beauty, watching me, its tail snake-strong as it flicked through the dry and raspy leaves.

I found a back door that opened into the kitchen. I peeked in a window and the kitchen was empty. I dug out my burglary tools and went to work. If there was a security system, he'd had to turn it off to get inside.

The possum watched me with great interest.

I was inside in less than two minutes.

The kitchen looked as if it had been borrowed from the set of a high-budget science fiction movie. Everything was chrome and glass and built in. Or suspended from the ceiling. It had the unused feeling of a print ad in a magazine with great social aspirations. This was the kind of kitchen that told you that you had not only arrived but that you planned to stay for a good long time.

I had my gun out. I didn't know what to expect. If he was really Paul Renard, he wouldn't be especially happy to see me.

I heard a noise upstairs. I hesitated. Listened.

Drawers being quickly opened and slammed shut.

Doors being flung open.

A frantic sense. Escape.

I walked through the house. Even given the circumstances, I had to pay it its due. An elegant black curved staircase wound from the first floor to the second, contrasting with the white and tan motifs of huge, open living area. With all the statuary, mostly running to medieval Italian it seemed, the place combined the feel of an art gallery and a home you'd never want to spoil by living in it. For sheer cold perfection, it was gorgeous.

More drawers slamming. Cursing now. The noises floating down the staircase.

I went up after him.

For all of its loveliness, the staircase didn't provide much in the way of cover. Even crouched down as I was, he could see me with no problem. I just hoped he kept busy in his rooms.

The noise stopped. Halfway up the staircase, I stopped, too.

What was he up to?

He stalked out of one room. "Where the hell did I put it?" Talking to himself the way we do when we're angry.

Just as long as he didn't decide to check out the staircase for some strange reason.

I crouched even lower. I had stuffed the faxes inside the pocket of my sport coat. They rubbed against my elbow. The sound seemed very loud suddenly. I quietly moved my elbow away. Crouched still lower.

He got busy again. His footsteps were heavy, angry on the carpeted hallway of the second floor.

A door opened. More drawers jerked open, shoved shut. More curses.

I started up the staircase again.

At the top, I hesitated and started to look to the left. And that was when he took his first shot at me.

He stood right in the center of the hallway, holding the weapon cup-and-saucer style just the way they'd taught him at the shooting range, and he let go a shot that came just close enough to knot up my innards and set my left leg to trembling.

I remembered some of my own training at that point. I pitched myself to the floor and rolled across the hallway into the open door he'd exited just a few moments earlier.

He kept on firing.

All the shooting apparently flattered him into thinking he was really in control of the situation.

He started walking slowly down the corridor toward me.

I was now inside the room, with the door angled half-shut.

"I can kill you anytime you want, Mr. Payne," he said.

I smiled. "That's bad movie dialogue, Dr. Williams. You couldn't get in this room if you wanted to."

He put three bullets into the edge of the door.

And scared the hell out of me.

"I know who you are, Doctor. And if I know, that means somebody else knows, too. What's the point of killing me? You're through here, anyway. You're headed to prison."

Long silence. Was he planning something?

I'd underestimated him before. He'd done pretty well putting those bullets in the edge of the door, only a few inches from where I stood. I didn't plan to underestimate him again.

"Shit," he said.

"What?" I said.

"I said shit. S-h-i-t. You're unfamiliar with the word, Mr. Payne?"

His tone confused me. More irritation—frustration—than anger now.

"How the hell did you find out about me, anyway?"

"I didn't. Kibbe did. The private detective."

"That fat bastard. As soon as my secretary told me he'd stolen that paperweight, I knew what he was up to. He wanted my fingerprints. He wanted proof of who I really was."

"You should never have come back here. It was a great joke—the escaped inmate running the asylum. But you were bound to be caught."

"What the hell are you talking about, the escaped inmate?"

"I'm talking about you, Renard. And coming back to the place you'd escaped from."

And then he was laughing. Not mad-scientist laughing. Not loon-crazed psycho laughing. No, this was an intelligent man genuinely amused, laughing.

"Why are you laughing?"

"Because," he said, "you and Kibbe are such stupid pricks. I'm not Paul Renard. My name is Wayne DeVries."

"I SEDUCED HER, and it wasn't easy. For one thing, I was her father's best friend. And for another, she hated me. At first, anyway. Here was this beautiful sixteen-year-old girl who drove around in a Porsche convertible and slept with all the right boys at school and was apparently trying to set a record with abortions. She'd had three before her sixteenth birthday. I had just turned forty. I was overweight and depressed and impotent. My practice was the only thing I had going. My wife had her clubs and her charities and my two boys had their computer games and the matching BMWs we'd bought them for their seventeenth birthday. Our house was very much a motel. Always very busy but always very impersonal. We didn't even have dinner together. The boys always ate in the TV room and more and more my wife wasn't home when I got there. I suspected she was having an affair but I didn't care. One drunken night, I tried humping the maid. You don't think that's embarrassing, especially when you can't get it up? I finally had to fire the woman—I gave her a great severance my wife didn't know anything about. I just couldn't face her every day with that knowing look of hers. 'He can't get it up.' That's what the look said. And it wasn't paranoia. Employees love to have their superior little secrets about employers. And that was the most cutting secret of all.

"So now we come to Ellie. I'm not good at describing people so I won't even try. All I can say is that she was beautiful. And gentle and graceful and subtle. I'd been hired to be her psychiatrist, and as such that was the first thing I noticed, the contrast between her soft personality and her hard life. She was a great fan of Debussy and Monet and Emily Dickinson. And yet at night she'd change into this totally different person. The sleaziest bars. Drugs. Alcohol. Every kind of sex you can conceive of. That's why she'd had three abortions before she was sixteen.

"I said that I seduced her. I'm not sure about that. It could well have been the other way around. After I'd seen her three months, I felt a shift in her attitude toward me. Oh, I don't mean she suddenly saw me as this paramour, but I think she did begin to see me as a person. A person she liked. I'm sure you know about transference, how the patient frequently thinks she's falling in love with her doctor. Ellie—the good Ellie, at any rate—seemed to be going through that with me. She'd write me poems. Brings me flowers that she'd picked. She even took me out for pizza one night. I tried to pretend that I was still in charge. Family man. Respected shrink. Wise and knowing sophisticate. Of course I was in charge. That's why, when it happened that first time in my office, I saw it as my doing, not hers.

"But by then it was too late to matter. I'd never been in love before. I'd never been handsome or dashing or anything like that, so I'd always been forced to be with the 'sensible' girls. Ellie was the opposite of sensible, of course. The danger was exhilarating. She taught me so much about making love. I fancied I became good at it. I saw now that I'd never pleased my wife. No wonder she'd had an affair. Or maybe affairs plural, who knows. I became saturated with Ellie. I wouldn't brush my teeth after we made love. I wanted the taste of her to linger as long as it could. When we were apart, I'd put her photograph next to a flickering candle and masturbate. It got so bad, I couldn't *not* be with her. She gave up the bad Ellie. So we could be together nights. I truly believe she loved me as much as I loved her. And then she told me she was pregnant.

"I spent a whole month pleading with her to have an abortion. We had terrible arguments. She actually wanted to keep the baby.

"I'd come to my senses. I looked at myself in the mirror one day and saw what a tremendous joke I'd played on myself. I was this chunky, nearsighted, rumpled cuckold who'd fallen in love with this beautiful but clinically insane girl who'd been under my care. My God, a quietly unhappy marriage in suburbia was just where I belonged. It was my fate, as the French would say, and I should embrace it. I wanted to be part of the same old monotony again. I'd destroyed my life and humiliated my family. I had to get rid of the baby. I even thought seriously for a time of killing Ellie. I came up with several different creative methods. But I knew I couldn't do it. I wasn't a murderer. I was too weak even for that.

"I kept pestering her, of course. We'd have these terrible arguments in my office. She'd always end up weeping and screaming at me to let her have the baby. My nurse would rush in and remind me that there were patients in the reception area hearing her scream. My whole life was coming apart.

"And then she got in that car wreck.

"By this time, her parents were very suspicious of me. She refused to talk about me to them. So when she died in the car crash—her car suddenly swerved into the path of a semi, whether intentionally or not we'll never know because the highway was very dark and icy—and when they did the autopsy and found out Ellie had been pregnant, all their suspicions were confirmed.

"I tried to lie my way out of it, but the medical tests proved my paternity. My wife immediately went back to Connecticut where her people are. Very wealthy people, too. They found a house for her and the boys. I speak to the boys at Christmastime now. On the phone. Very antiseptic and formal.

"My life was over. At least until I read this magazine article in *Esquire* about how, if you have the money, you can re-create yourself. A little bit of plastic surgery, a lot of forged documents, three or four forged recommendations, and you are a new person.

"I applied for three or four positions. One institution was about to hire me, but somebody on the hospital staff got suspicious and decided to check out one of my reference letters. I immediately withdrew my application.

"The third time, I got lucky. Here in Brenner. I was now Dr. Williams. Head of my own psychiatric hospital, an honor I'd never had before. And now, thanks to you, Mr. Payne, an honor I will have no longer."

"Quite a story."

"And all of it true."

"Sadly."

"Very sadly."

"The coffee's good, anyway."

We sat in his kitchen nook. The Mr. Coffee had done a decent job.

"I was going to run away."

"I know."

"I have a friend in Mexico. He's on the run, too. Sort of the same thing except it involved money instead of sex."

"Money?"

"He got this elderly woman patient of his to sign over several very valuable pieces of property to him. Which he promptly sold. He's got several federal agencies looking for him."

"You two just might give psychiatry a bad name."

He smiled. "If only you knew what *really* went on, Mr. Payne."

I said, "I'd consider going to the hospital and telling them the truth and seeing what happens."

"You mean they might keep me on?"

I shrugged. "Beats running and hiding the rest of your life."

He sipped some coffee. "I imagine you're disappointed."

"About you not being Renard?"

"Yes."

I shrugged. "Things happen that way sometimes."

"He's alive."

I had been stirring sugar into my coffee. I looked up. "You really believe that?"

"Absolutely. He's been taunting me for over a year."

"Taunting you how?"

"Phone messages. He tells me to go back through his records and look for little details he discussed with his shrink. We inherited whatever records survived the asylum fire, since some of the staff doctors are now employed with us. Whoever he is knows things only Renard could know. Names and dates."

"Why didn't you go to the police?"

"Put yourself in my place, Mr. Payne. You don't go to the police unless it's absolutely necessary. Absolutely. And since Renard—or whoever he was—wasn't hurting anybody that I knew of, I decided to overlook it. I didn't want to give the police any excuse to start nosing around in my life."

"I guess that makes sense." I gulped the last of my coffee.

"I'll think about what you said."

"I won't let the hospital know what I found out for twenty-four hours. Give you time to think it over."

"I appreciate that."

I still didn't like him. But at least I didn't hate him anymore.

☾

THE SUIT WAS Armani, the woman was bulletproof Professional.

"Hello," she said, offering a slender but strong hand, "I'm Courtney. Tandy has told me so much about you."

"She's inside."

"Ummm. Being interviewed. NBC."

"And, Courtney, you're with?"

"Pyramid. Pyramid Media."

"Ah."

"We produce Tandy's show."

"Ah."

"Since Laura is dead, the company told me to hustle my buns out here and cover for her."

Given her nice, humorless face, her sensational and probably real breasts, and her excellent perfect legs, I had no doubt her buns were also gapeworthy. I guess it was her eyes that spoiled the effect of the other body parts. Nobody had any right to look this happy in the face of Laura's death. But then, without Laura's demise, we wouldn't have NBC in Tandy's room, would we?

I'd gone up to my room. All her stuff was gone. The gentleman at the front desk told me that she'd been assigned a new room. Which was where I stood now. Facing the guard Pyramid had dispatched.

"Any idea how long you think she'll be?"

"I'm not sure, Robert. If I may call you that. But I'll be sure to have her call you if she gets the chance."

If.

Given that Tandy's fate was clearly in Courtney's hands, I doubted I'd be seeing her tonight.

"Tell her I need to talk about the drawing."

"The drawing," she repeated. "Got it. Now I'd better get back inside."

Oh, yeah, she would be sending Tandy right out.

I DROVE OVER to Wendy'sand got a salad in the drive-through. I stopped at a convenience store for a quart of Hamms. I drove slowly back to the motel. It was kind of a make-out night. All the hot small-town cars up, their radios illegally loud. I saw a college-age girl in an old battered Plymouth. She had a University of Iowa parking sticker on her windshield. She wasn't really what you'd call a babe—actually, I've always been attracted to the quiet, pretty, bookish types instead of the babes—but I made up a little history of her. Good-looking, bright girl from poor family has to work so hard she never has time for a social life. And then she meets the famed Right Guy, not unlike me, who eloquently and persuasively convinces her with his silver tongue, not unlike mine, that she is truly a beauty and needs only self-esteem to realize all the good and great things waiting for her. She looked over at me for a moment and I was tempted to roll down my window and tell her all the things in my head. But I figured with my luck, I'd get arrested and she'd run off with the bail bond guy or something.

There was a good Robert Mitchum picture, *Track of the Cat,* on TNT. I watched the whole thing. It was ten o'clock. Two hours since being deflected by the unctuous Courtney.

I decided it was time to try the Gileses'. See if they were asleep yet.

I dug out the phone book and called.

Mr. Giles answered on the first ring.

I hung up.

I tried Tandy's room. Busy. Tried the operator. She got a busy, too. Should she report it? No, thanks. Courtney had no doubt taken the phone off the hook.

Restless. Paced. Tried Tandy again. Busy.

Then somehow it miraculously became ten-thirty. Tried the Gileses' again. Mr. Giles barked "Who is it?" after the first ring.

I sat down and finished off the beer. And fell asleep. Tension was gone; exhaustion overcame me. I hadn't slept well in a couple of nights. Now I was drained.

The Exercise-in-a-Spray infomercial was on. That's right. No dieting. No exercising. Just spray this on your body and you magically begin to lose weight and tone up. Gee, and to think there were probably cynics who thought that the stuff didn't work.

I went to the bathroom and came out and tried Tandy. She surprised me by answering. "Wow. What a night, Robert. NBC."

"How's the drawing going?"

"Oh, that. I really haven't had time to get back to it yet."

"Oh."

Pause. "I'll try, though. I'm too wired to sleep, anyway. And I do keep getting these flashes. Just like the old days, Robert. Laura always said it would come back to me." Hesitation. "Every time I think of her, I feel like shit. I turned out to be just like her. I *like* all this celebrity stuff. And I was always making fun of her for it." Teary-voiced. "I loved her so much, Robert. Our relationship got so complicated by the end, I know. But the bottom line is that I loved her so much." Another hesitation. "I really will work on the drawing, Robert. Maybe something'll come to me in the middle of the night. You know, the way it used to."

"If you get anything—"

"I'll call you right away. Thanks for being such a sweetie."

We hung up.

I went in the bathroom and changed into dark clothes.

MOONLIGHT CAST LONG, gothic shadows over the Giles house. Every window was black with night. Inky clouds partially obscured the moon. Soon enough, it would be raining.

I'd parked half a block away and walked up the alley. When I reached the back of the house, I charted my course.

Back porch roof to a small, black, ornamental wrought-iron balcony built just under the attic window. Apparently, the builder had hoped to reenact *Romeo and Juliet* here someday. And then I'd get inside the attic. If Claire didn't scream, I'd be all right.

It was fairly easy work and I did it almost soundlessly. My palms got scraped up on the rope I lassoed the balcony with, but other than that there was no real difficulty. When I reached the balcony, I pulled myself up and stepped inside the wrought-iron enclosure. And felt the balcony start to collapse all around me. It hadn't been built to hold a 162-pound man. I moved carefully and quickly.

I pulled the rope up from below. A dangling rope was a sure giveaway.

I crouched and peered into the window. Saw nothing. Too dark. As I was waiting for my eyes to adjust to this particular darkness, the thunder started.

It was summer thunder, deep and vast, racing all the way down the sky to set objects and souls trembling. There was enough caveman DNA in me to recognize the thunder's booming warning of cosmic malice. This was when you went to the back of the cave and clutched your family to you and pretended that you were not afraid at all. But your wife knew and you knew she knew. You just hoped that the little ones didn't know. It was important that the chief hunter of the family be, in their eyes, anyway, fearless.

The rain came not long after.

I hunched beneath the overhang of roof as well as I could. But it wasn't much help. I still couldn't see much.

The layout started to take shape. Large, partially finished attic that was mostly a bedroom. I guess I'd been expecting one of those hellholes you hear about where children are held captive. The smells and the blood and the weapons of torture.

No such evidence here.

I could see a bed, bureau, small TV, toilet, sink, older-model refrigerator.

Not just a bedroom, after all. A tiny apartment.

Then I saw, in the center of the floor, the metal chain bolted to the floor. I followed the length of chain until it disappeared somewhere in the covers of the bed.

I thought of the chain-dragging noise I'd heard from the other side of the door.

I tried the windows. Locked tight. There would doubtless be a hook on the other side. And I doubtless wouldn't be able to lift it. The rain increased. Hard. Cold.

And the ornamental balcony began to shift beneath my feet.

I started to knock—hoping I could rouse Claire from her bed and her no doubt drugged sleep—when the spotlight caught me.

I turned and saw, through the silver rain slanting cold in the yellow beam of the spotlight, the unmistakable shape and colors of a police car.

"YOU GOING TO tell me what you were doing up there?"

"I'd rather tell Chief Charles."

"Well, I'd rather be home in bed with my wife. But that doesn't mean jack shit, does it, Mr. Payne?"

Fuller was in fine form. Ever since meeting in the interrogation room, he'd let it be known, none too subtly, that he didn't care for me, Tandy, or out-of-towners in general.

He was finally getting a chance to express himself.

"You going to attack her?"

"Who?"

"Claire. The woman who lives in the attic."

"Yeah. That's just what I was going to do. Rape her."

"It happens."

"Well, it doesn't happen when I'm around. I just wanted to talk to her."

"You couldn't go in the front door?"

"I tried that. Her folks wouldn't let me see her."

"Then that should've been that. You got your answer and the answer was no."

"Would you please call Chief Charles?"

"You know what time it is?"

"I'll take the blame. Just please call her."

"I'm afraid not. I'm going to take you to the shop."

"The shop?"

"That's what we call the station."

"Ah."

"Then I'll call the chief."

"Who saw me, anyway?"

"A good citizen whose headlights caught you about halfway up the back wall when you were climbing."

"I thought you worked days."

"I do. But Sullivan has the flu."

"Then at least call Tandy for me. Tell her where I am."

He smiled nastily at me. "You'd think a psychic could figure that out for herself."

HE WENT THROUGH the whole thing. Booking. Fingerprinting. Even a nice new photograph.

He was having himself a damned good time.

"Not often a lowlife local lawman like myself gets the chance to book an FBI man like yourself."

"I quit the bureau years ago."

He looked up at me from the form he'd been filling out.

"Maybe you left the bureau, but the bureau didn't leave you, Payne. You've still got the attitude."

"The bureau do something to you, did they, Fuller?"

"Yeah, me and every other hardworking pissant local lawman. They come in here and take over and push us around and never tell us what's going on. And if there's any credit, they take it all for themselves."

"How come Chief Charles doesn't seem to feel that way?"

"Because she's got the paper."

"The paper?"

"The degree."

"I see."

"Took all the courses. Kissed all the city council asses. What she wants to be someday is mayor. And so she has to play the game. FBI comes into a town like ours, all the people get all hot and fluttery. Like a teenager in heat. Oh, the FBI is so wonderful. Oh, the FBI is so professional. Like we're dog shit or something. Well, let's see the fucking FBI pull their fucking car out of a ditch in the middle of a blizzard sometime."

An angry man.

We were in Susan Charles's office. He sat at her desk. This was where he obviously hoped to be permanently someday.

He started to say something. A young man in a 1958 crew cut was pushing a wide broom down the corridor. He paused in the doorway.

"You want me to skip the chief's office tonight? This is when I usually do it."

"Just come back when we're done talking."

"Fine. I'll just take my break now."

When the young man was gone, Fuller said, "His break. Sonofabitch takes ten breaks a night."

"You could always fire him."

"The mayor's kid? You kidding? He flunked out of Iowa last term when we were looking for a night janitor. Mayor figured this would teach his kid a little humility. Cleaning toilets and shit like that."

I was tired of small talk.

"You call Tandy?"

"Yeah. She wasn't there."

"What the hell you talking about, she wasn't there?"

"Just what I said, asshole. She wasn't there."

"You call the desk?"

He sighed. "I figured you'd piss and moan about it, so I tried it direct one time and got no answer, and then I tried the front desk and *they* tried and didn't get no answer. That good enough for you, Payne?"

"Where the hell would she be?"

I got a terrible feeling about her not being there. This time of night. A slashing rain. Her exhausted from her day. Why would she be gone now?

He stood up. "Couple things I need to do. I'll be back. You want coffee?"

"I'd appreciate it."

"You got thirty-five cents?"

"This isn't on the house, huh?"

"You pay for your coffee same as I do. That's what happens when you're a real lawman, Payne. You pay your own way."

"You ever hear of Prozac?"

"You ever hear of gettin' a nightstick shoved up your ass?"

He went away.

I sat and listened to the rain and looked around the office again. He hadn't been kidding about Susan's public success. She had all the right awards and citations you need to prosper in a small town. Kiwanis. Rotary. The hospital. With her brains, style, and poise, seemed she could be mayor anytime she wanted.

I got up and walked over for a closer look.

I studied the family photos on top of the small bookcase. Young Susan Charles at various ages. The very youngest photo was so pretty, she could have been a face on baby food or baby soap. Curly dark hair, stunning green eyes, and already a kind of wry smile, as if she knew that her beauty would someday be defaced. The wryness being her way of dealing with it.

The cheerleading photo, despite the out-of-date hairdo, was still sexy. Definitely a trophy girl. The campus stars would have all vied for her. And she no doubt would have let them.

A high school graduation photo; a New York city vacation photo; a swimsuit photo in which she wore a goofy hat and looked like she was giggling.

And then no more.

No photos of her with her scar.

"Those were the good days," she said from behind me.

Yellow rain slicker, red blouse, jeans, wading boots, sprightly yellow rain slicker hat. Cute cute cute.

"BS," she said.

"BS?"

"Before Scar."

I smiled. "Sounds about right."

She sat down behind her desk. "You're in trouble, Robert."

"I know."

"Fuller is enjoying himself. It's sort of like giving a pit bull a side of beef."

I sat down, too.

"That's an apt description, Chief."

She leaned forward. "Why the hell were you trying to get into that attic?"

So I told her what Emily Cunningham had told me. I told her about all the false leads with Renard, though I didn't mention Dr. Williams. I told her that somehow all this connected up with a baby picture. Sandy used to clean up Claire's attic room and saw the photo and also saw it somewhere else. Told her about Tandy and her drawings.

"Why didn't you work with me?"

"I should have. I wanted to help Tandy, I guess. Keep her in the center of the spotlight."

"You're a good friend."

"She's a nice woman."

"Very neurotic."

"We're all very neurotic," I said.

She smiled. "Is that the lawman speaking or just the man?"

"Both."

She sat back in her chair. "I'll talk to Fuller and see what I can do. Explain things. Maybe he'll back off a little. But if he wants to go ahead with charges, there's nothing I can do."

If she blocked his charges, the Kiwanis and the Rotary would be most unhappy. I didn't blame her. I wouldn't have blocked the charges, either. Whatever my motive, I really had been trespassing at the very least. True, and thankfully, I hadn't gotten inside, where several other charges could have been brought against me.

She picked up the form Fuller had been working on and said, "Let me go talk to him. See if he'll agree to sort this out in the morning." She looked at me with an expression I couldn't read. "Despite the fact that you were carrying burglary tools."

"And let me go back to my room tonight?"

She nodded. "But we're talking fifty-fifty at best."

"That's what I figured."

Form in hand, she left the office. I went back to the photos on top of the bookcase. I felt a compulsion I couldn't explain.

"All right if I get in here now?"

The mayor's kid with his cleaning cart. He looked like a decent kid in a shaggy, slow-witted kind of way.

"Sure."

He grinned. "Fuller'll probably kick my ass out of here, he comes back."

"I'll talk to him."

He looked stunned. "Mister, you been booked. Why would he listen to you?"

"Let's just see what happens."

He saw the small framed photo I held in my hand. Cheerleader. "She was a babe."

"She sure was."

"Don't know how she ever got to be a cop."

"The times're changing, I hear."

"Yeah, I s'pose. But still and all, you sure don't expect your chief to look like *that*. I mean, boobs like that and everything." He lifted his dusty dry mop, as if presenting it to me. "Guess I'd better get to work."

He started in on the office. I stayed in my corner next to the bookcase. He worked around me. He missed all kinds of spots but I didn't want to be the one who pointed it out.

I looked through the photos and silently weighed my chances with Fuller. Zero to none, it seemed to me.

"That's the one Sandy always looked at."

"Sandy?" I said.

"Yeah, the girl that got killed by Rick Hennessy."

"Really?" I said, setting the baby photo down. "How do you know that?"

"This was where she was working when she died. She had my job. Saving for college. She broke me in. You know, showed me around my first week. Right after that, she got killed."

I hadn't known about her job here.

And then I thought of her other job. The one with Claire Giles.

"She ever say anything about the baby picture of the chief?"

"Don't think so. She'd just pick it up and look at it a lot. It's kind of a cute picture, for a little kid, I mean. She'd just keep staring at it."

"What the hell you doing?" Fuller said, bursting back into the office.

"Where's Chief Charles?" I said.

"For somebody who's gonna spend the night with us, you sure ask a hell of a lot of questions, you know that?" Wide face sweaty, angry, frustrated. Then, "Get the hell out of here, Ronnie. Payne and I need to talk."

"Where's Susan?" I said.

I was pushing him to the edge. I didn't have any choice.

"Some personal business came up, if that's all right with you. She told me to take over and do as I saw fit. Is that good enough for you?"

"She told me she'd ask you to let me go back to my motel tonight."

"She didn't say anything to me."

The way he said it, I knew he wasn't lying.

But why wouldn't Susan have kept her word and asked him to let me go, at least for tonight?

But I already had a good idea.

And now I had no choice but to run.

I was quick enough to surprise him. He cursed, jumped in my direction, slamming his knee hard against the edge of the desk.

Then he got entangled with Ronnie and his dry mop. Ronnie moved in sync with Fuller, and Fuller couldn't get past. Daffy Duck and Bugs Bunny executing a routine.

I was several feet down the hall by the time Fuller burst out with "Stop him! Stop him!"

And then he was running down the hall after me.

And then the whole jail was waking up from its rainy slumber.

More shouts. Slapping footsteps.

My chances of escaping weren't much better than those of Fuller letting me go back to my motel room.

SIX

BACK DOOR. OPENING just now. Patrolman coming through in rain poncho. Smelling of cigarettes and cold air. Didn't see me at first.

I shoved him out of the way. He bounced off the doorframe back at me. I had to shove him again. Ran into the night.

Rain was so hard it was like soft bullets exploding on my head, shoulders, and back.

Running out of the circle of light in the rear of the police station. Darkness. Had to reach the darkness.

Asphalt alley. Splashing through pooling water in the sloping center of the asphalt.

Garages. Tiny loading dock. Dumpsters. Two, three back doors of businesses. None offered much hope of a hiding place. They'd comb the alley for sure.

I needed a car. But hot wiring didn't happen to be a specialty of mine. I could do it, but it would take a long time. Too long.

The street. Small dark businesses on either side. Wind whipping signs and trees and overhead traffic signal viciously.

Had to have a car. And that meant Tandy. The car she'd rented would be at the motel. I couldn't take mine. Too easily spotted. The motel was seven, eight blocks from here.

I jogged three blocks over. If I stuck on a straight course, they'd find me for sure.

I wanted to stop and get out of the rain. Just for a second. There's an old Ray Bradbury story, one of my favorites in high school, about a couple of astronauts marooned on a planet where there's no escape from the rain. Eventually, they go mad. I knew the feeling. I hadn't been out in this stuff ten minutes yet and I was already starting to feel disembodied. Soon, I'd be nothing more than another puddle.

Night. Cold. Rain.

Alleys. Backyards. Streets.

Backed-up sewers. Wind tearing off tree branches. Lightning surgically severing the black sky with a shining silver blade.

Running. A hitch in my side. Slowing down. Gasping. Until this moment, I would have said that I was in reasonably decent shape for a man my age. That's what I told the ladies in the bars when they remarked on my slim body. Now I knew better. Slim wasn't the equivalent of healthy. It just meant you did a better job of *hiding* your unhealthiness.

And then it was there.

I was just coming out of another alley when it appeared, apparitionlike. Big, hot, heavy, throbbing in the rain.

A squad car. Fuller driving. Aiming a spotlight back and forth across the front of the alley. He must have glimpsed me. Or thought he had.

I dove behind three garbage cans set into a wooden frame. I had developed a nose bleed and the blood was flooding hot into my mouth. I was shaking all over.

I peeked up just enough to see the spotlight whip back and forth, forth and back a few more times.

Was he going to pull into the alley and search it?

The nose was becoming a problem.

I ripped a piece of my shirt off, wrung it out as well as I could, and then pressed it to my nose. Teach me not to carry handkerchiefs.

Fuller still sat at the head of the alley.

Why?

Then I was able to hear the squawk of the radio. He was talking to the dispatcher. I couldn't catch most of the words. But I did get a sense of the exchange.

I lay against the ground. I was already so wet, so cold, it didn't matter. I was so close to the garbage cans that the sweet, fetid stench of last week's dinner leavings were starting to gag me.

I had to get a car. I was sure I knew what was going on. But I needed proof. Fuller wouldn't be easy to convince.

And then he left.

Just as wraithlike as his sudden appearance had been, so was his leaving.

No siren. No quick acceleration. He just left. All that heat and power of the souped-up Ford just vanished.

I got up and started running again.

For a block or so, I got disoriented and had no idea where I was in relation to the motel.

But then I saw a small radio tower that was a block west of the motel and that set me right again.

Sirens in the distance. Probably for me—what could be more exciting than an honest-to-God manhunt for an escaped prisoner?—but then again maybe not. This was perfect fire weather, cops and firefighters alike often converging on the same scene.

I ran.

I was a block from the motel, in an alley, when the dog found me.

Wind, rain, and a ripped branch had worked together to knock down the fencing that was the only protection the civilized world had from him.

His barking was terrifying. All sorts of images of me as his dinner flooded my mind. I was paralyzed.

My fear, of course, was that he'd attack me. But just as the mutant rottweiler—or whatever the heck he was—started to think about moving on me, I saw a flashlight beam cutting faintly through the mist and rain.

And then a male voice calling, "Gretchen! Gretchen!"

He hadn't taken time to dress properly, a beanpole of a bald guy in a robe and pajamas, slipping and sliding over the muddy grass of his backyard to get to his precious dog.

"Gretchen! Gretchen!"

Gretchen was out to impress him. Demonstrate just how bloodcurdling her bark could be. If he had any sense, *he* would have been afraid of it, too.

I was pinned against a garage on the other side of the alley.

The flashlight beam found my face.

The rain hissed and hummed and hammered away. Soft bullets.

"Who're you?"

"My name's Payne. Robert Payne."

"What the hell you doing in my backyard this time of night?"

"I wasn't in your backyard. I was walking down the alley to my motel."

"On foot on a night like this?"

"My car got caught in a little flash flood. Sewer backed up. Couldn't get it started again. So I was walking back to my motel."

"Oh."

"Your fence got knocked down just enough to let Gretchen out."

"Oh, hell, I'm sorry about this, mister."

He was so trusting, I felt ashamed of myself for lying about my stalled car.

Gretchen growled.

He leaned down and said something to her in dog. She quit growling.

"She really wouldn't hurt you."

"Yeah, that's the impression I had."

He caught my sarcasm and smiled. "That's actually the truth.

She wouldn't hurt you unless you made some threatening move or something."

"I'll try to remember that."

"I'm going to dry off and make some cocoa. You want to come in and have some?"

"No, thanks. I'd better get back to the motel."

"Well, sorry if she scared you."

Headlights. Far end of the alley. Very good chance it was the police.

I started to edge away.

"Appreciate you coming out like that. Thanks."

Edging away.

"Busy night," he said, staring down the alley at the headlights. "I heard sirens earlier. Something must be going on."

"Well, see you," I said.

The headlights were starting up the alley now, malevolent in the rain-slashed night.

I didn't run. But I came damned close.

IN THE CUTTING rain, the motel looked shabby and beaten, age and relentless rain more than it could handle.

No sign of cops.

I went around the back way. I didn't want the old gent in the office to see me.

I spent a lingering moment under the overhang. No more rain except the beads that bounced off the cars pulled up to their respective rooms.

I leaned against the wall. Catching my breath. Enjoying the respite.

And then I saw the cop car at the far end of the motel. Starting toward me.

I jumped around the corner and took the stairs two at a time to the second floor.

At the rate the squad car had been moving, it would be just about below me right now.

I found Tandy's room. No sound but that of spraying wind and rain as I pressed my ear to the door.

Where was she this late at night? I needed to get in there.

The door wasn't closed. Disbelief, at first, as if somebody was tricking me. But it was true. The door was slightly ajar.

I went inside. Darkness. Perfume. Wine. I stood by the window. Intermixed with the rain was the raspy sound of a police radio. He was almost directly below.

The spotlight again. Angling across the door and window of Tandy's room.

Then he worked his way down the line of doors.

Behind me, a moan.

I couldn't risk a light. I moved through the shadows to the moan, which had been repeated now two or three times.

Soughing wind; rattling rain.

I knelt next to the bed. Groped for her face. Touched it. Blood.

"What happened, Tandy?"

"She tried to kill me. What time is it?"

"About five."

"I've been out for a long time. She beat me with her gun. I think she thinks she killed me."

"I'm sorry. I should've figured this out a lot sooner."

"It's not your fault," she said. Then, "Giles is Renard."

"I know."

"She was afraid it was going to get out and ruin her career. She has big plans. But being associated with Renard would end them."

The moan.

"And Susan Charles is his daughter. His daughter with Claire."

The moan again.

"The face was hers, Robert. She came in here and saw the drawing—the scar—and knew what was going on."

I stood up. "I'm going to call an ambulance for you."

"Please. I'm scared, Robert. She beat me pretty bad."

In the darkness, I found the phone. Dialed emergency.

"Where're your car keys?"

"You're going after her?"

"Yeah."

"They're on the dresser. She's crazy, Robert. Maybe as crazy as Renard."

"Yeah," I said. "Yeah, she is."

SEVEN

MANY OF THE streets had become wading pools. Shrubs and children's toys and even a lone garden rake carried away in the torrents. Huge branches lay at angles in the water. Fire sirens; police sirens. Rising water covering entire lawns, swirling water obscuring entire intersections. Yellow overhead traffic lights flashing bold and useless above it all.

Took me a long time to reach the Gileses'. Every other street had to be detoured. All I needed was a stalled car. I'd snuck away from the motel with no problem. I didn't want to get stopped now.

THE GILES HOUSE was dark.

I parked as close to the curb as I could get.

A steep hill was conducting heavy washes of water down onto the flat corner where the Gileses lived. Most of their front lawn was already submerged.

Some rain smells clean. This rain smelled dirty. I walked around the house. At first, I didn't see any sign of her.

Then I checked the garage.

Smart.

She'd run her car into one of the two stalls. Nobody would find her.

So she was inside and the house was dark.

Maybe she'd finally snapped, the years of keeping her terrible secret finally too much for her.

Claire was her mother. Claire had known Paul Renard and fallen in love with him. According to most of the locals, that hadn't been too difficult to do. A real charmer, they all said.

And she'd borne him a child. Susan.

And then had suffered her breakdown. And let her own mother, Mrs. Giles, care for the baby.

And then fifteen years ago, Paul Renard had returned. He hadn't worn well, and he'd changed his style entirely. Looked like a used-up workingman. The perfect disguise for a dashing former ass-bandit.

And now all of them were in the house standing before me in the cold, hard rain. Crazy Claire and her mother and step-father— and crazy Claire's daughter, Susan.

Tandy would have a story, all right.

The garage smelled of summer tools that hadn't been cleaned completely. Lawnmower and rakes and wheelbarrow all smelled of sweet summer grass. *Dry* summer grass. It was time for me to leave my roost again.

I walked outside.

THE FRONT DOOR was locked.

I went over to the window and peeked inside.

He sat in his armchair looking straight at me. His T-shirt was bloody. So was his face. A butcher knife had been plunged deep into his right eye. There was a .45 a few inches from his hand. He'd likely dropped it defending himself and his wife.

His wife lay sprawled on her back in front of him. The breast of her faded housedress was soaked with blood. She'd apparently been shot several times.

I tried the door again. Without my burglary tools, there was no way I could get in this way.

I went around back. Took my shirt off. Wrapped it around my fist. Punched out a pane of glass in the rear door. Reached in and opened the lock and pushed my way inside.

No sound but the rain.

Smell of tonight's dinner.

A cat creeping across the kitchen floor, not wanting to look at me. I probably scared him.

I started through the small house.

The living room stank. The bodies were in the process of purging. I picked up the .45 from near Giles's lifeless hand.

It was somehow melancholy seeing this creature of myth— this preening, diabolical, indomitable Renard—reduced to death inside the body and clothes of a worn-out old man. Evil existed, true, but it was rarely as romantic as we liked to envision it. It was frequently housed in the most mundane of minds and bodies and circumstances. We wanted the romantic evil because it kept the real truth from us. The truth of the grave, and rot and extinction.

The cat was back. An orange tabby. Edge of the living room. Watching me.

I went upstairs.

Their voices were muffled but I could hear them: they seemed to be part of the wall itself, the voices, muffled and ancient with their arguing and pain, as if they'd been entombed alive within the walls of this old house. I touched the walls and imagined I could actually feel them, the voices. One was shrieking, the other pleading softly, thrumming on the tips of my fingers.

A window at the far end of the dormlike second floor had been left open. The bottom part of the curtain was soaked with rain. The whipping, whistling wind chilled the entire room. The twin beds would be nice to slide into. Cold sheets to be warmed by a human body. Even with the window open, sleep would come.

I pushed on.

Up the short stairs to the attic, the attic door open, as if awaiting me.

THE ROOM WAS surprisingly spare.

Bed, bureau, portable TV, sink, toilet, stove, two small bookcases, one overburdened with paperbacks, the other with small framed photographs. Some would be of Claire and her parents, but others would be of Claire's daughter Susan.

Throw rugs on the bare wood floor. Insulated wallboard on the walls. A couple of space heaters for winter, and a large window air conditioner for summer.

The smell was terrible. Fresh air was unknown in this room. And so was life. The pretty but gaunt middle-aged woman who sat in the rocking chair, her weeping daughter's head in her lap, had not been alive for a very long time. This was not a room that would permit life. It suffocated you, like a time capsule.

She said, "Susan has been a bad girl and she's very sorry."

She wore a housedress faded to white, reaching to the middle of her calves. Her shoes were cheap, ugly sandals made from old tires. Her graying hair was tied back in a surprisingly cute and vital ponytail that relieved the dead gray quality of her face.

But it was the eyes that held you. Mad dark eyes; eyes that had felt and seen things that had destroyed its mind long, long ago. She was the only woman I'd ever seen whose face reminded me of Christ.

And then Susan looked up at me from her mother's lap—her lovely body stretched out at her mother's hip as if in supplication—and I saw the same eyes. The same madness.

And she said, "I can stay here with my mother, Robert. Nobody ever has to know. I'll live up here in this attic with her. And I'll never leave. Not even on sunny days when I want to be outside in the park or up at Thornton Hill at those old Indian burial sites."

She eased away from her mother. "I am very sorry, Robert. I just couldn't let anybody find out who my father was. I wouldn't have had any career then."

"The infant Tandy found buried by the trestle bridge—"

"My twin sister. She died very soon after she was born."

"And Kibbe—"

She shook her head. "He confronted me. Knew who I really was. He was going to blackmail me. I'm a peace officer. As if I have a lot of money."

So her story about having a judge for a father was a fabrication.

Claire reached out and started gently, fondly stroking her daughter's hair. "She got a straight four-point in high school and college both, Mr. Payne. She's always been a very bright girl." She said this hopefully, as if it would somehow brush aside Susan's murders.

"But I don't care about that anymore, any of it," Susan said. "I just want to be here with my mother."

She might be insane, but she wasn't stupid. A part of her understood that she'd killed people and would be held responsible for it. No wonder she wanted to stay here.

"Susan," I said softly, out of deference to this strange room and these two strange, sad women. "I need you to come with me."

"My mother was so ashamed of me," Claire said, "when I told her that I was in love with Paul. And then when I told her that I was pregnant by him, she slapped me, really beat me up. Even kicked me a few times. I'd never seen my mother like that. It wasn't till later that I realized he was sleeping with her, too. Here we were, both nurses at the asylum, and a patient was sleeping with both of us. I couldn't blame her, though. If you'd known Paul when he was a young man, he was so beautiful, so seductive."

I just kept thinking of the dumpy little man dead in the chair downstairs.

"When he came back fifteen years ago, she took him right in.

She'd never married since my real father died when I was six. She'd just waited for Paul. You couldn't recognize him. He'd had his face worked on and lost his hair and gained a lot of weight. But she didn't care. She still loved him. And so they got married. I had a breakdown right after I had Susan and my mother put me in an asylum. I'm schizophrenic. It can be controlled with medication. But I still have times when—" She shook her head wearily. "And then she decided I'd be better off here, in the attic. She was afraid I'd tell people who Susan really was. She was still in touch with Paul. She was afraid if I said anything, the police would start trying to make a connection between her and Paul. So I stayed up here. Susan knew who I was, of course, and came up here all the time."

She leaned over and kissed her daughter's head.

Susan clung to her mother, a child. "Please don't make me go, Mother."

"I'm afraid you have to, honey. They won't hurt you." She looked at me. "Will they, Mr. Payne?"

The rain rattled against the attic windows.

Susan said, barely audible above the wind and rain, "The older I got, Robert, the more comfortable I was up here. I wanted to be governor—but at the same time I wanted to live up here, too. The attic. With my mother."

And then she produced her service revolver. She'd hidden it under her right side, so I couldn't see it.

"No!" her mother screamed. "No!"

But it was too late.

In the movies, the detective would have tried a fancy shot. Knocked the weapon out of her hand. Saved her.

But I wasn't a movie detective. Nor a fancy shot.

All I could do was start uselessly forward, unable to take my eyes off the grisly sight before me.

The service revolver being raised. Reaching her temple. Her finger squeezing back on the trigger.

It wasn't as dramatic as it would have been in the movies, either.

No geyser of blood. Not that I could see in the shadows of this old attic, anyway. No violent jerk of the entire body, just the head sort of jumping rightward and then slumping to the shoulder. Not even a scream. Just dead. Animal dead. Human dead. Not movie dead.

Just weeping.

Just Claire weeping.

Just Claire in her rocking chair weeping.

FULLER WAS THERE in five minutes.

The first thing he said, seeing Susan dead on the floor, was, "Believe it or not, Payne, I really liked her. She was a straight shooter."

The cops were going to have another long night. So were the boys and girls from the state bureau.

"I guess you're the chief."

He said, surprising me, "That's what a shit I am."

"Oh?"

"That's the first thing I thought of when you called about Susan being dead. That I'd be acting chief and that the town council would probably appoint me chief full-time. I'm a selfish sonofabitch."

"We're all selfish sonsofbitches. It's our nature." I thought of how sanctimonious I'd been, at least in my thoughts, about Tandy. Celebrity had made her feel a little better about herself for not being as beautiful or bright as Laura. So who was I to judge her for that?

"I really did like her."

"Yeah," I said. "So did I."

AS MORE AND more officials came up the stairs, I led Claire downstairs. At one point, she whispered to me that she hadn't been down here in more than ten years, the last time for a Christ-mas Eve party.

We sat in the kitchen. I made us instant coffee. She said she was cold. I found her a sweater.

She sipped the coffee and said, "I don't know what happened to her."

"There's never any real explanation for anything like this, Claire."

"I watch a lot of TV up in the attic. Every time something tragic happens, there's always people on the tube explaining it."

I smiled. "Keeps them off the streets."

"I just keep seeing her when she was a little girl."

"She was beautiful. I saw those photos."

"She was sweet, too. She'd sit in my lap and I'd tell her stories for hours. She always smelled so warm and nice."

She started crying again.

I didn't even try to stop her.

EPILOGUE

THE STATE PEOPLE had a lot of questions, and since I had a few of the answers, I was asked to stay around for a while.

For all the gore of the past few days, the town was surprisingly sympathetic to Susan Charles. They seemed to feel that it probably wasn't her fault. What could you expect with the chill blood of Paul Renard in your veins?

Nobody knew why Renard had decided to come back here, and I doubted they ever would. The handsome heartbreaker of his youth had ended up a parody of low-rent sitcom grouch. Go figure.

I read a Brian Garfield western and a John D. MacDonald mystery and spent most of my time lying on my bed in the room. The rain was relentless.

I tried getting hold of Tandy, of course. But things were moving "very quickly," according to my favorite PR flack, Courtney-from-Chicago.

"Meaning what, exactly?"

"Well, meaning *People* magazine. Meaning *Dateline NBC.* Meaning Jay Leno."

Things were moving quickly indeed. And moving most quickly of all was Tandy. Away from me. I didn't expect, or probably even want, any of those long promises with short intentions one makes after being especially intimate with someone for a few furious days. We were both too pragmatic for that.

But I did want to hold her next to me and smell her hair and hear that little-girl laugh of hers. Maybe it wasn't love, but it was a nearly terminal case of like. I had fallen under her messy, self-conscious, insecure sway.

The phone rang just after I dozed off.

"Remember me?"

"Hey, I thought maybe Courtney baby had written me out of the script entirely."

"No way, Robert. Let's have dinner tonight."

"Great."

"In town."

"Great."

"I'll call you back to confirm." Then she cupped the phone and said, "Courtney says there's a call from the cable network I need to take."

I was elated. I lay back on the bed feeling sixteen again, all that sweet youthful promise, that best drug of all.

And indeed she did call back. A few minutes to six. I'd already showered and shaved.

And said: "Oh, shit, Robert. *Dateline* flew a producer out here already. He wasn't supposed to be here until morning. Courtney says I *have* to spend time with him."

"Oh."

"I know you're pissed."

I didn't answer.

"Hurt, then."

"I'm something. But I'm not sure it's hurt and I'm not sure it's pissed."

"Well, somewhere between them, then. How about lunch?"

"Great."

"See, you can't even say 'great' with any enthusiasm, and I don't blame you."

"Lunch would be great. Around eleven-thirty."

"Fantastic. God, Robert, please don't be pissed."

"Just do what you need to, Tandy."

I slept pretty well. I crawled all the way back in the dark warm cave of sleep and cuddled up in a ball and visited a variety of dreamscapes.

The call came at ten A.M.

"Now the *People* people are here, too. And Courtney says that I absolutely have to talk with them."

"It's all right. The local gendarmes are going to cut me loose after one more interview. Then I'm flying on home."

"To Cedar Rapids?"

"No. To the old house."

"The married house?"

"Yeah. Her birthday's coming up. I thought I'd spend it there."

"You know what? You're such a sweet, dear person that I'm going to schedule dinner with you tonight, and whatever Courtney says, I'm going to tell her no deal, I'm spending the night with Robert."

"You really think you've got the nerve?"

"Just watch me, Robert. Just watch me. I'll call you back midafternoon." I heard Courtney calling her name in the background.

I NEVER DID hear from Tandy that afternoon. I got in my rickety biplane and flew to the small town where I'd lived with my wife. The widowed woman who house-sat for me showed me the cardbox box filled with my mail, and then tiptoed me down the hall to show me where our three cats were sleeping on the double bed.

Two months later, at Christmastime, I got a card from Tandy. It was pure gush. Show was ranked at number one again in the syndication ratings. Her book was almost finished (she liked the woman writing it for her). And she missed me a great deal, and could I ever forgive her for not calling me back that afternoon?

Oh, and I shouldn't forget to watch her for the *second* time on *60 Minutes* the first week in January.

I wasn't sure what to make of any of it except that Tandy was happier. All her life she'd wanted approval. And now she had the approval of millions.

I felt empty, and then idiotically sorry for myself, and then I felt embarrassed for being such a child.

I built a fire, and picked up a collection of mystery stories, and let the cats throw my ancient and venerable house slippers around.